GAIA'S
REVENGE

J. A. BROWNE

www.jabrowne.com

Peahen
Publishing

Praise for Book One – *Hannah and the Hollow Tree*

'With real connections, problems we all face and simple truths
this book is one to warm the heart...I would recommend this
book to all who want love, magic and adventure.'
Susie, aged 10

'This story is so magical that it took me back to my childhood
reading stories of magic, beasts and all things fantastic.'
Sal – Amazon customer

'My children have loved this story.
Would definitely recommend.'
Amazon customer

'I loved the dynamics of the relationships between the
female characters – girl power at its best.'
M Stephenson

For Aaron and Stephen

"Nature favours those organisms which leave the environment in better shape for their progeny to survive."

James Lovelock

First published in Great Britain in 2019 by Peahen Publishing Ltd
www.peahenpublishing.com

Copyright © 2019 J. A. Browne
Illustrated by Darran Holmes

ISBN: 978-1-9161282-3-1

A CIP catalogue record for this is available from the British Library

Peahen
Publishing
Bringing your stories to life

THE EARTH CHRONICLES

GAIA'S REVENGE

J. A. BROWNE

CHAPTER ONE

Earth – Halloween: Hannah
Inferno

I am not at home in bed. I can't roll over and pull the duvet over my head or flick my electric blanket on. I'm a Northerner. Tough things out mostly, but sometimes, just sometimes, it's really nice to flick the leccy blanket on. But I'm not cold here, lying on the ground. Blades of grass tickle my palms as I entwine my fingers amongst them. Strange. October doesn't feel so cold today. I inhale the aroma of pines and the lemony scent of fir trees which triggers my hunger clock. As I roll over onto my stomach I imagine what delicious treats Gran can rustle up for us. I push myself up onto my knees, which brings me face to face with it. Etched words that can't be unread and I wish, more than anything else in the world, that I'd suddenly lost my ability to read.

Engraved into stone.

Burned into my brain.

These words have robbed me of my ability to breathe.

But she isn't dead…

HERE LIES
CAROLINE
WALSINGHAM
BELOVED
DAUGHTER AND MOTHER
TIME PASSES, BUT LOVE STAYS
BORN: 30TH SEPTEMBER 1976
DIED: ALL HALLOWS' EVE

I don't understand. I don't understand because she's not dead. My mother isn't dead. *She just isn't.* Gran wouldn't lie to me. *Would she?*

I crawl forwards. My hands register the sudden coldness of the grass. Dew soaks through my jeans. *How is that possible? It was warm.* I reach out, fingers connect and trace the grooves like reading Braille because my eyes just won't accept what they see.

"Here lies Caroline Walsingham." My voice barely audible.

That isn't possible.

"Time passes but love stays."

Of course love stays. It doesn't just go! Defiance awakens deep from inside me.

"But time hasn't passed. She's just sleeping!"

We interred Mum's body under Windsor House only a few hours ago. Me and Joyce and Gran. *Where is she?*

"Gran?" I call out through gritted teeth. I grip the headstone, steadying myself. Glancing around I see only trees, clustered together in a silence that slaps me.

But I felt Mum's heartbeat. That's how I'd known she was alive! Did Gran lie to me? Is Mum de...? My whole body trembles. *I need to run.* Like running will save my life. Or Mum's.

"GRAN?"

As I stand the stars blur against the night sky. It takes a moment for the world to return to stillness, but as it does, I register where I am: Windsor House. The front garden to be exact. *But we were inside the Hollow Tree watching Harriet. How did I get here?* I glance in the direction of where I think the Hollow Tree is but suddenly every tree looks the same, like sentries on guard in rank and file, Gran would say. There're so many. *Shouldn't I just know which it is?* It's *my* Hollow Tree after all. Or, did I dream it? Am I dreaming now?

Light travels faster than sound so I see the flash

millionths of a second before the wall of noise strikes my chest, launching me into the air.

Urgh!

The frosted ground steals every inch of breath from my body as I smack against it. *What the...?* I lie swimming in a sick-dizzy feeling. If I knew what being drunk felt like, I reckon this is it. Not wanting to throw up all over myself, I bite down and roll over trying to think of anything else but being sick. As I do a rush of warmth flows down my head. I clasp my hand against the back of my skull. It's wet and warm. I don't need to look. I know what's seeping through my fingers. Its metallic stench hits the air. Tears begin streaming, washing away the grit that has invaded my eyes. I try to focus on something. Anything. Something that looks like anything.

An intense heat stings my cheeks. I scramble back as the ringing in my ears begins to fade. My vision clears. I stand, feeling like David facing a Goliath-sized wall of fire.

No! No! NO!

"MUM!"

I dart towards the house but searing heat forces me back further.

"Help me! Someone! Please!"

Every second the human brain has one-hundred thousand chemical reactions and every single one of mine totals just one thing...Mum.

"Gran! Where are you?"

Nothing.

I'm alone.

The fire rages and spits as the house groans in defeat.

I spin around and scream out towards the mass of moonlit trees begging them for help.

"Hollow Tree, please, you have to help my mother!" I choke, but what can trees do against fire except crumble to ash and cinder.

Smoke billows up to mingle with the darkest clouds. Eyes closed, I push my thoughts out to Gran with every ounce of energy I can muster.

"The house is on fire. Please, Gran! Mum's insi...Joyce! Oh my God, Joyce! The foxes! They'll die...They'll all die! Do something!"

But she doesn't answer. Only the cracks and snaps of burning timbers speak to me. Almost as soon as my tears fall, the searing heat dries their track marks, imprinting upon my cheeks, tightening my skin.

I have to do something.

I'm Gaia's heiress.

I must be able to.

I charge at the house again through the smoke-filled haze engulfing it, but thick flames just lick and lap the air which feeds its greed as it grows and grows. It's useless.

I'm useless.

"No! Mum! Joyce!" I drop to my knees. Blisters form across my knuckles, as I smash my fists into the ground. Screams rip from my chest over and over...my eyes glaze against the glow of the fire destroying Windsor House. Destroying the place where Mum's body lies cocooned. *Will she feel it? Will her soul realise?* Even if it does, her body couldn't survive that.

She must be dead.

I collapse and feel the coldness of the Earth's bed seep through my skin. A blanket of smoke settles on my chest.

I'm dying.

Wait for me, Mum.

CHAPTER TWO

Dream, Remembered

"Hannah, wake up!"

It's not real.

A voice in a dream, that's all.

"Hannah, I'm coming to get you. Alpha, guard the portal and keep watch."

I suddenly feel hands. Their cold touch pulls at my limbs and places me against something soft. Then, the tips of fingers touch five points on my face. I flinch as my mind jolts against an invader. I peel my eyes open.

"Gran?"

I'm laid across her lap, propped against her shoulder. She doesn't move her finger tips from my face.

"You're dreaming, sweetheart. You won't wake up. Giving me quite a scare again, Hannah. Sorry for the jolt and for what's next..."

We share the need for shallow breaths as my body rises against her chest.

"You're in my head, aren't you?"

"Yes. As we're speaking together now, this isn't a dream. You've done what your mother has, only your conscience is still in this realm, unlike your Mother's."

"Gran, it felt so real. I thought..." I splutter fighting back the tears that seem to want to choke me.

"Shh, all will be well. Now, this is going to feel somewhat strange. For both of us. Different to last time because I used the lavender, but you need to get used to these feelings for many different reasons and I'm not going to force a slumber upon you after *that*."

I don't like the way Gran just said, 'that'.

Before my mind 'wanders off the beaten track' as Dad used to say, a pulling sensation sends heat ripples through my body. Gran's touch is clammy.

"Hold on, sweetheart," she warns.

I stare into a kaleidoscope of silver light, deep within her eyes, which fan out around us, gentle at first. My ears sting against the whistling sound that ricochets like a stray bullet. Gran's face fades as the light at the centre of her eyes engulfs her. It's so beautiful. I reach out to touch her cheek, but feel only a wisp of air. The light pulls at me, taking each limb in turn, lifting me from Gran's arms.

Snap!

Like being released from a slingshot, I hurtle into the brightness of the light, wincing...waiting for the impact... but there's nothing. Just a fading light and a sudden quietness.

"Gra-?" I pant against a fever of heat sweeping my body.

"I'm here," she says pursing her lips to blow cool air across my face.

"It really was a dream?"

"Yes, sweetheart. Your Mum and Joyce and the pack are safe."

Gran pulls me into her chest, cradling my head in her hands.

"Never have I gotten used to that. Ever. Glad I'm not a Visionheir. At least I have full control of cerebral immersions."

I have no idea what Gran just said.

Relief curls cat-like into the pit of my stomach and settles. Gran inhales deeply. Maybe relief is doing the same inside her. Alpha's nose nudges my arm repeatedly until I cup my hand over her face, which she tries to lick. Affection is good. Even the slobbery kind.

As the dots of light in my eyes fade, I drink in a welcome sight. *My Hollow Tree.* From its thick bark, full of deep crevices, every shade of autumn fans out. *Olive's still my favourite.* It's strange to think we're sitting where the heartwood normally is, but this is a hollow tree. *The Hollow Tree.*

Eventually, I feel Gran peel my sweat-soaked hair from my face. I shiver.

"You'd tell me the truth, wouldn't you?"

"Your mother isn't dead. I promise you. I won't let anything happen to her. *My* daughter, remember?"

"And Windsor House hasn't burned to the ground?"

"Is that what your dream was about?"

I feel Gran's body shudder underneath me. I nod, thinking Gran could do with a sip of camomile tea right now, never mind a sprig of lavender.

"I promise you, Hannah, your mother is fine. She's safe under Windsor House. Joyce and the pack are protecting her."

"But, I've had that dream before."

"When?" She looks startled.

"Yesterday. I mean, the other night, whenever it was. Right before the phone call woke me and Mum to come here. Well, to come to you. I couldn't remember it when I woke up the first time, which is strange because–"

"You always remember your dreams," Gran says squeezing my hand tightly. She looks exhausted.

"Always. Well, not so much lately. My head's kind of a mess."

"Tell me everything, and don't spare the horses. I need every detail. Everything that you saw."

"Can't you just read my mind like you usually do?"

"I can, but I want to hear it from you, Hannah."

As I begin, my empath gift – bestowed by Gran – awakens like birdsong at dawn and for the first time I feel something. It's coming from Gran. And that something is ice cold fear.

CHAPTER THREE

Memories

I don't know how long I slept, but I needed it. After telling Gran all about the dream, I'd felt exhausted so, as if it was nothing at all, she stitched a blanket of leaves together in seconds, pulled it over me and let me curl back into her arms; my feet tucked under Alpha, the foot warmer.

"How long have I slept?" My neck cricks as I stretch out the aches.

"From the amount of drool soaked into my gown, I'd say a couple of hours," Gran replies, wafting my makeshift pillow to let it air-dry.

Gran cups my face for a moment. "Gaia's powers are beginning to show, you know?"

"What do you mean?"

"There's the slightest tinge of new colours forming in your eyes. Still the green and blue, but the flecks of mauve and peach are a very pretty addition."

"Really? Is that normal?" I pull my phone from my pocket, but stop myself not wanting to waste the battery. Those photos, our silly selfies and her ring are all I've got left of her. For now, anyway.

"No, *that* is unprecedented, but when we find water, you can see for yourself," Gran replies as I push my phone back into my pocket.

16

I glance around the Hollow Tree then through the portal. The rush of excitement floods back as I remember watching Gran, fingers dripping with fire, singe the Earth's fabric just enough to open the portal after showing me how to get inside the Hollow Tree in the first place. Well, it was more of a face-plant to be honest, once I'd felt it pull at me like she'd said it would. Staring through the portal, nestled between thick blankets and white sheets, the little girl I can barely take my eyes off sleeps, oblivious to the fact that she is being watched. *I wonder how she found her way in here.* She can't be any more than eight years old. I envy her. She's peaceful. Snug. I still can't quite wrap my head around the fact that this little girl is Gran's grandmother.

"What are we waiting for?"

"Not sure yet, Love," Gran replies, patting my knee.

I have no idea how long we've sat here in the Hollow Tree but it feels too long. Not that memory stumps aren't comfortable. They are. I just hadn't quite believed Gran when she'd explained what one was. She shuffles across from hers – one of several scattered around – to share mine. "You weren't joking, were you? About the stumps being able to find their way home," I ask.

"Why would I joke? What a notion. Memory stumps have molecular-level memories. Like I said, trees remember where they came from, their families are rooted just as ours

17

are. These stumps have just come home."

There isn't the slightest hint of sarcasm in her voice. *Gran's not kidding. Trees with memories. Cool.*

"We humans are more like trees than many of us realise and so often do the exact same thing. In our last moments, we too want to be surrounded by family at home. So do trees. Nothing strange about that."

I swallow the peach-sized lump in my throat.

A strange *harrumph* suddenly reminds me that my new best friend, Alpha, lies at my feet. I shuffle them underneath her weight as she repositions herself. I push my fingers through her thick olive fur – her sign of contentment, Gran says – as she purrs. Whilst staring at Harriet, it dawns on me that I'm looking through a hollow – a Gran-made one – actually inside the Hollow Tree. As I settle back against her, my mind drifts back to Gaia and the whole other world I know nothing about, yet. *There's so much I want to know. So much I need to know.*

"What is it like in Gaian?" I have a sudden thirst that needs quenching. And, well, water just won't do.

"You'd really have to see it to believe it. Long before I became a grandmother, I used to spend days roaming the groves of its most westerly realms, picking muckleberries. They were always at their best in late autumn, like now."

"What are muckleberries?"

"Well, hard to say. I suppose they smell a bit like honeysuckle, but taste like minted blueberries, although perhaps a tad sweeter. They are the only Earthly fruits I can liken them to."

"Sound delicious, but weird."

"Well, maybe you'll get to try them one day. If you're very lucky."

"Go to Gaian? Seriously?"

Gran nods.

"Did you ever live there?"

"Yes, when I was about your age. Younger, in fact. I was a restless little thing back then. Always fidgeting and fussing. I would run through endless pastures looking for the brightest sprigs of lemon parsley. I loved absorbing its juice."

Absorb?

"Don't you mean drink?"

She shakes her head, the eyebrow arches.

"Tell me more."

"In Gaian, flowers and trees endure little fatigue. Unlike here. There aren't daily toxic battles from pollution. The air is so pure, it's quite a heady existence. Even though I'm autumn born, I adored springtime in Gaian. The warming winds brought symphonies of birdsong and sweet aromas. Lilies, honeybells and iriscus. Their scents kissed us.

Pollinated our senses. An old friend of mine, a changeling called Listle, used to take me across the Vulturian Valley."

"Across?" I interrupt.

"Flying."

"You don't mean on a plane, do you?"

Gran's shoulders shudder, as she stifles her laughter. "No, dearest."

I'm suddenly jealous of all the things that Gran has seen and done. But then she is ancient, I suppose, and I'm just beginning.

"Listle and I would climb the crags and rockeries and bask with lotus flowers and creamed daisies. Sun worshippers, the lot of us. I remember one particular day around the middle of a Wolf Moon..."

"A what?"

"Wolf Moon. Gaian doesn't have quite the same calendar as Earth does. Wolf Moon would be equivalent to July."

"This really does sound like the coolest place, ever. Will you take me?"

"I don't see why not."

Before I can burst like a squashed bilberry, Gran taps my shoulder, pointing across to Harriet. She stirs, but doesn't wake up. I'm secretly pleased because I want to know more about Gaian and what it's like. Excitement tingles across my shoulders.

"When I was very little, Listle and I used to climb Cook pine trees. They lean towards wherever Gaia is at any given time, and we thought if we climbed them and whispered out to her, she would hear us. Oh my goodness, what little fools we were, but happy ones! I would rest my head against their thin limbs and listen to the *thump-thump, thump-thump* of their heart beats."

Trees have heartbeats! Cool.

"Such a beautiful view. Gaia covered her lands in quilts of olive and lime, stitched together seamlessly, interwoven across patchworks of dandelion and vanilla fields. We used to holk them, day and night. 'Nurturing nature,' Listle would say. And so began the hum of Harvest. Everyone worked. From the first day of the Autumn Equinox until the last day of the Harvest Moon. All Gaians brought home delights. We'd fill panniers on the sides of the Shires with succulent fruits like pashions. You know, if you heat them, they leak cinnamon syrup. I loved the sweet nectar of the sugar maple but Listle liked what she called the 'sour bite' of the vapefruit."

Gran's eyes glaze, lost in thought as I clutch my rumbling stomach.

"Can I ask a question?"

"You've just asked one," she smirks.

I roll my eyes. Gawd, I'm just like her.

"Don't suppose there's a pizza tree nearby. I'm starving."
Gran laughs out loud, a real whoop of a laugh. It wasn't
that funny. Whilst she continues chuckling away and not
ordering pizza, I continue to watch Harriet sleep soundly.
After a while, Gran, quite 'spent of all her laughter' as she
puts it, says, "Alas, pizzas I cannot provide, but let's see what
I can rustle up." She glances around the Hollow Tree and
the scattering of memory stumps wearing her 'calculation
face' which makes her look just like...*Mum*.

I'm tempted to look at my screensaver, but don't want to
waste what little battery I have left. I'll just have to picture
her without a gadget.

"Ah! Got it!"

"Got what?"

Gran doesn't reply.

"What are you doing?"

"Come on little fella, nothing to be shy about. Help a
hungry old lady out," she says patting the floor. Slowly,
a thin liquorice-like root from the tree rises which Gran
gently pulls out. "Here you go. Suck on that."

"Eugh, gross. Thanks, but no thanks." I clutch my
stomach. *Urgh! Is she kidding?*

"I thought you loved liquorice? Or is that your mother?"

I suddenly want to wake Harriet and ask her to chuck
me a bread roll through that hollow. *So hungry.*

"Mum's favourite. Can't we go back to the house and get some more dates or apples at least? Joyce could make a flask of soup for us, couldn't she?"

"This isn't a stake out."

"Yuck, don't say steak. Veggie, remember."

"We must attend to Harriet," Gran says before sucking the liquorice through pursed lips. "Trust me, you're missing out."

Doubt that. Even if I am a plant-eater.

Gran dangles the length of the root in front of me and I cave. I'm just way too hungry. Oh, I'd give anything for Mum's homemade blackberry crumble and almond custard. I hesitate before taking the root.

Just like liquorice, right?

I dive in pulling it with gritted teeth. The root snatches back and whips away, vanishing underground. "What the Hel...I mean, seriously?"

"Hannah, I said suck on it, not devour it. Poor thing. It's trying to feed you and you take a chunk out of it. It won't come back out now."

She's not kidding.

"Here," she says shoving her liquorice root into my hand. "Don't bite it. Suck like a straw." I hold the root to my lips, sideways glancing at Gran who is cooing at the floor, apologising on my behalf. I guess trees really do feel pain.

I place the root between my lips, close my eyes – like I'm waiting for the dentist's needle to pierce my gum – and suck. Slowly, a warm thick juice begins seeping through. It's actually liquorice! But sort of raspberry-flavoured.

"Mmm, yum-ee." *Mum would love this.*

"Yes, I know," chips Gran, that brow of hers arching. Clearly, she's listening again. Note to self: Learn the art of reflection. Fast!

"Did you ever meet Gaia?"

"Of course." Gran smiles a sort of half wink like I've missed something I should've got. "Gaia would say, 'To see me, know me, believe in me, is just a matter of sensibility and the senses. In my Divinity, you can root yourself. Through me, you breathe. Through me, you grow. And through me, you will die.'"

Gran's face falls. I stare at her for a moment tracing every line and crease. She opens her mouth to continue, but a voice whispers, "Who's there?"

CHAPTER FOUR

Gaian – Hunter's Moon: Lilith
Visionheir

The first vision I had lasted only a moment. I knew exactly when it was going to happen because Gaia, our Almighty Mother, had stood at my side, holding my hand as she, herself, sent the vision. It was of a crystal clear lake, glistening in the sunlight which filled me with warmth. It vanished as quickly as it came. She explained that the next vision – a naturally occurring one – would feel quite different, more intense. Like water rushing through my mind. What Gaia failed to tell me was that visions feel like you're drowning. I would be submerged in the vision until it released me. I remember being filled with so many questions. Gaia assured me that Holt, my Elder, would answer them, being *his* visionheir.

"You're dreaming again," says Elric as his fawn coloured wings nudge my side, flex then settle. Elric circles me, his manner playful, amber-filled eyes glinting against the emerging sun.

"I was just thinking about Holt."

"More questions?" he asks. His smile radiates warmth.

"One or two." I leave it at that.

We stand in one of the small groves I tend to, surrounded by trees teeming with apples, apricots, betel berries and carissa fruits. The lime and mawberry bushes' offerings litter our lands and their crisp sweet scent rises with the warming air, but never have they flowered as late into the Hunter's Moon as this. Of all the groves in the western realm, this is my favourite. Not only because it produces an abundance of the juiciest bloom berries but because it provides the perfect vantage point to admire the green banks of the Logarian Valley.

"Must you tend today?" he asks, stroking lengths of hair from my shoulders.

"It is still the Hunter's Moon," I reply.

"Only just. There can only be a few more rises until the moon begins to frost."

"But you know full well that All Hallows' Eve has not yet passed. Harvest is not yet over. Don't expect that I'll just leave my duties. Gaia has entrusted these easterly woodlands to me. Besides, it isn't work when it's your destiny. And we should be very grateful we've made it to the Harvest, what with Gaia's fevers."

"I admire your loyalty to our Almighty Mother and her well-being, too. And, to your 'destiny,'" he replies, arching a thick black brow, glistening with sweat.

"Don't mock me. You know I love what I do. I protect these groves and forests. Every blade of grass and every fire flower needs my attention."

26

His eyes apologise.

"Maybe you should consider how you spend your days. Now that your training is complete."

Elric's gaze falls. *Have I injured his pride?* My question was not meant as a slight.

"You're not the only protector roaming these valleys, you know. I shall take up my place when the time is right."

When Eldred deems it so, that means.

His playfulness extinguished, Elric leaves my side and crosses the jet-pebbled pathway to sit on a jute-covered trunk of a redundant yoke tree.

"True. True. But, you forget, they protect me, too," I smirk, attempting to put right the slight. "My trees have ears." I run my hand along the plume of black feathers that cross his shoulders and sit beside him. Feeling the tickle from the emerging roots of a nearby sugar maple as they wrap around our lower limbs, I gently pat them away.

"Shoo! I am not hungry, but, thank you."

Elric, forever at the mercy of his insatiable appetite, lets the silky roots pierce his thick mottled skin. I watch as they begin pumping his muscles and veins with nutrients.

"I can't help but worry about you," says Elric. I sense his desire to wrap his arms around me, but a Gryphon's injured pride needs a little time.

"I know you worry, but I am fine."

"Since evoking your gift…I mean…those visions are…"

"I'm learning. It takes time. Besides, I have only had two visions."

"That second one floored you, Lilith. It tore me apart seeing you in pain," Elric says resting his forearms on his legs. I am quite struck by how much all this change is affecting him.

"I know it did. But I recovered quickly. I'm not some delicate little creature that needs to be swaddled."

Elric turns and takes my head in his hands. "You are, without doubt, Lilith, the most amazing being I have ever met."

"Elric?"

It's happening.

But he continues talking.

The vision pool rises. I feel it first in the nape of my neck. The tingling rushes like a fast-flowing current upwards, then submerges my cerebral cortex. Just breathe deeply. You can do this. I imagine a watery glaze filling my eyes as he realises.

"Lilith!"

But it's too late. He has to let me go.

Clouds swirl, faces flash in front of me. Faces, I do not know. A thick sound bubbles in my ears, muffling the world around me. I see the face of a human. Female. More advanced in years

28

than myself, but not of elder years. A woman. Cropped blonde hair. Her cocooned body plunges down into a sea of darkness. Not dead, but not living. Preserved? As the only light above her diminishes, I am overwhelmed with a sudden urge to reach it. I push, with every scrap of strength I have. I push up harder and harder, just as Holt told me. It's like swimming against a changing tide. There! Something…a figure. Another human. A girl. Blonde bedraggled locks. Tears swelling in bright green eyes that look through me, fixed only on the descending body. Such pain.

The image flickers like sprites' wings.

The humans vanish.

The vision, now opaque. Dread rushes through my veins. Shapes begin to emerge as the vision becomes clearer. Moving, forming, stretching, they create another figure? Female, for sure. The vision clearer, I see a body writhing in agony. She turns…

"Gaia!"

But does not hear me.

Her face, torn in pain; water droplets form across her brow, then drip down her caramel skin. The fever!

Watery bubbles burst in my ears as the vision spirals from sight…

My lungs inhale the crisp autumn air as I emerge from the vision pool. *Will I ever get used to the feeling of drowning?* Then I register his touch. I feel one arm around my waist as the other cradles my head.

"Lilith! Are you alright?" Elric helps me to my feet, but doesn't let go. I shake off my vision, like an animal shakes off rainwater.

"I am, yes. But...I think Gaia's dying."

CHAPTER FIVE

Earth – Halloween: Hannah
The Whisper

Harriet, her cat-like eyes wide, pulls the sheet up under her chin, her face just visible from a shard of moonlight peeking through velvety curtains. A familiar sense of dread from being woken in the middle of the night seizes me. I wonder if Harriet feels the same. That night, now, feels like a century ago. *Was it really just a couple of days?*

"Is that you, Jack? I demand an answer!" Harriet's exclamation interrupts my thoughts. She pushes her knuckles into her eyes, rubbing hard. I do that, too and Mum always told me off for it.

"Mum," I whisper. Even saying the word stings my lips.

It's hard to breathe when I remember.

Harriet, brow furrowed, calls out, "Jack, I'm warning you. I know it's you teasing, you monstrous rat! And when I tell Father, he'll leather you for certain."

"Who's Jack?" I ask, not daring to take my eyes off Harriet, who remains statue-still.

"Her elder brother. Constance, their sister, is the eldest. She'll be almost sixteen years of age or thereabouts."

I would have loved a sister. In fact, I would have loved a brother, too.

Evelyn's children.

31

Where is she?

Did she survive?

Questions hang like coat tails and I can't shake them off. Gran promised that we would find Evelyn, no matter what.

"It's not Jack, is it?" I ask.

"No," begins Gran. "It's Lilith. It looks like she's been the one assigned to protect Harriet."

I remember hearing her name being mentioned. And I remember by whom: *Galtonia*. That traitor! That witch!

My stomach churns – a bubbling cauldron of emotions. One, stronger than the rest. *Breathe*. I won't let that feeling burn me. Maybe now being an Empath like Gran means I can just calm myself down.

"Shh, listen…" she says, but I can't hear anything. Harriet clearly has though.

"H-a-r-r-i-e-t," echoes the whisper. "I'm in the Hollow Tree."

More familiar feelings gallop towards me on the back of the whisper. If I wasn't already sitting on a stump, those feelings would have put me well and truly on my backside.

NLR. NLR. NLR.

"Hannah, what do you mean 'NLR'?"

That 'ability' of hers to hear my thoughts never seems to fail.

"Well?" she prompts.

"It stands for No Lavender Required."

As Gran sniggers to herself, I wonder if Harriet's feeling the way I did when I heard a voice call out to me...flashes of the car spinning...Mum screaming...glass shattering. *Stop*!

Whoever called out to me, their voice wasn't gentle like Lilith's. How can Harriet think that's Jack?

"Gran, what is it with you supernatural types? All this echoing, chanting, projecting, whispering you do. You know that little metal gadget that Joyce offered to buy you recently? I'm going to get you one of those."

"We are a rather dramatic bunch, aren't we?"

"Just a bit."

"And point taken, re: the mobile."

"Embrace the tech, Gran. Open your hand to it."

She rolls her eyes, as I tuck my feet up to the side and lean back on her.

"I know it's you, Jack!" Harriet hisses pulling back the covers. I wonder if I can feel her, like I did Gran.

"So, what's the switch then, for the empath powers? I mean, how does it work?"

"This one is fairly easy. It's all about concentration."

"Isn't everything?" I groan and can't help but roll my eyes.

"Yes, so shush! Focus-"

"Using a synonym for 'concentrate' doesn't make it better y'know," I smirk.

Gran arches her eyebrow as high as possible. "Focus," she repeats, "on who it is you want to reciprocate with, and then imagine almost drinking in their energy so you can taste it. When you want to affect their energy, you pour whatever it is that *they* need into *them*. Does that make sense?"

"How do I *pour*, though?"

Uncomfortable on the stump, I slide down on the mossy carpet and rest my back against it, instead. Just as Gran is about to answer my question, Harriet moves to the window, pulling one of the curtains back inviting the rest of the moonlight in. I have a feeling the whisper will return.

Gran shuffles onto the floor beside me, leaning to massage her ankle. I push my fingers through the moss, which is so soft I want to rub my cheek against it. Disturbed, Alpha pads around before curling up underneath the hanging vision.

"Gran, can you sense Harriet's feelings like you can mine?"

"Yes, it's faint because of the time lapse."

Time lapse. Of course!

Maybe that's why I can't feel Harriet.

"She's furious. I'm sensing a lot of sibling tension there."

"So she really does think it's Jack playing a joke, doesn't she?"

Gran nods.

With the moon's pearl-coloured glow now filling Harriet's bedroom, I take in her surroundings and, well, her. Long, loose dark curls. *Unlike me.* And she's definitely about eight years old. Harriet's long cotton nightgown skirts her ankles. Pretty lace decorates the cuffs and collar. In the centre of Harriet's bedroom is an enormous four-poster bed covered in heavy looking red and brown quilts. The walls are lined in mahogany panels. I realise the room looks almost identical to the one that Evelyn took us into to perform her Light Keeper's spell.

Weird to think that's Windsor House.

How can the past still be living?

"What year is it, Gran? I mean, in Harriet's time?"

"Well, without checking a newspaper, I can't be accurate, but based upon how old Harriet looks, I'd say around 1820, 1821."

Harriet wraps a cream shawl around her shoulders, then laces her boots before edging her door open. She slips through the gap and pads lightly down the hallway pausing to listen at a set of double doors. Maybe it's Evelyn's room. *She saved my life. I have to know she's okay.*

No way! Is she really going to? Throwing one leg over the

35

bannister, Harriet glides silently down and down the two-tiered balcony, pushing herself as it levels out. *I wanna do that.* I can, actually – when we go back to Windsor House for Mum. Slowing at the bottom, Harriet dismounts the thick oak bannister.

"She's like a jockey or a little ninja."

"More like an isherbird, I think," Gran replies.

"An isherbird?"

"Yes, if you could cross, let's say the furious speed of a kingfisher, with the wiles and stealth of a cougar, but compact it into a creature larger than, say, a dormouse, but smaller than a guinea pig, well, you'd have an isherbird. And it has wings, of course."

I honestly can't picture an isherbird and I lost the plot with what it has to do with Harriet, who is now at the foot of the stairs. Then it dawns on me where she is standing. My eyes dart to the floor and fix upon the ruby-coloured rug under Harriet's feet. Anger flicks my chest. *Doesn't she realise?* Beneath the mauve floral centre piece lies the pentagram under which Mum is buried. My breathing becomes shallow as I'm overwhelmed with a sudden urge to rush towards the portal and crawl through it. I suck in air instead of the liquorice root, which falls from my grasp.

Mum!

I bolt towards the entrance, but it doesn't open. Balling

my fists, I beat against the tree's walls.

"Let me out." *I can't do this.*

Alpha darts to my side, tugs on my jumper. "Let go!"

But she doesn't. She rears up, flashing amber fur, her paws pushing into my stomach, forcing me back. I stumble. For the second time in as many days, Gran sweeps me up, only this time she's not a ghostly projection of herself.

"Remember, Hannah, your mother isn't in there. Harriet doesn't realise because she doesn't know. And your mother is under *our* Windsor House in *our* time, not hers."

Lavender definitely required.

I rest my forehead against Gran's chest. Alpha's wet snout nudges my hand. It's kind of comforting to know that she will protect me even from myself, as well as draconites and the like.

Now by the door, Harriet slides the iron bolt back, checking behind for any hint of movement. Lifting the latch, she edges through the gap in the doorway whipping a flat cap from the mahogany dresser as she passes out into the stillness of night.

"What happens now?" I ask twisting Mum's ring around my middle finger.

Vrroomph.

The vision through the hollow rotates, blurring everything until it repositions our view, like a cameraman resetting a shot. It takes a moment for the vision to focus and settle, leaving me with that just-stepped-onto-a-boat feeling. *Need to get my sea legs.*

"Is that normal, Gran?"

"You'll get used to it."

Doubt that.

Harriet now stands at the foot of the Hollow Tree bathed only in moonlight. I'm tempted to turn as if she should be standing outside here, just a few feet away.

"J-Jack?" she whispers into the small crevice then looks back towards the house.

"Gran, I think I can feel her. She's nervous."

Hesitating, Harriet places her hand against the coarse bark of the crevice, which shudders and expands.

"Harriet's never been inside the tree, has she?" I ask.

"It doesn't look that way."

As Harriet leans to listen, the bark under her hand gives way. She stumbles. "Oomph."

The vision surges forward. Alpha rises and growls at the portal, her hackles pulse from olive to amber. I rush towards the portal wanting to pick Harriet up and dust her off, but someone has beaten me to it.

CHAPTER SIX
Family Ties

Lilith pulls Harriet up under her elbows then guides her to one of the scattered stumps. I smooth Alpha's hackles down as she sniffs the edges of the portal.

"It's okay, girl."

At least I hope it is.

I glance back trying to work out which one of the stumps it was she had sat upon all those years ago. But, then I wonder, even though this happened like, 200 years ago, I'm watching it now. *Headache.* I guess it's like us seeing stars in the sky that don't exist anymore.

"Have you hurt yourself?" asks Lilith, her face catching in the rays of moonlight that seep from between the branches at the highest point inside the Hollow Tree. Her skin, like almond milk contrasts with her warm olive eyes. Around her shoulders rest swathes of russet-coloured hair which cascade down past her waist. It's as if the sunrise is painted into every strand. She looks so familiar somehow.

Lilith wraps the fallen shawl around Harriet's shoulders to keep her warm against the October chill. It's probably as chilly there as it is here. *Or, should that be 'then' and 'now'?*

"I am perfectly well, I thank you. I don't mean to be impolite, but who are you?" begins Harriet.

I feel a sudden tinge of nerves, unsure if they're mine or hers.

"Forgive me. My name is Lilith," she says before stepping forward, pulling her lemon-coloured robe back around her shoulders.

"How did you get inside the tree?" Harriet asks.

"Have you never stepped foot inside it?"

I hate it when people answer a question by asking one.

"No. I climb it almost every day, but I was not aware I could crawl inside it. I have never seen any sort of entrance."

Gran looks at me, raising an eyebrow. "Evelyn," she mouths.

Why would Evelyn stop Harriet playing inside the Hollow Tree?

"If you'll excuse me, I must return to the house," says Harriet about to stand, but Lilith takes Harriet's hand in hers.

"Before you do, I must share a confidence with you. That's if you will hear me and excuse the manner of our meeting."

Harriet pulls her hand away.

"Your mother and I are close acquaintances," adds Lilith quickly. "Has she never spoken of me?"

"No. Not once."

Harriet stares at Lilith and I imagine a deluge of questions overwhelming her as they did with me. I may not look like Harriet, but from that expression on her face, the one that says 'I'm calculating things', I have a feeling we're quite alike.

"May I ask *how* you and Mama are acquainted?"

"We grew up together."

Lilith's silky voice reminds me of someone. Joyce, perhaps?

Whilst listening to the insanely polite conversation bouncing back and forth between Lilith and Harriet, one question is marching towards me faster than all the rest.

"Gran, *what* is Lilith exactly?"

She hesitates and Alpha's head turns ever so slightly towards her releasing a feint rumble. *What does that mean?*

"Just wait. Listen. Let Lilith explain herself," she replies, moving to the other side of Alpha, who rotates her ears like sound-seeking satellites, whilst keeping her eyes fixed firmly on the main show unfolding in front of us.

"You're very beautiful!" Harriet exclaims.

I smile, liking her boldness.

"And so are you," Lilith replies, her cheeks flushing. "Your elder sister is very beautiful, too, I imagine."

"Everyone thinks Constance is beautiful. She will be betrothed in no time at all I imagine. I think Captain Pennington's eldest son has designs on her. Have you met my brother?"

"No. I have not had the pleasure, yet."

"Well, I wouldn't say meeting Jack was any sort of pleasure," Harriet sniffs. "He's a hobbledehoy, but once he grows up, I am sure he will become a gentleman like Father."

"I look forward to meeting him, but Harriet, I must explain why I have come. It is very important and I don't have much time."

"Shouldn't you speak to Mama?" asks Harriet.

"Not just yet. I felt it best to speak to you directly. I hope you can forgive me."

"Gran, why doesn't Lilith want Evelyn to know yet?" I wonder.

"Evelyn wishes to protect her children," replies Gran.

"Is that why Harriet couldn't get inside the Hollow Tree?"

Gran nods. "You're learning fast."

I glance down at Alpha who still hasn't settled and it worries me. If a silverback fox is on high alert, then why isn't Gran?

"What is it that Lilith actually wants though? I don't understand," I say hoping Gran will explain what on Earth is going on.

"Hannah, do you remember the car journey down to Windsor House?"

Gran reads my expression – eyebrow arched.

How could I forget?

"Yes, yes. Of course, you remember. Well, I'll be more specific then. Do you remember me mentioning the Elementals?"

I do.

The conversation floods back to me, but it wasn't the one from the car. I hate to repeat her words, but …

"Now, *that* expression," Gran begins, "is telling me you've remembered. So tell me, because I am doing my utmost to stay out of your private thoughts."

I'm thankful for that.

"And?" she asks.

"Galtonia," I spit. "She said it. At the nursing home, before the Typhon attack," I continue. "I remember now. Galtonia said it was Evelyn's children who were the elemental heirs."

My stomach plummets like a lift that's had its cable cut. I clutch it. Alpha stands and circles me. My hand trails across her back steadying both our nerves.

"Gran, what's going on?"

"It looks like Lilith has been assigned to protect Harriet. I assume Althea and Elric will be waiting to hear from her."

"Protect Harriet from who? Galtonia? The High Council?"

"Yes. Probably both. Harriet, indeed, all of the Elementals are in danger. We suspect Harriet because she is the youngest and perhaps the most vulnerable. A fledgling to be picked off which is why she must be protected. Lilith is the obvious choice to be her guardian."

Gran turns away unexpectedly.

What is she hiding?

"Tell me the truth, Gran."

"Evelyn will try to stop them. She doesn't want to risk her children," she says.

"Of course she'll stop them hurting her children."

"No. She wants to stop Lilith, Althea and Elric from taking her children to Gaia. It doesn't matter that they are the Elementals called upon. Evelyn will do everything she can to stop them being used to prevent a climate war."

War?

"That's a good thing isn't it? It's what mothers do. Protect their children from harm, no matter what?"

Gran casts a glance in my direction, then looks through the portal at Lilith.

"Think about it. Harriet, Jack and Constance each carry specific elemental gifts and those gifts are needed now as are yours. Gaia is still dying, Hannah. What do you think will happen to us if she does? And..."

"What?"

"You won't like it..."

Alpha stands and growls. I suspect she knows, somehow, what *it* is.

"Lilith is explaining to Harriet. Listen."

"Have you never heard of us?" says Lilith.

"Well, I can't say that I have, no. I mean, I have heard of fairies, but everyone knows they aren't real. But I've never heard of…what did you say you were, again?"

"A spirit of the forest. Our species are known as dryads."

Dryad?

I'm going to be sick!

I hear Harriet's voice, as I try to focus. "So you protect forests and all nature. Truly?"

Protector?

I want to spit the word out. My breathing quickens as I fight against a fountain of rage rising quickly from the darkest depths of my stomach.

"Hannah, calm down," says Gran.

I ignore her. "Lilith is a dryad?"

Gran grabs my shoulders. I smack her hands away. "You knew!"

"She is nothing like Galtonia. I promise."

"How do you know that? This is a trap. Galtonia failed to kill me and now, suddenly Lilith, another dryad, appears in the middle of the night seeking out Harriet. And you don't think that's strange?"

I move closer to the portal, desperation twitching in my legs.

"No, I trust Lilith."

"But you trusted Galtonia!"

"I admit I was wrong in that instance, Hannah, but I have known Lilith all her life. She is not directly related to

Galtonia through blood. You cannot tar her with the same brush, as the saying goes. That is unfair."

"What's unfair is that you lied to me."

"I didn't lie. I just never revealed the truth."

"Like that's different! And now Harriet's in danger! Even Alpha knows it."

She whimpers and places herself between me and Gran as if Gran is suddenly a threat. Ridiculous, of course, but I am grateful for her loyalty.

"Stand down, Alpha," orders Gran, but she doesn't.

"Stand down, girl," I say and immediately Alpha slides to the ground holding her Sphinx-like position and remains between me and Gran. Her coat – a deeper shade of amber now – tells me that she is anything but relaxed.

"Harriet is not in danger. Lilith is here to protect her. The Elementals need protection."

"We need to find Evelyn and tell her. She has a right to know."

That's if she's even alive.

"Yes, of course she has a right. I agree with you entirely, but we must allow Lilith some time. After all, you fought your mother for my sake to allow me to protect you."

"But you're my grandmother for Heaven's sake. Lilith is a dryad. They can't be trusted."

"*They*?" she scolds. "I won't accept that sweeping

statement from my own flesh and blood. Don't ever say that again! Do you understand, Hannah?"

I shrink back suddenly six-years-old again, ashamed of myself. I get it. I get Gran's point. But something inside me fears for Harriet's life. I'm not wrong. Alpha isn't wrong. Since I received Gaia's gifts as her heiress – the ones meant for Mum – I feel things I never have before. *I am not wrong.* There is a threat here. I know it!

"I'm sorry, Gran, but I'm going through the portal."

"You can't just chuck yourself at it, you know."

Oh.

"You expect me to trust you. Now, I'm asking you to trust me."

"I will. I do. I do trust you, Hannah. But just allow Lilith a fraction of time to explain to Harriet why she is here."

"Why do you trust her so much?"

"I have my reasons."

"And are you going to explain those reasons or do I have to guess?"

"You sound like your mother."

"Good!" I snap, but immediately regret it. Sometimes, just sometimes, the brat in me wins out. 'Sorry' I mouth.

Detecting the energy shift in me, Alpha returns to the hollow to keep watch over Harriet. I wonder if she can get through if I can't.

"Stay right there, Alph," I say. She doesn't turn, but her ears twitch then angle back once more. *Good girl.*

Gran strides over, huffing but still pulls me into her chest wrapping her huge shawl around the both of us. *I'm forgiven.* We face the hollow lingering for a while. I continue to fight the urge to rush to Harriet and protect her. *I know I could protect her.*

"That's very admirable, Hannah, but not yet."

"Didn't take you long to visit again, did it?" I ask as Gran's voice circles my mind.

"I was moved to. By this desire of yours to protect. That is why you are Gaia's heiress. The instinct you hold is beyond any force I have ever felt before, especially in one so young."

"Really?" I ask, pulling back from her, pressing the back of my hand against my flushed cheeks. *But I'm just a girl. A Yorkshire girl, of course, but...* A faint chuckle escapes from Gran. *Still listening, then.*

I just can't wrap my head around all this, though. I mean, I know I've been bestowed with a load of gifts from *the* Mother Nature; gifts I've thought very little about, actually. *I daren't.*

My pulse double-beats sounding like the *da-dum-da-dum-da-dum* of a high speed train. I try to focus through the moss-green mist that's descending. Then I feel her. Not Gran. Alpha. She brushes my side and lets the weight of her

48

body press against me. I lean down nuzzling my face into her fur inhaling her scent, spiced-oranges, frankincense and figs, like Christmas. *Mum's favourites.*

"Okay. You're right. You do deserve the truth so I shall explain," Gran begins. "There is a very particular reason I trust Lilith so much. Firstly, there are very few creatures left in either world whose soul emanates light like Lilith's does and that, in itself, would be reason enough for any native of Gaian to trust utterly and completely. But, there is another reason. A more personal one."

She pauses.

"The reason I trust Lilith is because I am her guardian. Humans would call her my goddaughter."

CHAPTER SEVEN
Infærald

"Seriously?"

I stare with a sort of blank expression that I can actually feel on my face.

"That question is ridiculous. Of course I am serious! I really don't understand why people have taken to using that phrase. It feels like no-one trusts anyone to speak an initial truth anymore. Yes, for all intents and purposes Lilith is my goddaughter."

I swallow the apple-sized lump in my throat. "So, *your* goddaughter has been sent to protect your grandmother?"

"Who better than family to protect family?"

"Depends on the family."

"That is, unfortunately, true. Certainly these days," replies Gran with a sort of sympathetic nod in my direction. She means Dad. I realise that he has no idea what's happened, either to me or Mum. Not that he would care about her. Or me, anymore. We went from being his *everythings* to his *nothings*.

I guess Lilith protecting Harriet makes sense. Not that I can actually understand how that works with the time lapse. Does it change how I feel about Lilith? I don't know. She's a dryad. But, she's Gran's goddaughter just as much as I am her granddaughter. All I know is that I can't shake

50

this...this...tarpaulin-sized blanket of distrust that's set up camp in my gut.

"Infærald," Gran says.

What?

"I'm demonstrating the fact that I trust you, too," she continues. "It means 'enter' should you feel the need to chuck yourself through the portal," she adds as her eyebrow vanishes under her hairline.

"Inf...inferrold?"

"In-fair-rald. Your pronunciation needs a little practise."

Infær...Infærald. I'm so going to just smack right into the hollow rebound like, well, something that rebounds.

"Got it," I lie. "And thanks. I think Mum says that's 'quid-pro-something.'"

"Quo. As in Status."

I have no idea what Gran's just said, but 'quo' sounds right.

Huh!

A sudden blaze of crimson flashes past me.

"Alpha!"

She lunges at the portal letting out a piercing, thin howl.

"Alph, what is it?" I say, spinning round and darting to her side as she rears up, hackles high, fur spiked like lightning conductors. She paws and scratches at the edge of the portal as if trying to climb up through it.

"I feel it, too," gasps Gran as she dashes to Alpha's side and places her hands on Alpha's temples. *Is she trying to read her mind?*

I look from Alpha to Gran, then through the hollow at Lilith who stands and, as if someone has flicked the lights off, stumbles around, her arms out-stretched.

"What's the matter?" cries Harriet. "What are you doing?"

Harriet stands and takes a step back from Lilith, whose body is convulsing, but in slo-mo, like she's under water, her lemon robes fanning out like lapping waves. I clutch my chest as a shower of fear pours down over me. It's not my fear but Harriet's that drenches me. She retreats from Lilith's suspended body and slams herself against the tree wall. Harriet's eyes scan her surroundings, searching for the exit.

"What's going on?" we chorus, her cry echoing mine across a distance two centuries long.

Alpha shakes Gran's hands from her head, turns and snaps her wide jaws shut, canines ripping a hole in my jumper. She drags me forward.

"She wants us to go through, Gran. We have t-"

"Hannah!" she screams as my knees buckle.

Help...me...

Icy shivers pulsate through my body swamping my senses as I vomit a fountain's worth of water. More retching. Water

52

spurts from my mouth, dribbling down my chin. Doubling over, I gasp for air.

"*Gran*!"

One hand clutches my wrist, as her other wraps around my waist, pulling me up. It takes every ounce of energy I have to remain on two feet.

I'm drowning!

"Hold on, Hannah!" Gran cries, as I clutch her gown.

What's happening to me?

The salty taste makes the vomiting worse. Over and over – water pooling around my feet – I double over again and again. This time, Gran pulls my arm up and over her shoulders keeping me upright.

"*Make it stop*! *Please*!"

"INFÆRALD!" cries Gran.

Our bodies launch up instantly into the air, like two stones catapulted from a slingshot. Gran's clutch tightens as I throw my free hand to my face expecting the vision to shatter as we hurtle towards the portal. It ripples upon impact, passing straight through. Startled by sudden swathes of heat engulfing us, I gasp between sobs and vomit. A blast of cool air hits as we emerge and begin to fall.

"Argh...Uff!"

Something cushions my landing, but the jolt forces

a tidal wave of water to erupt from my mouth, soaking Alpha, whose fur – now flashing between blood-orange and aquamarine – soothes the sting of prickly heat. A reaction of some sort?

Sliding off Alpha, I roll over onto my knees, I suck in air as fast as my lungs will let me, at the same time hearing another's gasp.

Harriet?

Through glazed eyes I try to find her.

"You're okay, sweetheart. You're going to be fine," Gran says, rubbing my back. "It's over. It's over."

How does she know?

But then I realise it's the empath gift and feel like the tide has turned and is no longer heading straight up my throat. I wipe my mouth with my jumper, but realise it's soaked from the sea of watery vomit which clings to my chest under the weight of the sodden wool.

"What…*was*…that?" I wheeze.

Gran, kneeling at my side, gives me the once over. "I've never seen anything like that before, Hannah." She hesitates. "I don't know, but I think it has something to do with being an Empath and what's just happened to Lilith."

"If that's…what being an Empath is…then thanks, but no thanks. Take it back!"

"That's…not possible," comes a voice.

I glance and am met with bright olive eyes.

Lilith.

Her body is close and I realise she's resting her hand on my knee, both of us on the floor, panting still.

"A gift once bestowed…it's like those water-filled eyes of yours, Hannah. Bestowed by your mother, I imagine. Or, a child with a talent for piano, gifted by parents or a higher power. Not something that can be…"

"Returned to sender?"

Lilith smiles. "Yes, that's very…concise."

"Concise. Yep that's me."

"Gran, what does 'conci…'

"Succinct."

"What's that mean when it's at home?"

"Gets to the point and is brief in doing so."

"Ah, right. Well, I am Yorkshire-born."

Still restless, Alpha, vomit-covered, stands and approaches Lilith, who holds her hand out, fingers down, exactly as all canine introductions should be made. Alpha sniffs, then with a lick of the fingers, turns and sits in the shadows to guard Harriet. *Good girl.*

"Are you feeling better?" Lilith asks.

I nod. "Are you?"

"Thank you, yes," she replies; her eyes smile at me. I half-smile back. My heart is like a flipped coin. Heads for guilt.

Tails for distrust. *I don't know what to feel anymore.*

Gran's listening. She winces at my words, and a tinge of sorrow swings to and fro between us. As Gran pulls herself up onto the nearest memory stump, I remember that we've crossed time into Harriet's hollow tree.

Pressed up against the bark, eyes wide, knees to chest, Harriet's entire body trembles. *Oh my God what have we done?*

I tuck my legs in to kneel up, but Gran presses my shoulder.

"No, no. She's terrified. We're strangers and what she has just witnessed…well."

"Can Harriet even seen us? Hear us?" I ask desperate to go to her, comfort her and tell her she's okay. I'll protect her now. Alpha, too.

"Yes, but she's in shock."

"I have failed," says Lilith, her voice breaking. "Eleanor, what are we to do, if what I saw was true?"

"What did you see?" I ask, without taking my eyes from Harriet.

Silence stretches out between us.

"Gran, don't keep me out of this. I have to know. Trust, remember?" I turn towards her, raising my own damn eyebrow.

"Lilith's vision showed an attack…on Windsor House."

"You mean like the fire? From my dream?"

"No, no. Something quite different."

"Is Evelyn here?" I ask.

"She should be."

"Then we have to warn her, Gran. Hurry!"

I fight the queasiness and pull myself up.

"It might be a trap," suggests Lilith.

Gran stands and walks to the inner wall of Harriet's hollow tree to rest against it. "Give me a minute," she says.

Jockeying for position, Questions One, Two and Three scream at me and I know they won't be ignored for long. But Gran needs a minute. Half of that is left.

Lilith stands and I get the feeling she wants to say something, but I focus only on Harriet. I don't mean to be rude to Lilith. Really, I don't, but I can't stand here waiting for something to happen like at the nursing home. *I refuse to feel that useless again. Especially now. I'm Gaia's heiress. I have to be able to do something.*

"Gran?"

"You're right, Hannah."

Listening again!

"So we stick together and go to the house and get Evelyn. That's if she's even there. Surely the protection spell still works?" I suggest.

"Light Keepers' spells are impervious," says Lilith.

"So, Harriet is safer in Windsor House than in here?"

Harriet rocks back and forth, her eyes fixed on the floor unaware of the large silverback fox just feet away.

"Technically, yes," replies Gran.

"Lilith, what did you see?" I ask.

She looks to Gran, like she's asking for parental permission. *Hate that.* Gran nods.

"Furies. The vision lasted seconds only, though."

Didn't feel like that to me.

"Furies? Like mythological stuff?"

"Yes. Three of them, but that is all I witnessed. Their arrival," replies Lilith. She's worried and I don't have to be an Empath to work that one out.

"Then we stick together and leg-it," I say.

"Agreed. Lilith, I need lavender," Gran says.

"Why?" I ask.

"Because that precious little girl needs her mother now more than ever. Something you well understand, Hannah. But she's in shock and I can't risk triggering a reaction that could put our safety in more danger."

"You're going to knock her clean-out aren't you? Like Joyce did to Mum back at the nursing home."

"Yes."

I turn to Lilith who – being a protector of the forest – can literally pull strands of lavender from her hair. Her fingers twist amongst her long russet locks pulling sprig after sprig of Gran's favourite flower out. Cool.

"I will administer the dose. Lilith, you'll carry her. Hannah, we'll flank either side. Alpha?" calls Gran.

She stands, puffs her chest out and pads towards Gran. "I need you to bring up the rear. Fork formation."

Alpha snuffs in agreement.

Gran crushes the lavender in her fist then blows her warm breath over it, making it more potent, she says. Releasing it into the air, she blows the plume of purple smoke until it settles over Harriet who slumps, powerless against it. Lilith catches Harriet's head, props her up against her knees then gently wraps layer upon layer of her own robes around Harriet's limp body. Finally, cradling Harriet, she lifts her from the ground.

"Positions, ladies," orders Gran.

I move to the left-side of Lilith, Gran to her right and Alpha behind. She nudges me.

"I'm sorry I threw up on you, Alph."

"Yip, yip."

I hope that means I'm forgiven.

I clutch my stomach, taking small shallow breaths and wonder if Lilith is still feeling the nausea like I am.

We face the wall of Harriet's hollow tree – our hollow tree – and approach the exit. Gran nods. 'Do the honours' that means. Stepping forward, I place my hand against the rough bark. *Does it know me?* A long thin crevice snaps and folds in on itself. That'll be a yes, then.

That October chill seeps in as we exit. *It feels like forever since we've felt the fresh air.* It makes me want to run. Scouring the skies, my heart suddenly races as we look and listen for a sign. In the distance, set in the glow of the moonlight, stands Windsor House. *It looks exactly the same.*

Gran's voice suddenly echoes into my mind, and Lilith's too.

"Ladies, can you hear me?"

We both nod and exchange brief glances.

"This is our only line of communication. The quieter the better."

"What can furies do, Gran?"

"Fly. They're strong. Not Typhon strong, but still, powerful enough. They're not impervious, but not easy to wound, either. Oh, and their greatest asset is invisibility."

"WHAT? How on Earth can we beat something we can't see?"

"That's why we stay quiet. We listen for them."

"Call Evelyn. Surely, she can pick you up from here?" I suggest.

"Can't risk her reaction until the last minute, but she'll pick us up soon enough."

"What can I do, Gran?"

"Those chains of white fire of yours will come in handy. Think

you can do it?"

"Hell, yes. If they touch one hair on Harriet's head…"

"That's my girl," Gran says with a wink. *"Now, shh."*

Each footstep brings us closer to home. Closer to Evelyn and safety. The grounds grow more familiar as we retrace our steps back, but not to our Windsor House. This is Evelyn's home now. Gran leads us to the right, away from the canopies of trees. Being out in the open, we can see what's coming. I ball my fists as nerves churn in my stomach and rise up but inhale deeply, swallowing them back down.

Grgh!

A low rumble escapes from behind Alpha's gritted teeth. Warning! I glance down, the sound magnifying as her coat fluctuates between silver and amber.

Crack!

From the gables of Windsor House, hanging Gargoyles burst from their tombs of stone and chorus together in sharp notes that pierce ear drums before fading. Gran holds up her arm for us to stop as she searches the skies. Stomach flip.

"There!" announces Gran glowering. Slicing through the moon's rays which fan out across the open grasslands in front of us, three thin figures sweep downwards, graceful in their landing. Stepping forwards into an arrowhead

formation, grey robes waltzing with the light breeze playing around us, blood-red eyes lock directly with mine.

"Galtonia sends her regards," cackles the first of the furies.

CHAPTER EIGHT

Fury

Witch!

A river of hate bursts its banks and floods my senses. My heart feels as dark as the night sky. It pounds. My body trembles. I do the only thing I can. Run. Right at them. It's as if I have left my body and am watching a rage-filled doppelganger charge down the furies, who stand goading me. They knew exactly what to say. Knew my reaction. She told them. But still, as I'm realising this, I can't stop.

I'll rip them to pieces…No, stop, you idiot. This is what Galtonia wants…But she's the reason Mum's gone…It's a trap…She's the reason Gaia is dying and our worlds are beginning to crumble… Shut up!

Behind me, Lilith screams for me to stop. But it isn't enough. Harriet's limp body isn't enough. Alpha's whimpers aren't enough.

For a moment, I expect a plume of purple mist to engulf me, knocking me out cold, but it doesn't. Gran can't eat *my* dinner for me, I guess. This is something I have to do myself. Send Galtonia a message back – show her what I can do. Wipe the floor with the furies. The first of them stoops like a crooked old woman; I know it's anything but… Stepping forward, it shifts side to side, casting spindly shadows against the waning moonlight which stretch out to meet me; *if only their shadows felt pain, too.* I sprint hard, then leap into the air, higher than I realise is possible. Our bodies slam together, then hurtle to the ground. I smash my fists into fury number one, but it grabs my arms, wrenching them apart. Yanking them free, I grab its arms instead, twisting skin, burning as my grip tightens. I press my whole weight through my knees into its chest. *Hold on!* The fury digs its blunt nails into my wrist forcing me to release my grip. It grimaces then slaps my face. *Ow!* I swear out loud, wincing against the sting. The fury shoves me back, but I react, stretching out to grapple with thick grey straggles of hair from its scalp; clumps hang from my fist as I fall back. I roll away, then scramble up all the time trying to conjure the white fire, but nothing happens. Concentrate! Cackles and wails from the furies echo across the night sky.

Distracted, I turn to see the other two furies, springing from foot to foot. The smallest, a toothless old crone wrapped in a sack-like cloth, rubs its hands together jeering and cackling.

"Kill her now, Tysaph! Kill her now!" it screeches sending a blade of ice down my spine.

"Silence, Alecta! Unless you want me to cut you instead," sneers Tysaph.

Alecta recoils.

Looks like there's a pecking order here.

Suddenly, Tysaph leaps, catching me off guard. It smashes its hands into my chest launching me across the gardens like a skittle struck by a wrecking ball. Argh! Landing hard, clasping my chest against the searing pain, I gasp for air. Hearing Lilith's cries and Alpha's barks, I expect them to appear, but neither do. Nor does Gran. *Why isn't she doing anything?* I pull myself up, but stumble back dizzy with pain, much to the amusement of the furies.

Tysaph's eyes of blood stare at me. A smirk curls from the corner of its mouth. Slowly, almost like some bat-crazed ballerina, it dances towards me. I focus on it, rather than the crushing pain across my chest. I *need* that white fire. I glance at my hands hoping to see a flicker.

"Come on!" I beg, feeling the blue of night closing in on me.

There!

It's starting...

Tysaph pirouettes, then pauses in front of me. Close. Way too close. Its putrid breath stinks. If faces aged likes trees, this fury would be thousands of years old. The warmth of the white fire glows against my skin, brightening, its power building, just like last time. It radiates upwards and I'm not afraid anymore. *My turn to smirk.*

Suddenly, darting forwards snatching my wrist, Tysaph

65

digs dirt-filled nails into my skin again and holds my arm up. I try to yank it away, snarling, but its grip is too strong.

'Not Typhon strong, but still, powerful enough,' echo Gran's words.

"Get. Off. Me."

"From the look in those pretty eyes of yours, you may well be ready to join us!" it begins, its voice sharp, like it could slice apart stone. "I can feel the rage pulsating through your veins. Galtonia was right. You have the power to bring the night crashing down on this Earth of yours and much faster than the rest of your pathetic species is already doing."

My heart plummets…

What?

No!

Her words slam into my gut like a freight train. *I am doing exactly what Galtonia knew I would?* No way! It's my turn to stare it down.

"Like Hell, I will."

"So be it," it replies, lurching forward and smashing its face into mine….

****

Feeling the tickle of something crawling across the back of my hand, I flick my wrist. *Hate spiders.* I peel my eyes open and am greeted by a crowd of stars. *Beautiful.*

As the dew seeps through my clothes and hair, I clutch my forehead registering a wave of pain and the wetness of blood across my eyebrow. I wipe my sleeve across my face, mopping the blood and salty sweat which stings my eyes. A smell that resembles the inside of a bin on a hot day makes my stomach convulse, then I realise there's another fury approaching.

"*Gran? Please,*" I beg, arching my head back to find her. *Why isn't she helping me?*

"Hmm, Hannah. Aren't you a little bundle of rage?" cackles fury number two, the youngest-looking of all three. Her white thread-like hair clings to her scalp and face like she's just walked through a waterfall.

"If I were, I'd be one of you by now, you thick witch!"

"And there's that spark again. What a sharp-tongued little vixen you are? We won't give up on you joining us. You could be s-s-s-o powerful, Hannah." The fury's fork-tongue flickers, the sound of her voice slithers down my spine.

Alpha lets out a shrill howl, but Gran orders her back. *Why isn't she letting Alpha help me, even if she can't?* The fury spits on the floor, scowling at those behind me. Taking advantage of the distraction, I kick my leg out aiming for the back of its knee but the fury reacts grabbing my ankle – piercing its nail through my jeans and deep into my flesh.

Argh! Glee glints in its eyes as it rags a nail down my shin, splitting the skin like a slab of meat under a butcher's knife. *Argghh!*

"Stop it! Stop! Pleeeeease!" But, the more I yank my leg, the deeper the fury presses into my flesh.

"Or what?" it growls, its face wrinkled.

Tears swell in my eyes, fear swells in my gut.

"*GRAN!*"

She doesn't reply.

"*Please Gran!*"

Why isn't she doing something?

Loneliness, the same loneliness that devoured me when Mum was…but before that thought leads me into darkness, a blanket of calmness covers me. She did hear! Then, as fast as a photo-flash, a picture of the draconite I defeated appears like a screenshot in my mind. I see it all but through Gran's eyes. Me, the draconite, Alpha and her pack surrounding it. My mercy. I didn't kill it. I couldn't do it. I'm the heiress to Gaia, the protector of all nature. I didn't do what it, even Gran and Joyce expected me to. The image fades and vanishes. *That's a memory-card.* Must be. 'Chess-move' Gran means. Just like she taught me all those years ago. *Think of a move, then find a better one.*

I try to block the pain. *Think!*

"But why…why…did Galtonia…send you here?" I cry

through gritted teeth.

The pressing of my flesh stops – *thank God* – but the cold rush of blood continues to drain from my shin.

The fury cocks her head – Galtonia-style – to one side, eyes narrowing.

"What does she want?" I ask.

"Little Hannah holds a world's worth of fury inside her. Galtonia felt it in you. I'll offer once more. Join us. Just say the word and it shall be so."

Screw that!

I tense, expecting more pain, but it drops my leg and retreats back to its position behind Tysaph. If my heart wasn't caged by ribs, I'm sure it would burst. I swallow my anger back down. I refuse to be beaten by it but push myself up and turn, limping back to Gran, who is standing in front of Lilith and Harriet, her arms spread out.

"*Lesson learnt?*" asks Gran with such a harsh tone I have to fight the tears and the fears from overwhelming me.

"What lesson? The one where you leave your granddaughter defenceless against three killer witches? Is that the one you mean?"

The furies cackle, pleased with the anger I can't hold inside.

I can't take this. How could Gran let them do that to me?

Tears flood my eyes, my head falls to my chest, but her

hand catches my chin. I look at Gran, but all I can think is, *where are you, Mum?*

Gran's eyes remain locked on the furies. *"Always…"* she begins, then waits for my reply.

"…*hold my head high.*"

"Lilith and Harriet were the primary targets, but they convinced you otherwise. They made their moves like Queens on the board and you became a pawn. Never let that happen again, Hannah."

"So it was a memory-card you sent, wasn't it?"

"It was. And you defeated that draconite with your head, not a rage-filled heart. Here endeth the lesson."

Gran drops her hand then places herself between the furies and us, raising her arms ready to conduct. As a light wind begins to swell, rustling leaves swirl up from the surrounding elder, hazel and ash trees. Gran conducts the leaves into an arc between us and the furies.

"You will not pass," announces Gran.

The third fury, with its stone-like smooth skin and black eyes, steps forwards again kicking at the leaves. Instantly, the line explodes showering it. Cursing loudly it brushes them off as if covered in spiders. *The leaves are protecting us!*

"I can heal that, Hannah," says Lilith with such a soothing tone, it feels like her voice alone could heal the wound. Alpha howls at the leaves' triumph then pads to my side as

70

Lilith rolls my jeans up above the knee, packing my wound with hazel leaves from the floor, holding them a second or two. A tingling sensation begins, then pulling, like the leaf is somehow knitting the wound back together. Lilith removes her hand, and it is exactly as I felt. An imprint from the hazel leaves covers the wound as it fades.

"Thank you."

I look at Gran. *"The furies like to play games. So?"* she says.

"Be the Queen. Like you taught me," I say although I feel very much like a pawn on this board.

"We haven't played chess since you were six years old. Time to practise, I think."

Gran winks, smirks, then takes my hand. The white fire flickers as we face the furies.

"You ladies ready to play?" challenges Gran.

They might be, but am I?

CHAPTER NINE
Evelyn 2.0

I hear *her* voice. Thundering out across the midnight sky. Evelyn. *She's alive! Thank God. In fact, thank Gaia.*

> "I am the Light Keeper. Hear my call.
> Those who trespass, will wither and fall.
> I give you blood, passed into light,
> Protect the sacred through this night."

"Those who trespass will wither and fall," she repeats, clutching a thin candle high in the air, blood trickling down her arm. *That's the line! They're trespassing.*

I begin to surge forward, but Evelyn holds her hand up halting me in my tracks as she descends the stone stairs from Windsor House – like a lioness – stalking the space in between us and the furies. Her deep blue satin gown catches the moon's light. Her dark hair, loose, skirts her waist. Her body is stiff, every step taken with care, ready to pounce.

She made it!

I turn to Gran, clearly as relieved as I am. No Evelyn. No Gran. No me.

Placing herself between us and the furies, Evelyn extends her arm out behind her offering me her hand.

"Hannah, come here," she orders.

I limp to her side. Evelyn doesn't make eye-contact, instead she interlocks her fingers with mine, warming them. She glances down at my leg, the imprint of the hazel leaf still visible and purses her lips.

"Ladies, tell Galtonia if she wants this daughter of daughters, she'll have to face me first!" says Evelyn raising our hands together for a moment.

"Where's the fun in waiting for Galtonia? I might just kill you now!" cackles Alecta wringing her hands, clearly the absolute nut-job of the three.

The jet black eyes of the unidentified fury bore like a drill into Evelyn's.

"Now that, you could never do," says Evelyn, flatly.

Tysaph laughs, then spits, "If only you knew what we knew, Light Keeper, you might not be quite so cocky."

A heartbeat of fear flickers from inside my chest as questions wake from their slumber and begin demanding answers.

"Chant the spell, Hannah. Now!"

"I am the Light Keeper. Hear my call.
Those who trespass, will wither and fall.
I give you blood, passed into light,
Protect the sacred through this night."

73

"Louder!" cries Evelyn.

> "I am the Light Keeper. Hear my call.
> Those who trespass, will wither and fall.
> I give you blood, passed into light,
> Protect the sacred through this night."

Evelyn raises our arms once more, then taking a deep breath, throws a blaze of light towards the furies propelling them high into the air. They slam into something. *The layer of the protection spell? Does it work like that?* Dangling in mid-air they thrash against the shackles of light, spitting vile language at Evelyn, threat after threat. A torrent of white fire rushes through us. I feel it in Evelyn too. *Ice-cold.* Knuckles turn white; but then I see it. The white fire cascades down my arms, glowing and pulsating. *But not from a place of rage or revenge.* Evelyn, circles her arm, then pulls it back like an archer before streaming my white-fire through her body, launching spear after spear upwards to ignite the sky. Dozens of spears pierce the furies' bodies sending them hurtling into the night, far beyond sight.

They're gone. For now, at least.

Our arms drop from the weight of the world. For a second, we stand, just holding hands. I love Evelyn, but how I wish it was Mum's hand in mine. She presses a kiss onto my forehead. *Like Mum. Like Gran.*

"Are you okay? I didn't know if you'd survived after…?" I whisper.

"I'm fine, Hannah. We Light Keepers are built to last."

Lilith rushes to Evelyn, delivering Harriet safely into her arms.

"Thank you. I take it you are the assigned protector?" asks Evelyn.

"Yes. I am Lilith." She lowers her head, almost ashamed to say her name.

"Very well. And who are the others we should expect?"

"Elric and Althea."

"Well, it will be good to have a gryphon with us. And from what I've heard, Althea can always be counted upon."

"Gaia's choices must surely be welcome ones," Gran says glancing across at me with warmth in her smile. *I've missed that.*

"But it is not my choice," begins Evelyn. "And, although I know the command must be obeyed, the elementals are and always will be, *my* children, Eleanor."

"Then you feel as I do," Gran replies. "And thank you again, Evelyn. You seem to be coming to our rescue almost every day."

"We are blood, Eleanor. We *both* have much to protect," replies Evelyn glancing down at Harriet laid across her arms. "Let's get in the house for I fear tonight's battle has only just begun."

"We have a Calling to perform. And truths to be told."

More truths? Ah crap.

"I heard that!" Gran announces loud enough for every creature in the surrounding woodlands to hear.

"I'm allowed to think it. Teenager. Hello."

"I suppose it could be worse," she says before calling Alpha over.

"Will you do the honours...?" But Alpha lowers herself even before Gran completes the question. I climb onto Alpha's back which is weird because she's Shetland-sized not Shire-sized.

I lean forward and whisper into Alpha's ear, "Am I too heavy? If I am, I can walk."

Alpha shakes her head, then yips and nods at Harriet.

"Evelyn, I think Alph's offering to carry Harriet, too."

"Thank you, Alpha, but no. I want her in my arms."

My lip quivers.

Mum.

"Right, home then," orders Gran.

But it isn't home. It's not York. It's not even Yorkshire. I love Norfolk. Always have. Always will, but...not knowing where Mum is...where her soul is splinters my heart.

Are the stars her companions now?

We approach Windsor House. Evelyn's Windsor House. Not *ours*. This is where Harriet lives with her brother and sister. Mum isn't in there. I feel a sudden urge to contact Joyce. Surely, she'll be able to hear me from here?

"Are you alright, Hannah?" whispers Lilith, her hand resting upon Alpha's neck.

"No. No, I'm not."

"Is there anything I can do?"

"Help me get my mum back."

"Why is she not with us?"

"She...she nearly died and now, well, I'm not sure where she is to be honest. Gran interred her body. It's being guarded here at Windsor House, but, well, not this one...I mean...I don't know what I mean."

"Interred, you say?" Lilith keeps walking at our side, but her face is fixed. "Is your mother's hair the colour of straw, like yours?"

I feel slightly miffed by her description, but nod before describing her complexion, hers isn't as pale as mine is, or was though. Whereas I usually look like I've just stepped out of a fridge, Mum's complexion has a warmness to it. Sun damage, she says. But we both have freckles, just across our noses.

"I saw her. Your mother."

"What? What do you mean you saw her? Gran!"

"And you. You were standing above her body as it descended. Crying. I couldn't believe how utterly heartbroken you were by it. I had never felt pain like it, Hannah."

"But, how? I don't understand!"

Gran double-backs, telling us to continue the discussion inside the house.

"There's much to do and our furious little friends will be back. Sooner than we expect, I imagine."

As we approach the house, the large oak door opens and a dark-haired man appears.

"William!" Evelyn calls. "Here," Evelyn adds offering Harriet into his arms.

Pushing his glasses back up on to the bridge of his nose, William rushes forward to take Harriet. Behind him I see two faces appear at the door, but Evelyn orders them back inside as we arrive. *Constance. Jack.* I'll finally get to meet them. *Do they even know who they are? What they are?* And, exactly what the four of us together may have to do?

CHAPTER TEN

Going Under

Constance rushes forward with blankets as William lays Harriet along a sofa in the hallway. The same one I lay on just a few hours ago, but now, of course, it looks brand new. Lifting Harriet slightly, Constance, perching next to her, pushes a cushion under her head, then strokes her brow. Jealousy brews in my gut like black coffee.

Near the foot of the stairs, I notice a boy, raven-haired with a paler complexion than mine. Must be Jack. Next to him, a plumpish woman with thick features and small kindly-looking eyes, dressed in matching white nightcap and gown, pats his hand.

"Mary! Jack! Fetch warm water and cloths," William orders. "Hurry!"

A sudden twinge, like those stitches you get when you run, jabs in my side. I press against the pain, like when you stub your toe.

"Gran, is that Jack I can feel?"

"Yes, I can feel him, too. Although perhaps not as acutely as you are."

Jack throws me a look of suspicion before he vanishes through a doorway with Mary. Charming.

"It is part of being an Empath, dear. Because the emotion you experience is not yours, it feels misaligned. That is how you can

detect the difference."

"You mean like trying to squeeze your foot into someone else's shoe?"

"I suppose so."

"Don't think I'll ever get used to it. It's like I'm a cut-out and his feelings have, well, coloured me in. He feels a sort of indigo. I know that sounds ridiculous, but, that's just how it feels."

"Not ridiculous."

Gran gestures for me to look back at the door. Alpha, hackles high, paces up and down, her coat a deep shade of indigo.

"Gran that's so cool. But I don't get it."

"Alpha has her own feelings, but you two have formed quite the bond. It appears she can reflect what you feel, too."

Love that.

I search for signs of the Windsor House that I know. Electric lights? Plug sockets? Internet hub? Nothing. I imagine a kitchen filled with copper pans and serving hatches. This really is the 1800s.

A sense of alarm seeps through the house, like when the school fire bell's triggered. Everyone hurries, but remains calm, forming lines. Registers taken.

Gran takes William's arm, then whispers something. Evelyn leans close to listen, then nods to Gran. Perhaps she's reassuring them. Crossing the hall, Gran heads over asking Lilith if she's okay.

I whisper, "Don't they know it's just the lavender?"

"Evelyn is letting them fuss. Keeps their minds focused on something they can handle." *As opposed to what they might not be able to handle shortl*y.

Can *I* handle it?

Knowing what's out there…waiting. Knowing that Gaia lies dying still and that it could be *our* fault. Maybe it isn't Galtonia and whichever of those creeps she's working for. I picture the four Lords sitting in the chamber arguing over how to save Gaia, what to do, and wonder which of them has betrayed her…which of them wants her throne…which of them poisoned her. Or, is it us? *If we are killing Gaia, then we're killing ourselves.* Panic hits me like I've stepped into quicksand with nothing to hold on to…

Huh!

"Hannah!" gasps Lilith seizing my wrist. Her stare fixed as she begins to fall…

"No, Lilith! Don't! Don't!" I grapple against her handcuff-like grip.

But it's too late.

All the light in the world fades…my body weakens as she pulls me under…

CHAPTER ELEVEN

Lilith
Unbreakable

Only the sound is familiar. Thick bubbles burst as I try to regulate my breath. I am not drowning, but it's hard to convince myself of that.

Opening my eyes, I realise where I am. Windsor House. Still on the stairs. Everything is discoloured, fragmented like broken glass. I scan the scenes looking for clues. Where is everybody? As I move, my fingertips brush her cool skin.

Hannah!

Grabbing her shoulders, I shake her.

Wake up!

But she doesn't. Maybe she can't.

No! Wait!

A pulling sensation vibrates through my body as the vision spins away. No! Hannah slips through my grasp. I try to fight it, but can't stop the room from becoming a kaleidoscope. My stomach churns until the vision settles.

Still lain across the seat, Harriet remains in the induced state Eleanor put her in. Mary, Jack and Constance tend her with cold compresses and concern. I shout out to them, but they can't hear me, of course. I know they can't, but still I try. Glancing round, I note the absences. No Evelyn, nor William or Eleanor. Where are they?

A sudden burst of light blinds me. Shielding my face until it fades, I feel the rushing of warm water around my cerebral cortex once more. Bubbling and gurgling, the vision spins, waves of nausea ripple through me. Ugh! I've never experienced a vision like this!

Please stop!

My body craves a stillness. An end to these feelings. A line of sweat trickles down my neck as eventually the vision grinds to a halt. I stretch out, reaching for anything to steady myself. Gripping the gravelled bannister which runs the length of the steps from Windsor House tightly, I stare out across the grounds as my eyes adjust. Blasts of light crack and fire across the night, stars vanish momentarily, before the darkness devours us again. I realise the vision has answered my question.

But that's impossible! How have they got through? No-one can break a Light Keeper's protection spell! Unnerved by the realisation that Evelyn's gift is not impervious, I grip the bannister once more with both hands; head spinning.

Between the rows of evergreens, two of the furies dance between blasts of light from Eleanor, goading her, tormenting her. Why don't they retaliate? Each fury swerves and ducks, but neither attacks. Tysaph darts from left to right, a moving target for Evelyn's orbs of light. Diversion! That's it!

Across the garden, William struggles with Megaera, the black-eyed fury. Knocking him across the grounds, it stalks towards him, but Evelyn darts across the clearing, leaving Tysaph temporarily blinded. The fury screeches and vows revenge before stumbling to the ground, but Evelyn doesn't look back. Megaera stands over William, poised to strike, but notices Evelyn charging towards her. Megaera, still holding her arm aloft, pulls it back as if to strike, but Evelyn stops, wags her finger and shakes her head menacingly slow. Megaera's eyes flick from Evelyn to William, who lies cowering. From the waistband of her satin gown, Evelyn pulls a dazzling diamond encrusted thread – the sharpest material in existence – and binds it around one hand before flicking her wrist to crack the air between them. Megaera flees, but Evelyn is fast. The thread, like a whip, flies out lashing the fury down its spine, tearing its flesh. Megaera falls. From the look on Evelyn's face, it is she who's the fury now. Taking each end of the diamante whip, Evelyn binds it around both hands and approaches Megaera, lowering herself over its body. It twitches and jerks, stunned by the pain, perhaps shocked at its own mortality then Evelyn wraps the chain around its neck…

Remember this.

Everything I see can be used against them.

"Lilith!" echoes a voice.

Hers is so distinct…"Hannah!"

I try pushing back towards the house to reach her, forcing the vision to bend to my will, but it fights back.

"Let me see her!" I call out, desperation filling my chest.

"Lilith! Wake up! We need you!"

Catapulting me forwards, air whistling, the vision blackens, shrouding me in darkness. Slowly, it reveals the entrance to Windsor House once more, illuminated by only a handful of candles. Through it, I see Hannah's body remains still and silent, Alpha curled around her. But, how did Hannah do that? I know it was her. I replay her words, all the while staring at her lifeless body. It was her…wasn't it?

A blast of ice hits suddenly, chilling every fibre of my being and every atom of air surrounding me. Breath billows out. As the plumes fade, a shadow emerges in the distance. A spectre, hanging as if impaled to the wall. Slowly, the hooded figure emerges from the shadows, but they don't see it.

"No! No! Constance, move!" I scream, but it's no use.

Alpha, her coat flashing every shade of red imaginable, hackles high, howls as the building begins to creak and shudder. Jack turns. Seeing the figure, he screams. It descends. Alpha leaps, jaws wide, teeth bared, but the figure strikes the silverback fox in its chest with the hilt of its sheathed blade. Alpha hurtles across the room crashing into the dresser sending candles flying; plates shatter against walls.

How will I remember all this?

How can we prepare for such an attack?

The figure lurches forward striking Jack. Taking the force of it across his fear-filled face, Jack hurtles to the floor. Seeing the shrouded figure unsheathe its black blade, Mary throws herself in front of Constance whose face hangs in horror. Mary's cry splinters my heart as the towering figure, now anchored to Mary's body, leans forward a little, inspecting the damage inflicted. Hateful creature! Then, as it extracts the blade from Mary's body, Constance lurches forward catching her, collapsing under her weight.

This is a vision!

This is a warning!

Constance's screams tear through the house as Eleanor and Evelyn appear at my side. Rushing past me, their pained cries pierce my heart. I remain unseen.

"Lilith! Wake up! Wake up!"

How can this be? Hannah? Through the tears, I see her, standing right in front of me, shaking me just like I shook her, plunging me once more into the vision pool...

My lungs scream for breath, stinging with the pain. Never have I been submerged for such a time. My legs falter, but Hannah's grip is strong, hot against my skin. Despite her efforts, I slump to the floor.

"Why wouldn't you wake up?" Hannah cries.

"The visions. I can't control them, at least, not much. I tried."

Breathe.

"You're too late!"

"What?"

I register the anguish on her face as the wails and sobs begin to surround me. I glance over to see Mary's dead body. Constance clutches her blood-stained nightgown. Jack, dazed, rocks back and forth, his legs curled into his chest. William, paler than death itself, sits clutching Mary's hand.

"It was a vision. This can't be real. It can't be."

"The vision was too late! You were too late!" screams Hannah.

Eleanor takes my arm as the reality of what has happened dawns. "Did you see all this, Lilith?"

"Yes. You were outside battling the furies."

"Did you see...*what happened?*" Eleanor, her voice, like a flat, calm ocean casts her eyes down at Mary.

"Yes. Yes! But I don't understand. It was a vision. It isn't meant to have happened yet."

"Well it *has* happened!" cries Evelyn. William, immediately places Mary's hand across her chest, then rushes to his wife. Wrapping his arms around her waist, he lifts her as her limbs lash out, forcing her back, before pinning her to the wood-panelled wall.

"Not now. Not in front of the children," William urges, but Evelyn pushes back, enraged, thrashing against his attempt at control.

"Eleanor, please," I beg. "I don't understand."

This isn't my fault.

Taking my hand, Eleanor leans closer and whispers, "Then tell me, Lilith, who has taken Harriet?"

CHAPTER TWELVE

Hannah
Black Blade

Lilith stands trembling, staring at Gran in disbelief.

"Taken?"

"Yes. Harriet has been…," Gran hesitates "…snatched."

The word 'snatched' triggers Evelyn's guttural cry and it's enough to shatter hearts and glass. William whispers something into her ear over and over, cradling her head. I choke back tears. First Mum, then Mary. And now Harriet. Gone.

"Mary was so brave," begins Lilith. "She threw herself in front of Constance." Streaks of dried tears run the length of Constance's cheeks as she cradles Jack, still sobbing quietly. Creeping across the distance between them and me like a murky fog, I inhale their sorrow which settles on my chest. I bend, resting my hands on my thighs overwhelmed by its weight. Like receptors on a flower, I open up and try to shower them with calm, but I can't feel it myself, so how on Earth am I meant to get them to feel it. *What good is this gift if I can't use it to help others?*

"And? What else? I need you to tell me everything you saw in that vision," demands Gran.

"I didn't see Harriet get snatched. The vision focused on Mary being…being…"

"Murdered!" cries Constance. Shocked at her own outburst, she clasps her hand to her mouth, rocking in tandem with Jack who remains shell-shocked, his stung cheek still flushed.

"It was the hooded figure. It struck Jack, then turned on Constance, and..."

"Did you see what the figure looked like? Anything, Lilith? Any detail at all that can give us a clue as to who has taken her, although I already have my suspicions."

"Diversion. I remember seeing you battle the furies, but it was like they were playing a game. And I remember thinking it was a diversion of sorts."

"So the hooded figure could attack at precisely the right time. What else? Please be specific because Evelyn's spell was incredibly powerful and Light Keepers' spells are impervious. I don't understand how furies broke through it."

Lilith stares down at Mary's body. "We aren't safe. We need Elric and Althea. Immediately. I know you said that it is *we* that should perform the Calling, Eleanor, but I don't agree. Jack and Constance need protection." Lilith's voice cracks. "Now...more than ever. Oh! Poor, Mary!" sobs Lilith. "She was so...br...brave. I hate knives. They cut life-"

"What did you say?" asks Gran.

"The hooded figure. It had a blade."

"Describe it." Gran's tone is almost as sharp as a blade itself.

"A jewelled hilt. I've never seen anything like it before. And it had a black blade."

Gran rushes forward, grabbing Lilith. "You're absolutely sure the blade was black?"

"Yes! Yes!"

"Then Gaia's fears have been borne out," she says exhaling deeply.

"What do you mean, Gran? And why's a black blade worse than any other blade?"

I'm suddenly plunged into a bubbling cauldron and cannot tell whose feelings are whose. It's like we are all drowning in fear. Alpha, her coat undulating black and red, leans into me, propping me up. Gran flashes me a look.

*Keep it together. I need you...*it says.

"There are only four black blades in existence. Carved in the fires of Vulturia. Bound in blood to their masters."

Four blades. Four masters.

"So it really is one of the High Council? One of the Lords that Galtonia is working with?" I ask.

"Working *for*. She's a pawn in their game, that's all. Whichever Lord it is, wants Gaia dead. And now that traitor has Harriet, an Elemental. Without her, Gaia won't survive."

"Where are the furies?" I ask.

"They vanished. One minute, there. The next, gone," replies Lilith.

"But that's what they do. Become invisible. So they could still be here, hidden amongst us. Listening. Spying."

"No, the gargoyles would have alerted us. And Evelyn's spell still stands, only now, it has one thin slit in its fabric. A point of weakness. We are all at risk. Our only warning system is the gargoyles and Alpha, of course."

"Yip, yip," acknowledges Alpha in her own special way, before whipping her thick tail as if she's ready to strike any further threat to our safety. I push my fingers into her warm fur as it fluctuates. *At least it's not black now.*

"Eleanor, fix this," begins William, looking down at his remaining daughter and son. "You must be able to find Harriet, track her or something."

Dropping Gran's hands, Lilith takes a deep breath, then steps forward. *What guilt she must be carrying.*

"I said earlier that we should not perform the Calling."

"And what makes *you* suddenly qualified?" snaps Evelyn. "How dare you! You were Harriet's guardian. The one assigned to protect her."

"Evelyn, calm down. Besides, that's our job," says William firmly gesturing with flat hands in front of her, but Evelyn glowers at him.

"And you, Husband, need to back off!" she snaps smacking his hands away. Evelyn's anger at William shocks me, but then she has just lost two members of her family in two very different ways.

"I have failed her. And you. But I believe, truly believe that she can be found."

"What makes you so sure?" Evelyn sneers, almost squaring up to Lilith, but William locks his grip on his wife's wrist, his now cold stare chills my blood. The tension switches between them, on/off, on/off.

"Let me go," she barks.

Suddenly, William shakes his head as if dazed. He glances around the room then to Evelyn. He pulls her wrist, now gently guiding her into his arms, his sobs stutter.

"Forgive me, Evelyn..." he begins stroking his wife's hair. *Overwhelmed?*

Who wouldn't be?

"I know," she replies.

Evelyn nods at Gran.

What have they said to one another?

"I cannot even begin to comprehend the depths of what you're experiencing," begins Lilith so quietly it's barely more than a whisper. "But trust me when I say Althea should be the one to perform the Calling. And," she pauses, "the reason I believe Harriet will be found is because of Elric. There is no greater tracker in all of Gaian. If anyone can find her, it's him. I need answers, too. I must speak with my elder, Holt. He will know why my vision failed or, at the very least, how it was tampered with. You see if this happens again, then we are all at risk and I may be a liability. We need answers and we need action."

Evelyn holds Lilith's gaze, and it sort of reminds me of Mum, and her 'calculation face' which is strangely comforting. *Maybe it's Evelyn we get it from?*

"I am inclined to agree with her, Evelyn. I can project to them just as Joyce projected to you. We should go," says Gran.

"Where?" I ask, as it dawns on me exactly what Lilith means.

"To Gaian."

"The other world?"

"That is where Harriet is, for sure. We cannot stay in the Hollow Tree. Gaia needs the Elementals. She needs you, too. We must go," says Gran. And with that, she places herself where Harriet had laid sleeping. Within moments, Gran's body slumps. I glance up to see her – hovering in front of the stained glass window, its moonlit colours glimmering through Gran's astral self. No ghostly sight this time. More angel-like. I rush to touch her, but she's just air.

"*Your hands are cold, Hannah,*" she says and winks, before vanishing.

"We must ready ourselves," orders Evelyn pulling out from William's tight embrace. She touches his cheek before collecting her children from the floor where they sit, silently rocking to and fro, eyes shut.

Evelyn begins her preparations because this time, we're the ones being called.

CHAPTER THIRTEEN

Departed

William kneels, staring at Mary's body before lifting her like a slab of butcher's meat. *Strange.* I mean, it's clear how much they loved Mary. Maybe it's just the shock.

Just as Joyce did, Evelyn twirls her fingers making a jam roly-poly of the rug. Revealed beneath are lines of emerald green and gold, cast against the familiar sandy marble floor. The pentagram. My stomach flips. *Mum's not under there.* I fight the feelings – too many to name – and push them back down, entomb them so they don't take hold of my heart in time to do damage. *I have to focus.* Harriet needs us.

Before taking her own place at the final point of the pentagram, Evelyn places a candle into our hands. She presents Lilith with the first, pinching the wick between her fingers, then clicks as if to summon the light; no matches required. She makes no eye contact with Lilith and I wonder if it's her level of concentration or her lack of forgiveness that doesn't allow her to. Evelyn continues to Constance and Jack, placing each unlit candle in their hands, again pinching and alighting each wick. Her sorrowful eyes flicker to each of them. *She hasn't forgiven Lilith then.* Both Constance and Jack draw a faint smile, barely more than a straight line, each of their brows creasing. I feel that twinge in my side return. It's not just Jack this time. Constance's fears form questions. She's thirsty for answers just as I was.

Evelyn steps into position, but leaves her candle unlit.

"Gran isn't back yet. We've got to wait for her."

"It will be any moment now, don't worry. William, please place Mary in the centre."

Strange. Why would we take Mary with us?

Jack, lip quivering, steps towards William clearly wanting to help carry Mary, but Evelyn holds her arm out, clicks her fingers and gives the slightest shake of the head. Reluctantly, he steps back, but his anger begins painting me in with huge brush strokes of ruby red. As I steady my breathing I realise Constance's gaze is virtually boring into the side of my head like Dad's old Stanley drill. She doesn't even know who I am. Everything feels rushed. I know it has to. We can't wait. Time isn't on our side. We've wasted so much of it already, but still, this just doesn't feel right. *I could really use that art of reflection right now*. I don't know how much more I can take. I can't even deal with my own feelings let alone anyone else's. Lilith squeezes my hand, offering reassurance, which I'm glad of as Alpha's tail brushes against my calves. *She always knows.*

Evelyn crouches down steadying her fingers over the final candle wick as William enters the pentagram carrying Mary.

Where is Gran? She's been way too long.

"Begin!" calls Evelyn. I look blankly at her. *Does she mean me?*

Then I hear those familiar words chanted by familiar voices. *Joyce! Gran!* The call echoes out around the house.

> "...hear our call
> *Those who trespass shall wither and fall*
> *William, Mary, come through this light.*
> *Protected be upon first sight."*

"Evelyn! No! What are you doing?" cries William.

"I'm sorry, my love. Trust me. It is for the best."

"Stop this! They're my children as well. I can protect them!"

William, pain etched across his face, looks to Jack and Constance; both cry out to their father. A bright light wraps itself around William as he clutches Mary's lifeless body, the strain clear on his face.

"Mother! Don't do this!" yells Constance. "Please stop!"

But Evelyn ignores their pleas.

"Something has affected you. Your aura has been tinged with darkness, William. When I sent you out into the night to light the lanterns, something happened. I don't know what and so until I do, I can't trust you."

"But that's insane, Evelyn. It's me. I'm fine. I feel fine."

"Joyce will inter Mary's body with Caroline until we return, but Harriet must be our priority."

Hearing Mum's name blindsides me like a stray bullet I never heard being fired.

"Don't do this to our children, Evelyn, I beg you!"

"I cannot protect you, William and I cannot trust you either."

"Dammit, Evelyn!"

"Joyce's alchemy skills will uncover what has happened to you. Do as she says. I love you, William. Forgive me!"

"Mama, stop it! Stop it! What are you doing?" screams Jack as tears bleed down his cheeks.

A sudden burst of light explodes. William and Mary fade away and the room returns to how it was before. Only, it will never be as it was before.

"Did it work?" asks Gran startling everyone, returning from the astral projection.

"You knew?" I snap.

"Of course I knew," she begins, crossing the room to stand between Jack and Constance, offering her hand to comfort, but neither of them accept. "As well as your father being human in the purest sense and what I mean by that is that he does not descend from any ethereal bloodline like each of us here does, makes him a prime target. Further, your mother sensed a change in him, which she later established as true."

She then looks at me. "It is better that Joyce and Alpha's kin figure out what happened when William lit the lanterns."

"Is Joyce safe with him if he is 'tinged with darkness'?"

"The pack never leave her. And if William tries anything..."

Gran doesn't need to finish the sentence.

"But, how did you know?" I ask Evelyn.

"Something he said triggered a suspicion. That night, after lighting the lanterns, I sensed a shift in his aura. But it was the following morning when my suspicion was borne out. I'd asked him about the woman's vote he had been working on and whether his draft had been approved for their rights to be awarded. He replied women had been given the vote, but according to my source, he was out by some 100 years," says Evelyn glancing at Gran. "William would never make such an error, so as he rested I read his aura. There was a darkness to it, a shadow devouring his natural light. I don't know what it is, nor do I know to what degree, but he isn't quite *my William*."

Constance begins sobbing so I grab her hand, "Please stop. You're hurting me."

"Stop what? Who *are* you?" she snaps, snatching her hand away, but I can't speak.

I watch Gran's feet march past and turn to look just in time to see her blow plumes of concentrated lavender into each of Constance and Jack's faces. It's not enough to knock them out, but instantly, the sharpness of their pain dulls. *Thanks, Gran.*

Constance bows her head and whimpers.

"What have you done to our father?" pleads Jack.

"He is safe. You have to trust me. I have a great deal to tell you," begins Evelyn. "But we have to leave this place. Your sister needs us. We must find her and we can only do that with Hannah's help."

I push myself back up. "I'm family. On my mother's side."

"What Hannah says is the truth. We are family. I promise you, I will explain what is happening, but right now, I need us all to stand in the centre of the pentagram. They are about to begin the Calling."

"Begin what?" Constance asks, but Evelyn doesn't reply, just holds her arm out inviting her to step forward. Constance looks at Jack. They hesitate before joining their mother. I follow and give Constance a sort of Mona Lisa smile out of politeness. 'I'm on your side' is what I want to say.

Alpha rubs her head against my leg, her coat flickers from olive to bronze. *I'm going to need a colour chart to understand her.* I stroke her neck needing her probably more than she needs me.

Gran takes my hand. "Begin!" she bellows, triggering an echo through the house.

And just as before voices chant, but this time, unfamiliar and unknown...

> *"...hear our call*
> *Those who trespass shall wither and fall*
> *Daughters and Sons, come through this light.*
> *Protected be upon first sight."*

Here we go again.

CHAPTER FOURTEEN

Gaian – Hunter's Moon: Hannah
Change of Climate

The fever rises, palms sweaty, nausea rushing towards me like a tsunami. It feels different. Not like before. Everything feels sharper, quicker. Strobes of silver and bronze light fan out, but rather than the pulling sensation, it's like jet propulsion. We hurtle towards a kaleidoscope of light.

"Make it stop! Gran!"

"It will pass," she replies.

Too scared to look into the light, instead I watch green water globules form and burst against my hot skin. Everything slows as the fever grows. I inhale an earthy scent which rushes to my head. *Ugh!*

"Gran?"

But now she doesn't answer and I can't see her or anyone else either.

Don't leave me!

All of a sudden the air whistles. I'm falling. Faster and faster. My arms flap like some graceless newborn bird.

"Help!"

Plummeting into the cotton wool clouds I'm hit by their lemon scent. It makes me want to bite them. Clumps stick to me like candyfloss. Emerging from their cover, I realise I'm hurtling to the earth. Only, it isn't Earth.

No! No! No!

Something's gone wrong!

Broccoli-shaped tree canopies grow larger and larger and closer and closer. But I don't fall through them ripping limbs on branches. Instead, I hit the crowns and spring back up as if they're trampolines. I can't react fast enough so bounce down from one to another.

Umph!

Landing on a flattish part of one of the crowns, I pull myself up and pant as lungs snatch for air. The tree shudders a little as my red-raw fingertips grip its greenery. I wince from both the sting and the scent. *Yuck!*

Hearing voices below, I peer down to where Gran and the others lay strewn across a clearing. *Thank Gaia!* Weaving out from the left of the clearing lined with what look like daisies – maybe the creamed ones Gran mentioned – is a stone path, which ends as the woodland begins. Crowded with hundreds of trees and hedgerows I've never seen before, the woodland's scent is like a pick n' mix, some sweet like caramel, some sour like grapefruit. There's an assortment of shapes and sizes; thin like my favourite silver birches, some with wide trunks like Shermans. *Wait, how did I know that? Strange.* That keeps happening. Like I've got a streaming subscription for botany.com.

Dotted around the clearing are strange half-moon

shaped bushes, which look like bright orange chairs with large walnut-shaped nodes for arm-rests. *They don't look comfy at all.* Gran and Lilith climb down from two of them. Nearby, Evelyn helps Constance dust herself down as Jack pushes himself up from the ground, rubbing his elbow and looking around. *How did they end up down there strewn all over the place and I get stuck up here?*

Then I hear it…beyond the edge of the clearing, to the east I think. From the cliffs, a wall of water strikes the surface of a nearby lake, creating a white watery picket-like fence that winds for miles and miles along the valley. Plumes of vapour rise. *Incredible. It could be the Valerian Valley, Gran mentioned.* After a moment, the waterfall eases to a trickle like someone's turned off a hose pipe and left it to drip, revealing a row of caves. Some have mouths like giants beasts, others narrow or small, a little like those in the Dales back home that you have to crawl into.

I hadn't really filled in the blanks of what Gaian would look like after listening to Gran talk of isherbirds and groves of muckleberries and carissa fruits, but now I don't have to. Remembering all the delicious things Gran mentioned, hunger hits me. 'But when aren't you hungry?' Mum would say. I'm desperate to try the fruits and imagine how sweet and juicy they are. Staring at the sky, dreaming of delicious things to eat, I can't actually believe the size of it. I know that sounds ridiculous, but the sky here feels enormous. It's probably no bigger than our sky. *Maybe I'm just used to concrete towers eating away at the share of sky's pie*. It's awash with huge swathes of blues and crimsons and filled with peach and lemon coloured clouds trailing across it. *I can't believe they actually smelt of lemons!* The sky reminds me of a Monet painting, making me think of the canvas above our fireplace. *Mum's favourite.*

I really am in Gaian…I drink it in like I want to drown in it. *It's beyond beautiful. And strange. I've gotta get Mum here somehow.*

"Do you plan on joining us?" calls Gran.

"How do I get down?"

Pop!

Some of the broccoli-like foliage bursts beneath me catapulting me into the air, arms and legs flailing. Birdie still hasn't learnt how to fly, I guess.

"Gran!"

A flash of silver streaks beneath me.

Ooph!

Oh Alpha! Squashed again! I push myself up, slide from her back and catch my breath.

"Yiiip, Yiiip!" she gasps.

"Oh! I'm sorry, Alph. You really shouldn't dive under me like that y'know."

Yanking her bushy tail from under my leg, she turns and slobbers across my face. *Lovely. Thanks.* Before turning away and settling down, she winks. My jaw actually drops. Her coat flickers a sort of pinkish colour. *That's new.*

"Thanks for the...nudge," I say glancing back up to the tree. Its broccoli-crown bows ever so slightly. *Cool.* As it does, a few leafy baubles clunk to the ground like conkers.

"Thanks," I reply before picking one up to shove in my pocket. Must be autumn here, too.

"I wouldn't do that," says the silhouette of someone I can't see against the brightness of the sun.

"Why not?"

"Like all trees, they all have their own specific defence mechanisms. And, well, brocknut trees are from the same family as sandboxes and they're lethal. Just place it back down on the floor very, very carefully."

So I do and as far away as my arm will stretch.

"Isn't it dangerous to leave it there?"

"Leave things where they land. It's nature's purpose."

"Here, let me help you," she says offering her hand, which I take.

Jerked up onto my feet, I steady myself checking my arm is still in its socket, rubbing my shoulder. Then I register her face. *Seriously? Another Gaian goddess?* I should create a hashtag for that. I mean, first Galtonia – even though I hate to admit it – was beautiful. Then Lilith and now…

"Althea. It pleases me to make your acquaintance, Hannah." Her voice is like a melody.

"Thanks. It's nice to meet you, too." *I sound so lame.*

Realising we're still holding hands, I shake hers and notice a crescent moon curving across the back of it from her thumb to her index finger.

"It is the mark of my tribe. Would you like one?" she asks, olive eyes, glinting. Politely, I pull my hand back. Still, it looks really cool.

"She's a little too young for that just yet, Althea," interrupts Gran, pulling me into her side and pressing a kiss onto my temple, her honeysuckle scent reminding me of home.

"Not too queasy from the journey I hope," Althea says. I shake my head.

The moon tattoo isn't the only mark on her cocoa skin. Two long white streaks with arrow heads and four small dots line the apple of Althea's cheeks. Tribal, I think. Painted down her nose and spreading under her eyes is a thin white triangle. A bronze band with a purple jewel in the centre holds cable-thick strands of braided hair from her face. Woven with ribbons and what look like vines, her hair trails over her heather-covered shoulders reaching her waist. Strapped across her shoulder and bound in thick bamboo-like reeds, are two crossed swords, each with jewelled hilts, but nothing like what Lilith saw. Each has a wide silver blade.

"I'll get my sea-legs, thanks."

"I have heard that phrase before. You will most certainly need them here, I can assure you."

"Welcome to Gaian, dearest," says Gran. "Isn't it everything I described?"

"More, Gran. Much more."

She nods. "I'll give you a minute to take the rest of it in."

I'll need more than a minute.

"Everyone make it out alive?" I ask, wiping Alpha's slobber from my face and instantly regret it. *Alive!* Why did I say that! *Idiot! Poor Mary!* I hope Constance and Jack didn't hear me.

"What is the current state of the climate here?" asks Gran.

"It fluctuates," begins Althea. "But we have been reasonably steady for a few days now. However, tremors are being felt across the Western Isles and it's spreading. Gaia is entering another phase of the fever. Sometimes it fades and never materialises into anything more than the ground grumbling, but the frequencies are growing. We experience immense heat, which you know, Eleanor, scorches the ground. At the start of the Northern Wolf Moon we noticed changes. Instead of the usual blistering cold, temperatures were mild. It wasn't until reports of heat storms as early in the year as the Southern Blood Moon when we suspected something more serious was going on. The heat storms lasted for days, rather than the few moments they normally do."

Heat storms? Blood Moons?

It's not just happening on Earth, then.

"I cannot tell you how much it pains me to hear this Althea. Truly," says Gran.

"The Vulturian Valley has experienced the worst of the flooding, being so close to the Nileanic Ocean. A great many Rusalkas have been lost. Drowned by their own gift. What was once a calm, epic ocean became a tidal hurricane. We have never experienced anything like this, Eleanor. Your wise counsel is most welcome here."

"The signs of suffering are not only felt in Gaian, believe me. On Earth, there has been much destruction. A summer unlike any other before it. Swathes of land scorched by wild fires. Crops and cattle dying. Famine rising in our Southern Hemisphere. Mass migration to the north and humanity has neither the infrastructure nor...I was going to say the understanding, but perhaps that is too harsh. The people seem to. But not the powers."

"Now I am the one that is pained, Eleanor."

"On Earth, coastal towns and cities flooded last winter and the water continues to rise year upon year. London and the East were worst hit. Goodness knows what we may face this winter…that's if we even make it to the Equinox. And by 'we' I mean Gaia in all her forms."

Gran's face looks drawn from tiredness.

Across the clearing, Evelyn now sits with Constance and Jack, all three are deep in conversation. At least Evelyn is sitting down to explain to them what is happening, unlike Gran turning into some creepy spectre and scaring me to death. I can't help but roll my eyes at Gran who doesn't have to listen to my thoughts to understand why. She looks sheepish.

Nearby, Lilith lingers, plucking leaves from what looks like a hazel tree. *She's probably going to treat Jack's bruises. If he'll let her.*

"I thought Elric would be here already," Gran adds.

"He is scavenging in the grove. We will need the sustenance. He won't be gone long. Especially now Lilith has returned to him. I must say, your contingency plan is a wise one," says Althea throwing a glance my way.

"Will people stop calling me that, Gran! I hate it. I'm a person, not a plan. Not some weapon or shield, or whatever it is you think I am."

"I know what you are, Hannah. My granddaughter."

She always knows the right thing to say.

"Alas, I cannot take the credit. Gaia commanded it. And, that is something to be discussed later. For now, our priority is Harriet. Whichever Lord has her, could use her gift to plunge our worlds into fire and everything our worlds are experiencing now, will be nothing compared to what could be brought to pass. Harriet was picked off because she is the fledgling, but that does not mean Jack and Constance are any less a target than her."

"Naturally, that target will be Constance. Air feeds fire," suggests Althea.

"Exactly."

"So, you suspect a Lord?" asks Althea.

"Not suspect. We have proof. It may not be beyond reasonable doubt, but whoever snatched Harriet took her by slicing into the fabric of Evelyn's shield. That can only be done with a black blade."

Althea's expression is one of horror. *That can't be good.* I concentrate hard to see if I can feel her, but my empath gift doesn't respond and I've no idea why.

"Lilith witnessed it. Her visions are being tampered with or were tampered with, but that is what she saw and what came to pass before she could warn us."

"A black blade? And tampered visions?" asks Althea. "I shall send Kimbiah with a message to Holt. Lilith will need

112

his guidance now for certain."

I've been so engrossed with Althea, that I haven't registered the argument now raging between Jack and Evelyn.

"No, mother! You're lying!" Jack cries. He turns and runs heading right for the edge of the cliff, where the valley drops.

Whumph. Whumph. Whumph.

Sweeping from the shadows of the woodland an enormous creature, half-man and half-I-really-don't-know-what glides over Jack's head, dropping what looks like a giant palm leaf, scattering the fruits and berries from inside it. With his path of escape blocked, Jack freezes. Like before, he colours me in. Grey. That feels like nerves. Understandable. Jack backs away.

"Gran?"

"No, no. Elric must be heard," she replies taking my hand and leading us over to Lilith, who, standing with Constance and Evelyn, doesn't even try to hide her delight. Althea nods at Elric as he folds his enormous sun-kissed wings back. Each tipped with black like they've been dipped in ink, sway in time with Elric's rising chest. Golden feathers line his sides and despite his obvious bulk, he seems graceful.

Clip. Clip. Clip.

Elric has hooves! But then his muscular legs are sort of horse-like. His thin whip-like tail swishes between them. Had I not seen Gran as a Firebird, then Elric would have probably been the coolest thing I'd seen yet.

"Get out of my way you, you..." screams Jack.

"What?" asks Elric, his voice gruff, deep like there's too much bass and not enough treble.

"How on Earth should I know what you are?"

"Ah, but you are not on Earth any more. We are in Gaian, so I will forgive you for not having heard of me, little man. I am Elric, son of Eldred, leader of the Gryphons of Valeria."

"Elric's a Gryphon? I thought they were, like, half-eagle, half lion."

"There are many breeds of gryphons. And before you ask, no. I don't know which breed Elric is. You'll have to ask him yourself."

"St...st...stay away from me! I mean it. I'll do something terrible," threatens Jack, looking behind Elric to the cliff edge.

"Now, that would be very foolish, I think," says Elric, flexing his wings which expand blocking any chance Jack might have had of getting past.

Jack turns back to Evelyn and begins to sob. "Where is our father?"

"Jack, come here!" begs Constance. "Mother, I insist you tell us what is going on."

Doesn't sound like Evelyn's told them much at all.

"She's a witch, Connie, don't trust her. Our mother is a witch!" Jack yells. "Let us go! Take us back."

All of a sudden, Elric pushes off from the ground, sweeps low and scoops Jack up under his wing. Jack's scream echoes across the valley as he kicks out and beats his fists against the feather-filled arm clutching him, but Elric is fast and drops him at the side of his sister. Looping up and over them both, Elric then places himself between Evelyn and her frightened, but angry offspring, in a 'you've-gotta-go-through-me-first' kind of way. *Not that Evelyn needs protecting.*

Folding his wings back, he asks, "Is that how all you humans speak to your mothers?"

My heart suddenly plummets. Guilty as charged. I feel Gran squeeze my hand. I've got to find Mum just as much as we've all got to find Harriet.

"No, of course not. But what has it got to do with you?" Jack snaps.

"Your mother is a dear friend of mine and I shall not…I repeat…" Elric nears Jack a little, his voice a shade deeper than before. "…*not* hear her spoken to in that manner."

Elric then turns to Evelyn. "You have much to explain to your children, but you are a mother of three, not two. Our priority now is to locate your youngest and together we shall attend our most Sacred Lady."

"Let me guess, Gran. A lady that is sacred."

Gran smirks. "Like I told you, a sacred circle is…"

"I know, a circle that is sacred. You're not funny y'know.

"Yes, I am dear."

"He does mean Gaia, right?" I ask.

"Indeed. He does. Sacred Lady. Almighty Mother. They're all terms of endearment, here."

Elric holds Evelyn's shoulder for a moment, nods then joins Lilith who is perched on a thick brown trunk segmented like the body of a caterpillar. They interlock fingers as Elric presses his lips to hers. I realise I'm staring and look away only to find Constance staring at me.

How do I talk to her? If she had a mobile, I'd send her an emoji. Puzzled face. Question mark.

Constance leads Jack – still sobbing – away from Evelyn telling her they just need a minute. Maybe this is my chance to speak to them. Together, Jack and Constance find a place to sit. Pulling aside a curtain of butter-coloured vines, which hang from a mushroom–shaped crown, Constance guides Jack to the base of the tree. It's a banyan tree. I'm sure it's a banyan tree although I don't know how I'm sure. *All this random knowledge, which I'm beginning to enjoy, is definitely since the gift retrieval.*

Watching them huddle together, jealousy pinches me

again. *I wish*…but it doesn't matter what I wish. I just have to help them understand somehow. I mean, their Dad's gone and so is mine. They've lost Mary. I've lost Mum. Perhaps not in quite the same way. I guess we've more in common than just a bloodline and an apparent ability to save the world, or whatever. Just as I'm about to go and speak to them, Constance calls me over. Jack looks unimpressed. I defeated a draconite for goodness sake. Well, I had a lot of help, but I mean, how difficult can this be? I don't know why it suddenly feels strange. Maybe it's because they're family. Or maybe it's because they're about my age. *Awkward or what*. I smile at Gran and leave her to talk with Evelyn. It's clear that everyone needs a moment.

"Look, I know this all seems like some crazy dream," I begin, crossing my legs beneath me. "Nightmare, even. I thought exactly the same and felt, well, it's a lot, I know. I'm not sure how much your mum's told you, but you have to believe this, believe her. Evelyn adores you and will do anything to protect you, but she also wants to protect everyone's future. Mine included. And like she said, your father's with my friend Joyce so he'll be taken care of, I promise. And Mary, too."

"Why should we listen to you?" Constance asks.

"You don't have to. But I think you should because, well, we're family. I don't care if you don't believe me but

Eleanor is my grandmother. Your sister is *her* grandmother. And so, somewhere down the line that makes you my aunt and uncle, I think. I know that sounds utterly crazy, like, I can barely get my head round it myself."

"You're lying!" snaps Jack smacking his hand on the ground.

"Look, calm down and open your eyes. This is real," I say pointing over at Elric. "It's happening whether we like it or not. We can't change what's happened, but that attitude of yours Jack, well, that can."

Jack's scowl doesn't fade. It's going to take more than a few words to calm this torrent of anger down. *I hate feeling it.*

"Gran, you've gotta teach me how to deal with this. I can't cope with much more from Jack."

"It comes with experience, but, yes, there are things we can do to mitigate the impact. For now, when you feel his anger rise, deep breath and imagine you are pushing his energy away from you."

I smile at Gran from across the clearing. At her feet, Alpha stands to stretch out, then stops, letting out a deep rumble from her chest, her hackles prickle into blades of silver cresting down her back.

"What is it, Alph?" I call as her hackles blacken.

Evelyn stands and begins approaching, but the ground

shakes, sending her hurtling to the floor. Trees shudder. Leaves tumble. From the waterfall, chunks of rock splinter and crash into the lake, spraying water high into the air.

"Gran! What's happening?"

She holds her arm out. "Don't move! It's probably an aftershock."

"Stay close to the trees!" shouts Althea as a rumble like thunder hits, but far beneath the ground, like a waking beast from a deep sleep. "It's Gaia's fever! Now you'll experience it for yourselves."

CHAPTER FIFTEEN
Global Warning

We're surrounded by the echo of creaking trunks. Branches break like fragile bones, tumbling to rest in their ready-made graveyard. Scrambling up, I push Constance and Jack behind me close to the banyan's spaghetti-like trunk. The grumbling ground settles, but looking out at a sea of lush grasses, its colour suddenly flickers. Gone are the bright tones and breathing plants…all that remains is an ocean of dust, scorched corpses of trees hanging against a grey sky. *What the…*

Click!

Nature flicks its switch and returns to the lush land it was when we arrived. Every leaf is brighter, larger. Trees are taller. Streams of sunlight stronger. Waves lap splashing the luscious green embankment lined with water poppies and lilies. Across the sky a crested lark zips, its wings furious in flight.

Flick. Flick. Flick.

As if the world is a book whose pages are being flicked, the scene changes descending us into darkness. Thick, white smoke billows all around and like it's hit a wall of fire, the lark's body disintegrates to dust, scattering in the wind, its existence erased. I sign to Jack and Constance to pull their clothes up over their faces, not knowing if it will stop us choking to death. Water fills my eyes fighting against the clouds of ash. *Can't. Breathe.*

It isn't stopping. Black skeletons of trees set against a searing white sky crumble as the heat stings our skin.

Flick. Flick. Flick.

Lungs inhale clear air. The smoke clouds gone. But it's hot. Where the trees once stood, now remains a vast desert of dried, cracked land covered with thousands of colourless spikes, all that's left of the stems of wheat and corn. Carcasses of lizards and flying foxes scattering the ocean of dust. *What have we done?*

I bend to touch the nearest pile of remains to see if it's real. It crumbles like the lark did.

Flick. Flick. Flick.

Gaian pants dog-like. Dehydrated and sick.

Jack scrapes his shoe across the ground as Constance steps forwards to drink it all in; the dehydrated, sickening earth. She turns to me as if to search for answers to questions I can't bring myself to ask.

CHAPTER SIXTEEN

Sugar and Water

Lilith charges across the clearing to a cluster of thickset trees as Elric swoops in behind her. The backdraft from his wings sends shivers across my skin. The tree is covered in emerald spheres with not a branch in sight. *Of course! Lilith's a dryad!* Taking a huge breath, she pushes her hands into the spheres. Colour drains from everything she touches – the tree, the ground, even herself revealing everything in X-ray vision. Lilith begins pumping a luminous green liquid from her own body into the bulbous tree. It bleeds out into the ground. *Is that her blood?*

"What is she doing?" I shout.

"Trying to stabilise their insulin levels. It might abate Gaia's fever."

A flashback to the Hollow Tree hits me like a truck.

Trees feed trees!

Looking at the ground under Lilith's feet, roots pump sugar through their veins.

Come on Lilith!

Elric bellows, "Enough!" But Lilith doesn't stop. Her body trembles.

Flick. Flick. Flick.

"Lilith!" shouts Althea. "It's nowhere close to being enough. Stop! It's a death sentence!"

Instead she pushes harder, her face splinters like a branch under too much pressure. Elric grabs her wrists and strains against the force as he pulls her free. She collapses into his arms.

"Foolish!" snaps Althea.

"She tried, didn't she," Elric says just loud enough for everyone to hear. He rests her against his body and wraps his wings around her as she lies panting.

"It's too late for gallantry, I am afraid," announces Althea. "Everything we have tried…it is not enough, Eleanor. Our only hope is the Elementals."

Althea stares at Evelyn, who only has eyes for her children. But for a second, her gaze flickers to me. I nod. We can do this. *We can save Gaia and we can save Harriet. I have to believe that!*

"Which is why we need to get Harriet back. As soon as this passes, we move," calls Gran.

All of a sudden, large splodges of water smack the grumbling ground. One, two, three, then hundreds and thousands more. Gran and the others are forced back under a kauri tree. Water droplets the size of fists slam through the dense canopy above us, but the banyan's inner layer of vines pop like an umbrella and take the worst of the pounding. I've seen rain storms before, but nothing like this. I look out to find Gran and Evelyn, but can't see them through the wall of water.

"Gran, what's happening?"

"It's Gaia's fever. It will pass. This will pass. Stay under the tree. Do not move. And for goodness sake, don't let Jack out of your sight!"

"I promise."

The banyan's foliage begins to bend under the water's weight. *It's not going to hold!* Out beyond the curtain of vines, the flickering seems to have stopped, but now the grasses and plants are swamped as the water rises. *Flashback. Just days ago. Home. York. The flood. The trees! Trust them.*

I turn to the banyan as Gran's words boomerang back to me. *'Don't let Jack out of your sight!'*

Placing my hand on its trunk, I have no idea if this will work, but they listened to me before. Maybe they'll listen again.

Through the thunderous sound of the water, I whisper, "Bind them. Bind the Elementals. As Gaia's heiress, I ask this favour of you. Bind them."

"Hannah, what are you doing?" begs Constance.

"Can you trust me?"

She hesitates. "Yes. Yes. I will. I do."

There's no point in asking Jack.

As I peel my hand from its trunk, the banyan's vines rise fluttering like ribbons in the wind. They approach from either side. I take Constance's hand, interlocking fingers, palm to palm, staring into each other's eyes.

All of a sudden, the banyan's green umbrella splits, rain pummelling down and within seconds we're drenched. It's so cold it hurts. I've asked too much of it. But the banyan doesn't stop. Hundreds of threads from its hanging vines and strands of cables from its trunk, slithering like snakes, wrap themselves around Constance and Jack binding them to its trunk.

Soaked through in seconds, I look to Jack, his face turned upwards, fists balled.

"It's...pr...protecting you, Jack!" shouts Constance, her teeth beginning to chatter as a chill seeps into her bones. But he doesn't answer, just continues staring at the sky, ignoring us now. Constance's cold grip tightens.

"You're safe," I say wishing rather than knowing that was true.

Water laps around the base of the trunk. *Think! How can I stop this?*

I can't see anyone. Not even Elric and Lilith.

A sudden crash, sends water spraying over us all as Alpha bursts through the waterfall of rain, panting. She shakes the water from her fur before howling a blistering howl that stings my eardrums.

"Stop it, Alph!"

Her coat fluctuates between red and black. *Not good.* Alpha lunges at me, grabbing the cuff of my jumper between her teeth and drags me sideways to Jack. He hasn't moved. Hair matted to his face, his gazed fixed upon the sky. *He must be petrified!* I grab Jack's head to look at him.

Oh. My. God!

Frosted blue eyes pierce me. He's in some sort of trance.

I daren't show Constance, but she screams at me to tell her what I've seen.

It's not Gaia. Not now. It's…it's…Jack!

"Constance, listen to me. You're an Elemental. You have powers, like, crazy, amazing, scary gifts. And your gift is air. You can control air. Harriet's element is fire. That means Jack is water. *He* is doing this. The rainstorm! We have to stop him."

"But how? Rain doesn't just evaporate by itself, you know!"

"What did you say?"

"Rain. It doesn't just evaporate," she repeats.

"Of course! Okay, Constance, I need you to do exactly as I say. Just keep blowing warm air over Jack."

"Why?"

"There's no time to explain," I shout, feeling Jack's rainwater rise around our ankles. The banyan releases Constance from her bindings. She immediately takes Jack's

126

hands and begins blowing warm breath over his face again and again. *Okay, now for my part.*

I press my hand against the banyan's trunk as hard as I can. *It happens faster than I thought possible.* The bark begins to consume my hand, bleeding into my skin and veins, which glow a luminous green, just like Lilith's did.

"I'm right here, Hannah. You've got this, my darling girl. Bring Jack back to us." Gran's voice echoes around my head.

How does she always know the right thing to say? How do grown-ups do that?

With my I.V. style hook-up into the banyan's cluster of cables, I grip Jack's wrist and like the furies did with me, press my fingers into his veins. Thin lines of blood trickle from his arm as I channel the energy into his body.

"Keep going, Constance! More, if you can."

She takes a huge breath and blows warm air over his face.

"Jack, I know you can hear me and I know you're angry with your mother, but you have to forgive her. You have to trust her."

Taking the sugar from the tree, I continue to funnel it into Jack's blood stream.

"We have to save your sister. Harriet needs you. She needs her big brother." My voice cracks. "Please, Jack. Help us save your sister. She'll be so...so scared. Harriet is all alone. We can't do this without you."

"It's working, Hannah!" Gran says.

I look around to see the rain begin to ease a little, but it's not enough.

Without me saying a word, Constance begins, "Jack, I never told you this, but you were my first ever best friend in the whole world."

Tears spill from her eyes. "Help me save our little Harriet. I know she loves her big brother very much. And I need you. I will always need you, Jack."

I'm hit with an avalanche from Constance and have to hold back her feelings with everything I have.

My grip tightens on Jack's wrist as Constance raises her hands and takes one more huge breath and blasts it into Jack's face, his hair now dry. His body begins to tremble. All of a sudden Jack gasps for air as an enormous plume of smoke billows around us. *Water vapour.* Jack's frosted eyes fill with mist. He blinks once, twice as it vanishes revealing his chocolate button eyes. I release my grip from his warm, clammy skin and gently pull my hand free from the depths of the banyan tree.

I pat it.

"Thank you. But mostly, thank you, Alpha. How did you know?" I ask, bending down. But then how does any animal know? I guess it's because they're so tuned to the environment, their environment. *Why aren't we more like that?* Maybe we were. Once. I stroke Alpha's muzzle relieved as her coat settles to a warm olive tone, then back to its natural silver. Shaking the rest of the rain from her coat, Alpha sneezes right in my face. *Great!*

After using my wet sleeve as a flannel, I turn back to the banyan tree as it unravels its vines from Jack's body. Constance and I take his weight, placing his arms around our shoulders as he slumps, feet struggling to co-ordinate.

"What happened?" he says drowsily.

He doesn't remember?

As the air begins to clear, Evelyn, Gran and Althea rush across to us and Evelyn takes her son in her arms.

"Thank you, Hannah," she says.

"Don't thank me. It was Constance's idea."

"It was?" Evelyn asks taking her eldest daughter's hand and smiling to which Constance shrugs as if what she did was nothing at all.

"You're learning fast, Hannah," Gran says stroking my hair from my face just like Mum does.

"The heat is returning. We shall all dry out shortly," says Elric, carrying Lilith as she begins to come round. "And that young man needs a little recovery time."

Evelyn takes her two remaining children to sit and rest against a pile of mushroom-like rocks, or are they rock-like mushrooms? I really can't tell. I hear Constance fire questions at her mother, which Evelyn begins to answer. Who she is. Who they are. And who I am.

"She really is quite extraordinary, Eleanor," begins Althea and I know instantly who she means. I remember snapping at Galtonia for how, what was it Gran said...yes, that's it, how she 'exulted' me. I hated it then and still do now but I bite down and don't say anything.

"Althea, how long has this been happening for?" Gran asks.

"I cannot be precise, but it has been for quite some time now," she replies.

"Then this makes no sense to me. If one of the Lords has poisoned Gaia, all these climate events would have occurred recently, yes?"

"What are you getting at Eleanor?" asks Elric.

I pull back from Gran as a familiar feeling of dread swirls in the depths of my stomach.

"Maybe it isn't one of the Lords of the High Council that has poisoned Gaia at all. What happens if it is, in fact, humans? And all this is a guise under which to destroy Gaia when she is at her weakest."

"You think it's us, Gran? Really?"

"I am starting to suspect it could be a very real prospect indeed. And whichever Lord has snatched Harriet, has seized an opportune moment, rather than concocted it."

Could that be true? Have we weakened Gaia so much that she has become a target for annihilation? My heart suddenly feels twice its weight. I can't help but think Gran could be right.

"Humanity is the author of its own misfortune," says Lilith as Elric sets her down.

"But it's not just humanity's misfortune, is it? It is all of Gaian too. Never mind the millions of species that inhabit our worlds," says Althea balling her fist. She turns away and stares out across the valley.

A wave of shame crashes over me. For the first time ever, I hate the fact that I am human.

 CHAPTER SEVENTEEN

Caroline
What Lies Beneath

Weightless and powerless, the violent undercurrent forces me to submit. Entombed within its dark realms I float as the pressure rises once more stealing what little strength I have left as my body is pummelled and scratched. Flesh rips against the thick bracken and rocks and the coldness of dark water stings. I'm only thankful nothing appears to be broken. Daylight arrives taunting me, showing me evermore inflictors of pain. When forced into narrow waters, embedded flint tears my skin, rocks bruise as chattel-like pondweed, rushes and reeds entwine limbs intent on denying my release. Trapped within an ocean-sized mausoleum, I ready myself as a new dawn signals the battle's commencement. I fight. I fight every day to free myself and get back to her. *Hannah*.

I have given up asking why. I don't know why I'm trapped beneath the waterline unable to surface or why I can breathe here, but I will never stop asking… *How? How did I get here? How do I find my daughter? How do I get back to her?*

Today's light is bright, making me wince, but as my eyes adjust, I can see clearer than any day gone before it. The shimmer of the water makes the peachiness of the clouds

132

sparkle.

Something brushes against my hand. The pygmy seahorse, so tiny, so delicate, covered in radish-coloured mounds floats past. Clearly lost, I offer the tip of my finger upon which it cautiously climbs on. *Come on little fella. Let's get you home, so that I can get home, too.* Scouring the nearby reefs, I locate the sea fan and carefully rest it upon one of its corkscrew limbs.

I must be nearing shallow waters again as my hands crawl crab-like across layers of pebbles, rocks and I can even feel the sand beneath my feet. I should be able to stand and emerge, but can't.

Along the edge of the grassy embankment, brightly coloured plants bloom, swaying against a breeze I long to feel against my skin. I can just make out the rustling leaves. With a gentle tide, I move easily along the seabed, my fingers feeling between each crevice removing potentially harmful debris until I notice an enormous cluster of trees, their canopies just visible from this constricted angle. I have no idea how long it takes me to navigate the stream but I use every advantage I'm afforded to orientate myself to this new landscape.

Shards of sunlight penetrate the water's surface and my body welcomes the warmth, wishing to store it like a stone.

Crack!

The sharpness of a snapping sound brings me to a halt. A branch maybe? I push my face as close to the water's surface as possible, hands pressing against the glass-casket of water entrapping me, straining to see where the noise came from.

Oh my God.

"Hannah!"

How is that even possible?

I bang against the water's hard surface, slamming my fists against it over and over until a numbness throbs through them. *Can she see me?*

"Hannah, help me! Please. Get me out of here!"

My limbs thrash against the rocks until I find a footing and push hard desperate to smash my way out. Fresh water washes away salty tears bleeding onto my lips. I cry out, pushing hard against the surface.

"I'm here, Hannah! It's me!"

She bends down to the water, dipping her fingers in then splashes her face. I react but not fast enough. Her fingers, so close, vanish back to the other side. A voice in the distance calls to her.

Her freckles are darker and there's a golden glint in her eyes.

"Just a minute," she shouts, but stares directly at me.

Why can't she see me?

I'm right here!

"Don't go, Hannah. Please stay! Help me. Get Gran. She'll know what to do!" I scream until I choke on tears. *Don't go. Don't go.*

Hannah lifts her head and looks out beyond the water. The sunset's haze casts a rosy glow to her cheeks. From a pocket, she takes out her mobile and clutches it tightly staring at it. *What was her screensaver?* I try to picture the image she'd last shown me the night before that damn phone call summoning us to Norwich. *Was it last summer in Stratford feeding the ducks?* She smiles as she looks at it then closes her eyes for a second remembering. It *was* Stratford. Tucking the phone back into her pocket, she begins to stand then I realise…she's seen me.

"Mum!" she screams plunging her hand into the water searching for mine, but without warning a rushing sound fills my ears. "Gran! Mum's in the water!"

I reach out to her, but can't make contact. I begin kicking hard, but suddenly feel the pull again…

"No! Please, don't." I cry as I'm pulled down far deeper beneath the water's surface. "Let me go!" I kick and thrash and reach, but remain shackled to the weight of an anchor I am powerless to hoist, only descending further into the depths and into the darkness. I flounder.

Help me, Han!

CHAPTER EIGHTEEN

Hannah
Muckleberry

"What on earth is it, Hannah?" Gran asks rushing to my side and pulling me up.

"I saw Mum! She was in the water." My whole body shakes.

Gran looks down as the ripples settle. "Are you sure?"

"Yes, I saw her!"

Didn't I?

Gran bends down and scans the water for any sign of *her* daughter but sees only her own reflection her. At least that's what I see.

"Are you absolutely certain?"

"Yes. I mean, I think so. I *really* thought I saw her in there."

"Was she..." Gran pauses allowing silence to rise and stretch between us. *She can't say it.*

"She was alive. She looked right at me."

"It's not that I don't believe you, but I'm thinking it's perhaps all this drama and tiredness affecting us all."

"Can't we check somehow?" I ask.

"Other than wading in there..."

I pull my shoes off, but she orders me to stop. "Not a chance. Way too risky. Elric?" she calls.

Swiftly, silently, Elric glides across to us.

"Elric, I think I saw my mum in there. Could you sweep the waters for us?"

He dives in. Everyone joins us, staring out across the waters, waiting for him to break through the surface, holding Mum in his arms. Ripples from Elric's dive eventually merge back with the gentleness of the waves. *I guess Gryphons can hold their breath a really long time.*

Suddenly, Elric bursts out like a dolphin about to jump, but his arms are empty. His wings flap creating a huge draught as he glides back towards us, landing next to Lilith.

"I'm sorry, Hannah. Your mother isn't in there."

"Are you sure? What if she's trapped under a rock or something and can't breathe. She'll die."

"She's not there. These waters are shallow enough for me to scan the seabed. My eyesight is very powerful. I scanned wide. There's nothing."

"I'm so sorry, Hannah," says Lilith like it's her fault. It isn't, of course, but I've been so desperate since Lilith told me of the vision she had of Mum...it meant something.

Strobes from the fading sunlight, catch the water's surface as I look back searching for Mum's face among little lapping waves. Maybe I did imagine it. It's then I notice my own reflection. *Gran was right.* My eyes are colourful. Still the green and the blue, but now filled with rainbow swirls.

There's even a spark of gold. My hair seems wilder, longer, with emerald highlights catching in the light. Even my skin seems less cow's milk white and more like almond milk.

"I can try again if you wish," offers Elric.

"No. It's okay. You're probably right," I say trying to hide both my disappointment and astonishment. "But thank you for looking."

"I'm sorry my darling. We will find your mother. I want my daughter back too, you know. Come on…," Gran says linking her arm with mine and leading us back to the others. "Our minds do play tricks on us when we're exhausted. My goodness, what I wouldn't give for a cup of Earl Grey."

That reminds me of Dad. Early Grey was *his* favourite. Dad. He doesn't even know where I am.

I don't really feel exhausted. Hungry, but not exhausted. And, as if on cue, my stomach rumbles. I guess Constance and Jack are too. They dive into a circle as Lilith holds up a bottle green leaf the size of an elephant's ear.

"Elric's brought treats for us all. We shall eat and then decide what to do next," says Lilith.

"Everything alright?" asks Althea her eyes still scanning the woodlands as we approach. I hadn't realised she'd stayed at the clearing.

"Yes, we think so," says Gran sucking in a deep breath of air. She's probably right.

With the ground dried out from the rising temperatures we all sit in a circle passing around the fruits that Elric had gathered before Jack's whopping strop. I pick at all different kinds and colours of berries wondering which the muckleberries are that Gran mentioned. They sounded so yummy. *Didn't she say they were like minted blueberries?* So, if I pick the one that's minty-coloured...I do and remembering what happened with the edible roots, nibble on the flesh of the fruit. *Yuck!*

"Urgh, that's horrible."

Elric takes it out of my hand and peels back its skin, smirking. "Try now."

"Oh. Thanks."

The scent of honeysuckle seeps out. *Definitely a muckleberry.* Again, I nibble at the fruit's flesh.

"O.M.G." I say out loud as juice dribbles down my chin. I wipe it on my sleeve, then hear a '*tsk*' sound from across the circle and know exactly where it's come from.

"*Use a leaf, Hannah for goodness sake! I know perfectly well Caroline taught you the basic rules of etiquette.*"

"*But that's around a dinner table!*" I argue.

I look round for one, but other than the giant leaf acting as our plate, there's none on the ground. Then a leaf floats past my nose into my lap. Looking up, I see half a dozen helicopter leaves swirling down from the sycamore tree close by.

"*Cool, thanks, Gran.*" But it wasn't her. Clearly, Evelyn overheard Gran's level of disgust at my serious lack of picnic-level etiquette.

Wiping my mouth with the leaf, I notice one last muckleberry. *I don't think anyone will mind.* They are so yummy. But it's not just me that thinks so as both myself and Jack dive at the last remaining one.

"Oh sorry," I say. His hand touches mine then pulls away. "No, Jack, it's okay. You have it. They're really delicious."

For a second, Jack holds my gaze kick-starting the empath engine, only this time he's not colouring me in using furious reds which is such a relief. It's so different that I have to catch my breath. Slowly and cautiously a straw-like colour fills me in. *What does that mean?* Geez, I need a colour chart for Jack as well as Alpha.

He takes the fruit from my hand. "If you're certain?" he asks to which I nod. "Thank you," he adds.

"You're welcome," I say letting a gentle smile rise into my cheeks. "And if you don't like it, you can chuck it back. I'll still eat it." I shrug. My gentle smile is now a massive grin. A faint flicker of a smile crosses his eyes, but never quite reaches his mouth. It's a start.

Constance, who is sitting as close as possible without actually being on my knee, whispers to me. "You said three letters. What did you mean?"

"What?"

"You mean pardon," she replies.

"Oh, yeah. Pardon."

"The three letters. You know, O, M and G. What do they stand for?"

"Oh my God."

"Excuse me?" Constance looks, well, horrified. "You shouldn't take the Lord's name in vain that like you know."

"I didn't. At least I don't think I did."

"Why say it? And why use an abbreviation?"

"I don't know. People use it all the time where…I mean *when* I'm from and it's used in a good way. Well, a dramatic way. It means, delight, I think. Or disbelief. Yeah, that makes sense. And we say the letters so we're not being rude using the word, g-o-d. Or it might just be laziness. In fact, I'm really not sure why."

"Well, we can all delight in the Lord."

"I don't think that's how we mean it, but, like I said, not really sure why."

Actually I'm pretty certain it has nothing to do with delighting in the Lord, but I won't tell Constance that.

"When we've all finished," begins Elric. "We'll head east through the woodlands, but stay close to the valley's line until we reach the Ffenlands. And it makes sense to stay near water."

It's been a while since a flurry of questions has descended upon me, but I daren't ask him. *He won't bite though will he? And it's nothing major.*

"Elric?"

"You have a question, Hannah?" he replies as the fawn and black coloured feathers running down his arms twitch.

"I do. What valley is that?" I turn behind me and point out across the rolling hills and distant mountain ranges, beyond the stream.

"It's not a valley in the truest sense, but the Dereland Vale stretches right up to where those mountains begin. It is one of the flattest valleys, if you will, in Gaian. It borders the Ffenlands, which is where we're heading," he replies before sinking his teeth into a small lemon-like fruit then spitting pips out into the palm of his feathery hand. He tosses the pips over his shoulder which sink straight into the ground like they're ready to be germinated.

Gran stands and brushes herself down. "So you think the Ffenlands are the best place to start?" she asks.

"I do." Elric replies. "And the reason is simple. They're crop farmers and understand every inch of this land and more importantly because of their trading posts, they hear news from all across the east bank.

"That would make sense. Let's move," says Althea

standing and tucking a thin gold blade back into the lining of her boots.

"Formation?" asks Lilith.

"Elric stays with Jack. Your speed needs to be in the right place. You'd best head the formation. Lilith and I will stick with Constance and Hannah. Evelyn, Eleanor, bring up the rear."

Constance smiles and steps closer to me, "You can teach me all about your time. Has the world changed much?"

Er...

"A bit. Yeah," I nod as Alpha appears at my side. Two peas in a pod, Mum would have said.

"Your fox is beautiful, although I must say I've never seen one so large."

"Neither had I. And, Alpha isn't mine. She's not my pet."

"Well I did think it was a little strange."

"Yeah, I guess it would seem that way. She's my friend."

Alpha shoves her back end into me nearly knocking me off my feet, but Constance catches my hand to stop me tripping. "Thanks."

"You're quite welcome."

"I think someone wants us to be friends," I say. *Or family. Either's good.*

CHAPTER NINETEEN

Fever

Light from the sunset runs through the maze of rowan trees as a haze of heat rises and falls. I didn't know it was a rowan woodland. It's all these random nature fact notifications popping into my head.

"My patch is very close by. It's in the most northerly part of the Logarian Valley, but to the east," says Lilith.

"North East. Like Newcastle."

"I'm sorry, I don't know that place."

"It's okay. I get it."

Although it feels like we've been walking for some time, we can't have as the sunset hasn't faded to dusk yet. Unless sunsets last longer in Gaian. The flow of the heat rising and falling little by little is so soothing, like finding patches of warm water in the sea when you swim.

I can't quite hear what they're saying as they're too far ahead, but it looks like Jack has found a new friend. Elric keeps rubbing his head, messing up Jack's hair.

I hadn't really noticed it until now but the march of the questions had faded into the background like a white noise app, but with Althea now between me and Constance, I suddenly have a shopping list of questions I want to ask her.

What can warrior witches do exactly? This question is at

the top of the list and has been since she started speaking about her tribe.

"Althea, what exactly can you do? I mean, I know what witches can do – at least the human version of a witch and I know what warriors can do, but warrior witches?"

"Look, I wouldn't worry about what *I* can do."

My heart flutters. I need to worry about myself, she means. Mum used to say that if you've taken care of yourself, then taking care of others is easy.

Why aren't I worrying about myself? Why aren't I asking a million questions about what I am and who I am?

I know the answer, but I won't tell myself it. Not yet. It's like something won't let me.

"And, Hannah," begins Althea. "When it's necessary, you'll see a demonstration of what a warrior-witch can do. Of that, I am certain. And then you can answer your own question. I always find that is the best way."

I wish I could be as confident as that.

Althea suddenly halts as does Elric. Turning, they both raise their hands, but say nothing. Jack steps forward to move but Lilith hisses, "Stay still!"

That comforting patch of warm sea water I was feeling now bubbles; its temperature rising fast. Too fast. In seconds, my skin shimmers with sweat as perspiration trickles from my brow letting salt seep into my eyes.

A woozy sensation turns the woodland into a green blur. *How do I stay on two feet?*

"It's Gaia's fever," broadcasts Gran. "*My goodness, this is what you're all dealing with?*"

Somehow we stay upright, apparently paralysed by its intensity. All we can do is wait it out. I will my feet to move. Come on!

"*Althea, how long will this last?*" I ask.

Constance's eyes widen, realising it was my voice she heard ringing around inside her head.

"*It varies. There've been periods much worse than this rendering us immobile for hours, even days.*"

Days!

"*But this is not as intense, so it will pass soon. At least, based upon past occurrences, that is what should happen, but 'should' is a dangerous word.*"

In the thick air, a woody scent lingers not unlike Dad's old aftershave. We all just stand, waiting, wilting like parched trees. The woodland is so quiet, still. Above my head, on one of the rowan's branches, a tiny chaffinch-like bird pants, its yellow chest heaves with the effort against the heat. Birds love berries, but this one isn't even tempted by the cluster clinging at the end of its branch. It's too small to be the isherbird, Gran mentioned.

"*It'll be okay little fella.*"

The tiny bird looks straight at me.

Did it hear me?

Its walnut-sized head nods just a fraction then it rests its eyes.

"Are you okay?"

Stupidly I expect an answer. The yellow chested bird bows its head low and tilts forward.

It's going to fall.

It'll break its neck if it does!

The bird's claws slacken, its weight falling forwards.

No!

I lurch forward, throwing my arm out cupping my hand to catch it and I'm instantly hit with the woozy feeling again. Startled by everyone's sudden gasps, I realise from those I can see, that everyone is staring at me and I really don't know why. *All I did was catch the bird.*

I stay still letting the fire of the fever pricking my skin start to cool. Elric and Lilith are still staring, mouths wide open. *Awkward.*

As the air cools I stretch against the stiffness.

"Okay, everyone sit whilst we can move. It's cooler down there. Heat rises remember," orders Althea. "This should be the beginning of it passing."

Elric pushes on Jack's shoulders until he crumples to his knees, then flops onto his side. "He's okay, Evelyn," he adds raising his hand to stop her struggle to move.

Althea's right. A coolness kisses my skin. Surely the worst's over? I can't imagine that lasting hours or days. The yellow bird slowly stirs in my hand and Alpha's nose appears to sniff it.

"Hannah, how did you do that?" asks Lilith, perching down on a small black rock.

"Do what? Catch the bird?"

"Yes!"

"I don't know. I...just put my arm out and sort of lurched forward."

"But we were all held in the grip of Gaia's fever. Even *I* couldn't move," Althea adds, her tribal marks creasing across her forehead.

And she's a warrior-witch.

"*Oh.*"

"Eleanor?" prompts Althea.

"She's the real deal," replies Gran raising a small smile. "Gaia's blood courses through her."

"It certainly does," adds Evelyn. "You should have seen her try to tackle the furies."

"Furies?" asks Elric.

"Yes, they attacked at Windsor House shortly before we came here. Galtonia's doing."

Elric casts his eyes out across the woodland and listens.

Everyone stays silent.

"If the furies have been awakened, then we're going to need more help."

CHAPTER TWENTY

Eleanor
Aquarius

Hannah passes the yellow cresta bird to Constance. Taking it in such a delicate manner, she whispers something as she strokes its head. Jack, recovering from his heat exhaustion, meanders over to look at the little creature Hannah rescued from certain death.

"Evelyn, something is plaguing me and I could use your wisdom."

"Of course. Is everything alright with Elric?"

"Yes, he's going to send word to Eldred. He's the closest."

"Sensible. So, do tell."

"Back at the clearing before we sat down to eat, Hannah was certain she'd seen Caroline in the water."

"Did you see her?"

"No. Both myself and Elric checked, but there was nothing there."

Evelyn pauses for a moment, smoothing the torn remains of her satin skirt down.

"But Hannah wouldn't lie about something like that. Not that I'm insinuating she lies about matters of less consequence, of course. You really believe there's something to be explored?"

"I do."

Evelyn looks through a network of branches to the

sky as the sun descends further. Flocks of nightgayles and sparrowsparks emerge from their slumber, soar into treetops and sing the sun to sleep.

"*Eleanor, look!*" says Evelyn pointing up beyond the tree canopies. "*The first night star.*"

"*Beautiful, as always.*"

"*Yes, truly. But that is not what I meant.*" Evelyn turns me to face her. "*When the draconite attacked what exactly happened with Caroline?*"

"*We were huddled behind what was left of an old stone hut, but she panicked and kept screaming about Hannah and protecting her. Whilst I was plotting an escape with Joyce, she sneaked around the far side of the hut and began to run. I screamed out to her and as she turned the draconite swung its tail and whipped her off her feet. She landed so hard, Evelyn. I didn't need to see it to understand how badly she was injured. The sound alone...*"

I need a moment to swallow the tears.

"*When the draconite took to the skies, I projected over so that Joyce and I could drag Caroline's body to a safer place. Joyce continued the onslaught at the beast whilst I created a prism to encompass us both. Her heart was still beating, but there were no other lines of life than that. I searched the stratosphere for her, Evelyn, but I couldn't detect anything.*"

I turn on the stone facing away from Hannah so she

doesn't see the tears I cannot hold back, even if she feels my sorrow.

Evelyn takes my hand and twirls the emerald ring on my third finger.

"That used to be mine you know. I am certain, absolutely certain, that you will be in a position to pass it on to Caroline. I have no doubt of that."

"Thank you, Evelyn."

"Do you know how I know that?"

I shake my head and let a deep sigh escape.

"Because I don't think Caroline is in the stratosphere at all and that is why you cannot find her there."

"Really? Explain."

"Remind me, when was Caroline born?"

"The end of January. What are you getting at?"

"So her element is air, isn't it? But if you searched the stratosphere for her and couldn't detect her on any air-realm, then Caroline unconsciously did the only thing she could – retreat to what she knows is a place of safety. She knows the zodiac. She's Aquarius."

I stifle a gasp.

Aquarius! Of course!

Caroline *is* in the water.

CHAPTER TWENTY-ONE

Hannah
Forewarned

My empath gift is getting stronger. I'm certain of it. Gran's trying to shield me from it, but whatever she's deep in conversation with Evelyn about has upset her. She's definitely using that art of reflection I so desperately need to practise. *Maybe I need to learn how to break the reflection, too? Does it work like a mirror?* But that would be spying, wouldn't it? I mean, it's not like I need to know everything that happens, but I don't want Gran being sad.

Constance coos at the...

"Gran, do you know what sort of bird this is?"

"Cresta. It's from the chaffinch family, like on Earth."

"Thanks."

Cresta bird. Cute. That explains the little orange crest on top of its head. Constance holds up her hands and encourages it to be brave. *She is so gentle. So much like Evelyn, except when Evelyn's not kicking the furies' backsides.* With a little push the bird jumps up in her hands then it's off, flitting between the rowans' canopies.

"I'm going to talk to Elric. I want to know about the rest of the gryphons," says Jack, then leaves.

"Hannah, if I'm not being too rude, may I ask a question that has been plaguing me a little while?" says Constance, looking somewhat sheepish.

"Yeah, course."

"Why isn't your mother here with us?"

I swallow hard and breathe deeply for a moment. Mum's face under the water flashes back to me then vanishes. I can't shake the feeling that it was really her. I mean, I'm not going mad, am I? So, surely there's a possibility it's true.

"I'm sorry, I didn't mean to upset you," adds Constance seeing the look on my face that I clearly can't hide.

"A creature attacked us, but I stopped it. Mum got injured pretty badly so she's staying with Joyce where your father has been sent to be looked after."

Constance flinches as I mention her father. I guess we've got a growing list of things in common.

"I'm so sorry. I do hope she will be okay."

"She will. I know it. And, you don't need to worry about your Dad. He's safe with Joyce. She's amazing and will work out how to help him and that aura thing that's well, gone wrong I guess."

"If you trust Joyce, then I will too."

Even though Constance is three years older than me, I've kinda got 200 years on her. I don't know if that makes either of us the wiser, but what I do know is this family feeling that's growing inside me – I like it.

"And *you* stopped the creature that attacked your mother,

you say?"

"Well, not just me. I had a little help from some friends," I say nudging Alpha who, as always, remains curled at my side.

"The fox helped you?"

"Yeah, Alpha's really cool. She literally never leaves my side."

"How did you defeat it?"

"Well, I used the gifts I've been given. I wasn't *really* sure what I was doing with them, but I guess it's something I felt. You know, like your instincts. I'm always discovering more and more."

"Does it scare you having such power?" Constance interrupts. "I mean, to have killed a creature, you must be *very* powerful." She places her hand on her chest as if to steady her heartbeat.

"Oh, I didn't kill it. God no! I stopped it. *We* stopped it. And, yes, the power-thing, these gifts? Definitely scary. Really scary, in fact, but I'm just trying to deal with it."

"So the creature is still alive?"

Swoosh!

Elric flies past us, leaps up onto a boulder nestled between two trees and listens.

"It's getting louder," says Gran and she and Evelyn rush to join me and Constance.

"What is it?"

"The water. And this time it isn't Jack," he replies. We all turn to look at him. I dart across and grab his head to check his eyes for any sign rising in them. *Nothing.*

He yanks my hands away. "Get off me!"

"Sorry, but I had to check."

"An attack?" asks Althea, hand curled behind her back, no doubt clutching a sword once more.

"Possibly," replies Elric scanning a wall of trees for any movement.

"But who knows we're here?" asks Evelyn.

"No-one knows. Unless my message to Eldred has been intercepted which is a possibility."

Pricks of fear jab at me from every angle as the rustling of leaves grows louder. I can't tell if it's all of *them* or just me.

"Gran, it's too much."

"I wouldn't have bestowed the gift of the Empath upon you if I believed for one second that it would be too much to bear. It's new that's all," she replies. I hope she's right.

"The heat's passed. Let's move," orders Althea taking Constance's side. Lilith joins me, trailing her hand across my back and asks if I'm okay. I say yes to be polite. I'm getting fed up of being asked if I'm okay or not. *Is anyone okay these days?*

"Pick up the pace," orders Elric.

I glance back to Gran to see a dozen roots extract themselves from her ankles and feel my jaw drop open. She notices my expression and says, *"Here the roots feed us just as trees feed each other on Earth. I'm all topped up. Let's go."*

Althea takes my arm and pulls me with her as we all march through the woodlands, dodging hedgerows and stumps and all sorts of plants I've never seen before.

Argh!

I duck as rows of crab-like plants snap their thick leafy shells wide open trying to nip us as we move past. Elric accelerates the pace. *How are we meant to keep up?*

"What does he think it is?" I pant.

"I'm uncertain and he hasn't said," replies Lilith leaping over a large fallen trunk.

"Can't you just read his mind?"

"Not all Gaians have that gift, although many species here do have broadcast receptors, which is why we all heard your grandmother and yourself as well."

Wow. That's like human inbuilt Wi-Fi or something.

Elric keeps the pace high at the front with Jack fixed at his side. We gallop through the woodlands with Elric every so often pausing to listen and track the sounds from the nearby river where I thought I'd seen Mum. Weaved amongst the rowan trees are silver birches and elms just like the ones on Earth. There are dozens of trees I've never seen before, too. Many look ancient, their branches gnarled and twisted. Some with wide, dark brown trunks. Some with spindly glass-like ones which look like they'd crack if you touched them.

Elric, wings unfurled, kicks off from the ground and hovers overhead, scouring the woodland once more. Alpha twitches then lets out a shrill howl which hurts my ears. I throw my hands up covering them.

"Alph, what is it?" I yell as Gran and Evelyn appear at our side. She pulls Constance behind her. Alpha's howl fades into a low rumble. Her sharp teeth tug at my jumper and I let her reposition me. Protective, as always.

In one long row we face the trees and wait...

"Whatever it could be, I feel like we're sitting ducks, Elric," says Gran.

"There is something out there. And as the humans say, 'Forearmed is forewarned' which is more than sensible. This comforts me that there are some *sensible* examples that walk amongst your species, although I fear they are few in number," says Althea.

"The furies?" I ask. "Gran, you said they can make themselves invisible so they could be stood right in the middle of us for all we know listening to this and trying not to cackle their freakish little heads off."

A twinge of hatred rises just thinking about them but I squash it back down. *If that ever gets the better of me, I'm theirs and everyone's lost. Mum, Harriet, Gaia…and if she goes…*

"No, their egos are well and truly bruised. They won't strike again for a while. And not without Galtonia, I imagine," says Evelyn.

Let that witch try it. I'll be ready.

Gran, clearly hearing that, raises that judgemental eyebrow of hers.

"Althea? What is your counsel?" asks Gran. I realise she's clutching an orb again, hidden beneath her bell-shaped sleeve. She hasn't used those since we fought the draconite, at least not that I've seen.

"We have to travel east, like you say. The Ffens will know something of what has happened to Harriet and they'll share it willingly. But the question is, which line east? We can retreat deeper into the woodlands bordering Logaria and by doing that Lilith can seek out Holt. We cannot trust any future vision she provides us until we know if she is still compromised. The alternative line is that way," she points, towards where whatever it is that might be about to attack us awaits. "We can either face what it is or realise the fact that it could be nothing at all and continue tracking the river into the Ffenlands."

I don't like the sound of either.

"Can't we just stay on this line?" asks Constance, beating me to it.

"Yeah, I agree. What's wrong with this line?" I add.

"Our Earthlings have a point," replies Elric gliding back down to land at Jack's side, who ducks as Elric's wings sweep backwards and fold away. "But whatever we decide, let's get on with it. Inertia makes me nervous."

Gran lifts her hand, "May I suggest we each ready ourselves?"

Easier said than done.

"Gran, I'm not sure I can just conjure mine like you can yours. Newbie, remember?"

"Try to get the white fire into your fingertips to start with. It's just a matter of?"

"Concentration," I say as she teases out my smile.

Lilith and Evelyn both produce brightly coloured orbs. The emerald glow from Lilith's reflects like a buttercup under her chin. Evelyn's are violet and pick out the light in her chocolate button eyes just like Jack's.

"Mother?" begins Constance.

"Just stay here at my side and follow every instruction given please my darling," replies Evelyn.

"Althea, choose a pathway for us. You are the elder here of the Gaian-born."

"Not now Eleanor is with us."

What? Gran wasn't born on Earth? I don't know why I'm surprised but I am. It makes sense. I mean, she is a witchy-supernatural granny that can turn into a giant bird of fire.

"True, but I have not spent the years on Gaian as you have, Althea. We shall follow your lead."

"Very well," she nods. Althea doesn't have orbs in her hand like Gran suggested. Instead, she crosses her arms behind her head then slides out the huge silver blades from their sheaths. Althea's gloved grip tightens as she lowers the swords out to the sides, her bronzed biceps bulging.

Elric hasn't produced any weapon of any sorts so I guess he is the weapon.

I glance to Constance and mouth, "Okay?"

She nods shakily. Jack, on the other hand, seems to be loving it. He cannot takes his eyes of Elric, still awestruck I think.

"Don't I get a shiny ball to throw?" he asks.

"I don't have a 'shiny ball' as you put it to throw, Jack. Why do you think that is?"

"Well, you're massive and have wings so I don't suppose you need glowing balls and blades to protect yourself as the ladies do."

As if.

"Er, excuse me," I blurt.

"Hannah, leave it. Jack isn't from your time, remember.

He meant no slight," says Evelyn. I glance across the group of female faces. Lilith smiles as if to say it's okay. It's not, but I guess we've more important things to focus on.

"*Exactly,*" Gran's voice echoes into my head. "*Safety first.*"

"We shall stay on this line for the moment, but I want this pace quicker as there's less than an hour's sunset left. Lilith, Elric, in position and stay alert. Move."

🍂 CHAPTER TWENTY-TWO 🍂

Sleepless

It feels like forever.

Forever since I've seen Mum. Forever that we've been running through the woods. Amazingly the sun is still setting, which seems to take a lot longer here than it does back home. *We really aren't on Earth anymore.* I know we aren't but Gaian is so much like home, only nicer. No smog. No birds bound in plastic netting, their remains littering shore lines. No concrete blocks packed with people living virtual lives. Gran was right about the air here. It really does make you dizzy it's so crisp and clean. Maybe this is what Earth was always meant to be like...

It's our fault. Humans. I'm sure of it. Surely, one Lord isn't powerful enough to do all that damage?

I hate admitting it, but maybe Galtonia was right. 'Usurpers' she called us. Beating the nature out of the world at all costs. Don't people get it, yet? The image of the girl from this year's global march flashes before me. She clutches her t-shirt and screams its words at the cameras – her image plastered over every worldwide screen, 'No Planet B,' she chanted.

But there is a Planet B.

It's just that no single human can ever find out about it.

****

Everyone, including Gran has been very quiet. I worry when she's like that because that means there's too much going on in her head. Occasionally, Elric throws up his arm and we all stop, listen before continuing. My stomach flips every single time.

In places the woodland becomes denser. Alpha leaps over the enormous trunks of felled trees. *I wish I could do that.* I'd be a fox. Well, if I could be a fox living here, not on Earth. Some people never stopped hunting, despite the worldwide ban. *Scumbags.* A tingle runs down my fingers and I realise what's happening. White fire cascades down my hands, slowly growing in brightness. I pull my sleeves down gripping the cuff to cover them. *Calm down. NLR, remember.* Gran's probably sensed it, but I don't want the others seeing it. Not yet.

After a while Elric signals to slow the pace once more, his wings unfurling to sweep to the sky. Cascades of cool air from his backdraft brush against my skin, helping the final shimmer of white fire to fade.

"We will rest here tonight," begins Elric. "We cannot make it through Val Mir in time. The sun's rays will be gone any minute now, but at least we are closer."

"Is it much further?" asks Jack his shoulders slumping.

Please don't be a whinger.

"No little man. Would you like to see?" asks Elric.

"Yes please!"

Elric grabs Jack under his arms and darts upwards through the trees canopies. Jealousy pinches.

"Well, nothing unusual about that then," says Lilith.

"What do you mean?" asks Constance.

"When there's work to be done, the males of our species suddenly just disappear," she replies rolling her eyes.

"Well that's good to know it's not just on Earth then," responds Gran.

"Still?" asks Evelyn.

Gran nods.

"I would have thought after 200 years things would have equalised."

"Not quite. Still plenty of room for improvements."

Note to self: Males – don't bother.

But then a thought hits me in the gut expelling every molecule of air within me...*That's if there's a future to bother with.*

I turn to look for Alpha who is out front sniffing the air. I dart to her and fall to my knees throwing my arms around her neck. *What if there's no future to bother with?* My heart races like its lapping Cadwell Park. I snuggle my face into Alpha's fur and feel her paw connect with the back of my hand.

Thump-thump-thump. Thump-thump-thump.

I pull back from her. "What's the matter, girl?" If my heart's lapping, hers is off the track!

Her snout points over my shoulder into the woodlands.

"Have you heard something?"

Alpha's amber eyes narrow, her head drops almost like a royal bow, but those eyes of hers dart at every little sound and probably the rest that my ears can't detect. The fur spiking between my fingers is tinged tangerine. *Warning.*

"Alph, *is* something out there?"

One nod.

"Can you stay on guard until Elric's back?"

One nod.

I press a kiss into her muzzle.

Huh!

A hand presses on my shoulder. "Gran! You scared me."

"What is Alpha sensing?"

"I don't know, but she's picked something up. Like Elric, I guess."

Gran kneels down stroking the hackles across Alpha's back.

"Good girl. Always working. Always alert."

"Alpha," I begin. "Do you think it's what Elric detected earlier?"

One nod.

"And do you recognise the sound?" asks Gran.

Alpha shrugs her nearest shoulder. *That's new.*

"Not wholly recognisable?" Gran continues.

One nod.

"Okay. Thank you, Alpha. Stay with..." But Gran stops then says. "She knows."

"Lilith, get Elric back down here please."

Lilith looks up and whistles. It's nothing like a human whistle. No *wit-woo* or referee blast signalling full time. It kind of zings like someone going for it air-guitar style, but on a harp.

Flurries of leaves sleet down as Elric's wings brush the layers of canopies, Jack clutching onto Elric as if his life depended upon it. *Which I suppose it actually does.*

"My apologies. I shouldn't have left," says Elric scanning the line Alpha guards. "What has our foxy friend picked up?"

"Probably the same threat you first felt," answers Gran.

"We're very blessed to have a silverback with us. Their senses are some of the keenest known on all Gaian," says Lilith taking Elric's arm.

"I think it is best if Alpha stays on guard first, then we can each take our turn through the night. She will need *some* sleep," begins Althea, pulling her swords from their sheaths. "I suggest that everyone beds down for the night."

"We're sleeping on the floor?" asks Constance, wrinkling her nose. "Or should that be lying on the floor attempting to sleep?"

Constance's question surprises me, irritates in fact. Like the floor's not good enough for her. I never took her for a snob, but I might be wrong about that.

"Constance, if it helps you can rest against Alpha with me. I'm sure she won't mind, will you girl?"

Alpha nods over her shoulder inviting Constance to join us before returning to scan the woodlands as the last of the sunlight fades.

"Oh. Thank you. That's very kind."

"No, that's Yorkshire hospitality."

Conjuring a golf-ball sized orb of light, Evelyn sits down at the side of her eldest. "Here, you'll want this. A little nightlight."

Gaia's fever must still be burning with the air being a little warmer again.

Constance and I curl down, hands for pillows and face each other. *She has more questions, but I don't know if I have answers.*

I think she's probably right though; we've all got a sleepless night ahead of us.

🍂 CHAPTER TWENTY-THREE 🍂

Treason

Thirst wakes me.

There must be something here I can at least sip.

Alpha sits staring out at the woodland. I whisper to her that I'm going to get some water. Her ears rotate, but she never glances back. I tiptoe past Constance curled into a ball and past Evelyn and Gran. It's so strange to think that Evelyn is Gran's great-grandmother. This time lapse thing kind of messes with your head.

I trek back along the path we walked trying to remember if I saw or heard even a trickle of water. Maybe left, I think. Turning off the path and pausing, I listen for any sound of rushing water. *Yes!* I knew I'd heard it. Pushing through giant elephant-ear leaves and kola-nut plants, it takes only a few moments to reach the edge of the stream. I bend down against the fur-like grass. I realise it's the very first time I've ever seen a Gaian moon. It looks so much like ours. Even the man-in-the-moon shapes look the same. *Maybe it is. Is that even possible that we share the moon? Is Earth on the other side?*

I cup my hands into the water and drink, lapping like a thirsty cat. The air is still warm. Wiping my sleeve across my mouth, I watch the ripples I created vanish with the flow of the stream. *Not an ounce of plastic to be found.*

Huh!

All of a sudden a shoal of silverfish leap from the water as if playing a game, each giving chase one after the other. Their scales sparkle and glint. *So beautiful. But, wait. How did I know they were silverfish?* More randomness, I guess.

Just as I turn to leave, something in the water catches my eye.

Mum?

My stomach plunges.

"Argh!"

Arms burst from under the water's surface, grabbing my wrists and pulling me in. Water fills my mouth as I splutter. *No!* I fight for breath as my legs kick to resurface, but the grip is tight. Too tight. Vision blurs leaving only blocks of shapes I can't make out against a wall of seaweed green.

The grip drags me down.

Let me go!

Thrashing against my captor's clutches, I beg for release but only choke on the water filling my heavy lungs.

Someone help me, please.

"Gran, I'm drowning!"

Arms yank and tug, legs kick. I know it won't be long before my body tires. As my eyes adjust to the blurred darkness of the depths her face emerges.

Mum!

What is she doing?

Her wide stare screams at me.

"Mum, I can't breathe! Let me go!"

I don't even know if she can hear me...hear thoughts like I can.

"Mum, don't do this! I don't want to die!"

The crushing pain in my head starts to fade, thrashing limbs, chest heaves. There's little space for life left in my lungs. Mum's face starts to fade, but not her grip.

"Mum, let me go! Please! You're killing me!"

Her grip tightens yanking me forward through the thick water. Mum screams but every word bubbles to the surface.

"I can't hear you!"

I can't hear anything...

So tired.

But just then her grip loosens leaving cold handprints against my skin as her face fades...

"Don't kill me, Mum."

Suddenly a huge force propels me back and upwards, surging against the cold water. Hands press into my shoulders.

Up.

Up.

Crisp air greets my waterlogged body as we break through and surface. I slam into the ground, spluttering. Hands are on me compressing against my chest and stomach to expel the unwelcome water, clearing my lungs.

"Breathe, daughter. Breathe!"

Mum?

I'm rolled onto my side to continue vomiting river water for what feels like an eternity. Eventually strong arms pull me upright. *No honeysuckle and lavender scent. No brush of soft fur. Nothing familiar to cling to.*

I try to register the face of the one who extracted me from a watery tomb. Focusing on silver flecks in her bright emerald eyes – it is a *she* – she dabs the water from my chin as I vomit the final thick, tar-like dregs from the river.

Is she real?

Thin lime and olive veins highlight high cheek bones and temples against caramel skin. Pink lips part, letting out a deep sigh as her hand finds mine, fingers interlacing.

"My daughter of daughters," she says.

It's her!

"Gaia?"

"Rest daughter."

Why does she keep calling me that?

"I can't believe it's actually you. I thought you were dying!"

"I still am. And I need you now more than ever. Promise me you'll help me, Hannah?" Her eyes narrow as her brow furrows.

"I promise. Of course, I'll help. I don't want you to die."

"Nor I, you. That is why I am here."

But how?

"I am left bewildered and perplexed. I do not understand why Caroline tried to kill you, Hannah," she says stroking strands of hair from my face just like Mum does. "Your own mother! This will not go unpunished."

What?

No!

"No, please Gaia! She didn't mean to. I know she didn't mean to. This can't be real. We're mistaken!"

"But you almost drowned. You saw her for yourself."

"There must be some other reason. She wouldn't do that! Mum wouldn't do that!"

"An attempt on the life of an heiress is unforgiveable. Caroline made her choice and her abdication was an insult."

No! No! No!

This can't be happening!

Gaia pulls me close, her warm breath kisses my face. I stare into emerald eyes watching swirls of amber and scarlet cloud the bright silver flecks within them as her face darkens.

"Your mother committed treason, Hannah. A price will be paid!"

🍂 CHAPTER TWENTY-FOUR 🍂
Watton

Alpha's gravel tongue laps the tears running down my cheek. I push myself up and feel Gran's hand resting upon mine. I scan the familiar faces searching. *Mum? Gaia?* I'm right where I was. Where I fell asleep. No sopping wet clothes. No pools of river water I'd thrown up.

Constance wraps a woven-leaf blanket over my shoulders just like she had for Harriet not even a day ago.

"So, you met Gaia?" asks Gran.

"It was a dream, wasn't it?"

"We're not sure. But what I am sure of, is that your mother would never, ever hurt you. You know that don't you?" Gran assures.

Am I having visions like Lilith? Please no. I can't. I just can't.

Lilith crouches down at my side. "We may need to deviate before reaching the Ffenlands. I *have* to speak to Holt," she begins, her voice quivering. "As my Visionheir, he is the only one who can make sense of this. When you were pulled into my vision, I nearly killed you. Now, a dream nearly did the same."

"Lilith is right. There's something we're missing. Holt will know," assures Althea, but her chest heaves as she exhales a huge sigh.

Exchanging glances with both Althea and Elric, Lilith

opens her mouth to speak but hesitates. Alpha's body tightens around mine and like a stem holding up a flower head stops me flopping from the pressure of Lilith's nerves. *I'm nowhere near being used to an Empath, please don't add Visionheir to that list, too.*

"Lilith, you must speak plainly," begins Gran. "Do not fear the words if they must be spoken."

"Very well, Eleanor," she begins then crouches down, facing me. "What are you afraid of?"

"Me?"

She nods just once.

"Not finding Mum, I guess. Not being able to save her."

"Are you afraid of dying?"

I'm beginning to think questions are tricky little creatures. Sometimes you don't even notice them when asked like a bee crawling through your hair. Other questions are like swarms that you can't outrun, but sometimes, just sometimes questions aren't like creatures at all. They're like sledgehammers with just one purpose and Lilith's sledgehammer did its job.

Breathe.

Suddenly the anger surfaces. "Of course I am. Isn't everyone?"

Stupid question.

"But what of your primal fear, Hannah?"

"What do you mean 'primal'?" I snap.

"What Lilith is asking is, when faced with death, how…" but Gran can't finish the sentence.

How?

"I can't say I've given it much thought. I'm sort of at the beginning aren't I? I haven't really thought about the end."

My end.

"I don't exactly want to know. I mean, who does?"

"Leave her alone," snaps Constance. "How can you ask that of her?"

"What is it Lilith? What aren't you saying? Have you seen something?" asks Althea stepping forward clearly concerned.

"No. No. I haven't had any more visions; just my own summations," replies Lilith, barely taking her bright eyes off me.

"And what exactly are these summations?" enquires Gran. "You must speak them."

"I won't have her pressured," Elric says moving in front of Gran, but Gran just raises that brow of hers like she's about to tell off a naughty school boy. Elric gives way, reluctantly. *Gran seems to have some weight to throw around here.*

Lilith's face falls to the floor before her bright eyes find mine once more, "You're afraid of drowning, Hannah. Even though you're a good swimmer, it's what you fear the most.

Even more than *not* finding your mother. I believe these fears are linked and they're manifesting. Like grief can and for all intents and purposes you are grieving her loss. Permanent or temporary. Loss is still loss."

Before it crests, Lilith strokes the single tear from my cheek.

Is my own grief trying to kill me?

I stare at the ground feeling everyone's eyes resting upon me. *Run. Just run away.* My calves twitch. Alpha stands then rubs her faces against mine. I pull her close.

"Can we run away together? Just you and me," I whisper into her ear. A little snuff comes from her snout.

CRACK!

Everyone turns trying to pinpoint where the sound came from. No-one moves. No-one had moved.

Crack! Crack!

Alpha springs up, sniffing the air, a deep rumble fills her chest, her coat a constant warning beacon. Lilith drags me up but Alpha's tail curls around my waist forcing me back behind her. I take Constance's hand and pull her close, Gran and Evelyn flanking us.

Elric lifts Jack up and actually throws him through the air – his arms and legs flailing – to Althea who catches him like a rugby ball then sweeps him behind her. *Damn, she's strong.* Jack gasps as if to speak, but Evelyn stretches out to clasp her hand over his mouth. Jack's brow furrows as he peels his mother's hand off. Evelyn presses a finger to her lips with a stern look and Jack huffs.

Flicking his gigantic wings, Elric darts forward, bounding from one jagged rock to another before landing between two pine trees. The backdraft from his wings spreads their scent across the balmy forest air like butter. Just beyond the pines a figure staggers and sways, a strange wailing sound cracking the quiet of the forest.

"El...dred!" calls the stranger, its arm reaching out. "Is that you?"

As the figure stumbles, Elric leaps to catch its rail thin body, cradling it. "It is I, Elric. What happened to you?"

"Gran, who is that?"

"I don't know my dear."

Lilith and Althea move slightly closer to where Constance and I wait.

"Elric?" asks Althea scanning the woodlands beyond where Elric rests the weary figure, propping it against a mound of grass and moss.

Jack, still behind Althea, traces his finger across the edge of one of her silver blades.

"Ow!" hisses Jack. Althea turns so quickly grabbing Jack's wrist. "Never touch the blades of a warrior witch again. Do you understand, child?"

He nods furiously. Althea returns her focus upon Elric and the new arrival, but without letting go of Jack, bends down offering the palm of her own hand. Into it coils a blade of grass until there's a faint snipping noise as if the grass has cut itself. Althea bandages the blade around Jack's cut, then throws his arm back down. *Not just my nerves he can get on then.*

Elric carries the limp body towards us. Nerves twitch in my stomach. *What if it's a trap?*

"It's Watton!" he calls.

"Watton!" exclaims Lilith. She squeezes my shoulders, before leaving my side. "Goodness! He looks most unwell," she continues. Lilith scours the nearby grasses and shrubs eventually locating whatever it is she's needing. Squeezing a bluish-coloured liquid from the trumpet of a dandelion-like flower onto her fingers, Lilith then moves to a nearby pine tree and brushes its bark with the back of her hand. A few of its needles fall to the ground.

"Elric, those rocks, there."

He takes the pine needles from Lilith and crushes them between the rocks creating a fine-looking powder within a second or two. Lilith dips her blue-tinged fingertips into the powder before kneeling at Watton's side and pressing the mixture onto his pale lips.

"Watton, take this tincture I've made," she instructs.

"Hannah, do you remember me raising the roots?" Gran asks.

"Yes," I reply. *How could I forget?*

"Your turn."

"What?"

"How many times have I told you, it's pardon, not what."

"You want me to raise the roots?"

Following Gran's instructions, I kneel close to Watton's feet. He smells. Like old wood or something. *I did ask the Hollow Tree for help. And the banyan tree. I just didn't coo at them like Gran had as if they're newborns.* I pat the ground around Watton and ask the roots politely to help.

Nothing happens.

"I feel stupid."

"Dearest, get over it," orders Gran.

Pretend it's a puppy. A puppy with freaky tentacles that pierce your skin.

"Let me show you," says Lilith and begins cooing and coaxing the roots up from the ground. "Now you. You do that side. The faster we go, the faster Watton can recover, yes?"

I nod.

Here goes.

"Come on little fellas. Up you come. Someone needs your help. Come on."

"You're doing great, Hannah," calls Constance. She looks at her mother who nods in our direction and then joins my side.

"Jack. You're an elemental too so you should be learning."

"Isn't that woman's work?" comes his reply and I suddenly feel the urge to want to pat him, really, really damn hard.

"I'll pretend I didn't hear that!" I snap.

"Hannah! Even with a mother like Evelyn, battling against the societal norms will take work and patience. Teach him."

"O-kay!"

"Your sister's right. Come and help."

Jack kneels at Lilith's side and we all continue cooing and coaxing. Within seconds, dozens and dozens of little white roots shoot up and pierce Watton's limbs pumping in a milkshake-like liquid.

"Why he has strayed so far from the Ffens? They rarely leave the borders," says Althea, still clutching her swords. She glances over her shoulder checking the pathways behind us.

"I think we're about to find out," Elric says gesturing to Watton as he opens his eyes.

"Who are you?" squawks Watton, pushing back against the boulder and pulling his knobbly knees to his chest. His skin is so thin it's almost transparent. He recoils as his straw-coloured eyes dart from face to face. "What you all lookin' at?"

Having completed their task the roots snap free from Watton's limbs and vanish beneath the grass once more.

Suddenly he recognises a face, much to his relief. Watton launches himself at Lilith and clings to her like baby orang-utans cling to their mothers.

"Where've you bin? I've bin searchin'! Oh, it's terrible, Lilith! Terrible, I say!"

"It's okay. We're here now. Try to calm down and explain," says Elric as Lilith places Watton down on the ground, his sackcloth clothes hang loose on his slender frame.

"Oh, Elric. We need you and your father and your whole bloomin' army."

"Gran, can't you waft some lavender over him?"

"Good idea."

As the lavender mist floats over and settles across every one of us, Watton turns to see who has sent it.

"Is it really you? Eleanor of Walsingham! You're here. You're really here!"

"I am, Watton, yes."

"This ain't no coincidence then is it? Freya said you'd come. She was right."

Watton knows Gran! I guess she's going to know a lot of... well, everyone.

"Tell us what's happened. Why are you so far from

Ffenland?"

"Take a breath, my friend," Elric suggests placing his hand upon Watton's shoulder. "Is Freya okay?"

"I dunno. I bin out, see, roundin' up last'at flocks; some had strayed onta Rushan's lans, so I went to get 'em. Can't leave 'em, can I? When I got back home, every blinkin' one on 'em, out cold they were. I thought they's all dead. But the ones I checked, their hearts were still beatin'. What if they never waken up? They're my kinfolk, Elric. They've gotta wake up. They've just gotta!"

I know exactly how Watton feels.

"So you're the only Ffen left ali...awake?" says Althea.

"I'm not sure. I ran to check on Walt and his family and that's when I realised Frey was missing. I went to all our fave-rit places, but she wasn't there. Nor was she with her family at their den. I searched everywhere for 'er but couldn't see 'er for love nor chickens."

Chickens?

"Elric, you gotta help me."

"I will. We all will. Alpha, can you smell Freya?"

Alpha circles Watton sniffing for what, I guess, is Freya's scent. She sniffs his hands and clothing, but then shrugs a little.

"Too many?" asks Althea.

Alpha nods.

"Watton, do you have anything of Freya's? An item of clothing with her own scent on for Alpha to track?"

"No, nothin' like that," he replies, sheepishly.

"Watton?" begins Elric accusingly. "I know that look," he adds before glancing at Lilith.

Watton's cheeks flush, but his eyes sparkle.

"I is a proper Ffen and will not speak on it!"

Gran steps forward, placing her hand on Watton's bony shoulder. His eyes widen and mouth falls open like he's been touched by a goddess or something.

"What you tell us Watton will remain private, I can assure you of that and remember this: it might just save Freya's life."

"She kissed me! Right there," he blurts pointing to his cheek.

Aw.

"Alpha," invites Gran.

Watton pulls his head back creating a ripple of chins as Alpha begins to sniff and lick his face.

Welcome to my world, Watton.

Gran glances aside and smirks, clearly overhearing my thoughts. I can't help but smirk too. Eventually, Alpha drops and nods to Elric.

"Right, we stick together and follow our tracker," orders Elric as we assume our formations once more.

CHAPTER TWENTY-FIVE

Earth – November: Joyce
Funerals and Autopsies

William hasn't moved. His cup of oolong has long since gone cold. Curled into what was probably his own armchair all those years ago, I watch the rain pelt the windowpanes, resting my cup and saucer on my knees. There is little else I can do. Forcing William to accept what is will serve no purpose. For this new reality is something he must come to in his own time.

I stand and remove William's cold tea from the table and return to the kitchen followed by the pack, passing Mary's body on the chaise wrapped tightly in wool blankets. I promised Eleanor that Mary would be laid to rest before dawn with or without William, but I cannot imagine she had any clue as to William having such a reaction as this. Anger? Rejection? Yes, but not this catatonic state? I linger by the doorway certain that the news of his children's purpose is weighing heaviest of all.

Leaving the door latched, I collect a pan, fill it with cold water before adding four eggs and bringing them to boil. Pulling out a large tub of poultry from the larder, I toss the silverbacks enough to satiate even their appetites. That's the thing with gargoyles. Once awakened they tend to gorge on delights they've missed out on for years or even decades.

I set two places, butter the bread and wait in the hope that William's appetite will eventually control his actions rather than his emotions. Just as I finish the second egg and reach for a third, the latch clicks.

"Ah, William. At last. Come and sit. Here, these should tempt you."

He steps down into the kitchen and lunges at me. The chair scrapes across the stone floor as I push myself back but neither of our human reactions compare to those of silver foxes. Beattie and Delta launch at William striking his chest with brute force sending him hurtling across the kitchen. He slams into the dresser. Teacups fly and shatter against walls as plates roll and smash. Sprawled on the floor, dazed, William clutches his chest.

I signal for the silver foxes to stand down.

"Stay up front though my darlings," I say to which Delta snuffs and nods holding the ground between me and William. Clearly the darkness in his aura has surfaced, as I suspected it might.

"Urgh. What…what happened?" William groans rubbing his chest and wincing.

"You tried to attack me so the foxes put you down."

"I feel like I've been struck by a locomotive."

"Yes quite. I apologise for the blunt force, but it was

necessary. I am here to help you, William. That is why you have been sent to me, but I will defend myself by any and all means even if you are the father of the Elementals."

"Forgive me, Joyce. I don't know what's gotten into me."

"Well, that's why you're here," I say picking up my dining chair and resting over the back of it.

"Truly, I beg your forgiveness."

Sensing a level of normalcy in William's demeanour, Delta and Beattie slide downwards resting upon the cold floor.

"That must be earned. Like Evelyn said, at present you aren't to be trusted which pains you and me both. This is not your fault or your doing, that I understand, but still, precautions are necessary," I reply gesturing at my protection squad. "And there's more out there should the need arise."

"That won't be necessary. Look, I knew what Evelyn was when we married, but never did I imagine what would become of us and our children," William says pushing himself up onto a dining chair, grimacing through the pain.

"Your dedication and belief in Evelyn is most commendable. To commit to her, love her as you do, that is an act of selflessness knowing what she is. But now there is much more at stake, William," I warn.

His head falls into his hands, "So this woman, Gaia, she

really is dying and my children are…" but he falls short of repeating my revelation.

"Yes, and yes."

"Then I have to do something!" William stands, but so does Delta.

"And you shall."

The kitchen falls quiet except for the tick-tock of the carriage clock.

"Why am I feeling like this? This darkness you say, that has attached itself to me. What is it doing?"

"What it's doing is infecting you, turning your soul dark and against those you hold dear. If left unchecked, it will consume you. We all have it inside us. Mostly, dark and light are balanced. Some creatures, some humans have a greater capacity for light, but what is equally true is there are those who hold little or none and darkness dominates. And finally, there are those that become infected by it and once an imbalance occurs it can be very difficult or impossible to rectify once certain trajectories are set. Like the spillage of ink. No amount of blotting paper can undo the spillage, but it could have been avoided altogether."

"What do you propose?"

"There is one thing, but I dare say you will not like it. It will, however, give me the most definitive picture of what has caused the shadow on your aura."

William paces the kitchen for a while then rests against the large mantelpiece above the fireplace, staring into the flames. "I am not sure I want to hear this."

"Well, technically, you don't have to. I can put you into a state of suspended consciousness which would allow me to perform the…"

"I won't be put in any type of suspended state. I have a right to know what is being done to me."

"Good. That settles it. The procedure is known as an astral autopsy."

"Autopsy? No! No! Absolutely not!"

"Then you will never see your children again, William. We could never put them at such a risk."

"But you can't do that!" he cries turning and slamming his fists against the table making the eggs topple from their cups, roll off and smash on the floor, leaving the yolks to bleed out. Delta leaps up on the table and stalks towards him, baring razor sharp teeth, and emitting a threat deep from his chest to which William instantly throws his hands up in surrender.

"Alright! Alright!"

"You could never live with yourself if you hurt them and you know that," I try to reassure.

"Very well," he sighs accepting defeat. "You have my permission. Whatever it takes. I will not let anything come between my family and I."

"Wise choice. I am glad you've come to this naturally," I say looking at the silverbacks allowing just the faintest smile to rise into my cheeks.

"Well, if you call being threatened by unusually large foxes, natural."

"Quite. But before we begin the procedure, there is something most pressing which must be done."

"Lay Mary to rest," he nods.

"She will be safe alongside Caroline."

"That is Hannah's mother, yes?"

"Correct. She has been interred under Windsor House. Completely safe."

"Very well."

"Delta and Beattie will remain at your side for your own protection. And you want to be thankful, William, it was the foxes who put you down just now, and not me."

His jaw drops, disbelief walks across his face.

Hmm, if only he knew.

Once back in the reception, I remove the large rug to reveal the emerald and gold pentagram. William passes five pillar candles which I light and then invite him to place Mary's body in the centre.

He hesitates. "The last time I was asked to enter a pentagram, I ended up here."

"And here you shall stay, but Mary cannot. She deserves an appropriate send-off wouldn't you agree? After all, she has been with your family a great length of time, I understand."

"It is most befitting that she is laid to rest here. Mary has been with our family since I myself was a little boy," he says placing her body down with great care. He takes a moment to kneel at her side and holds her hand to his cheek. "Goodbye dearest, Mary. You were loved."

"And still is, I imagine."

William steps out from the pentagram as I light the final candle, flanked by Delta and Beattie.

"Almighty Mother. Here lies a daughter. A protector of the Elementals. Stalwart in her commitment to the sacred lineage of the Walsingham line – your line. As only a mother so benevolent can, encompass her in your light, envelop her in every protection you can afford until such time as she is ready to reunite with us all. Anchor her spirit to this sacred place, this house of worship, binding her forever to it, forever yours. Conceal her being from those who would trespass and seek out this protector. This we ask of you, Almighty Mother with hearts filled of everlasting light. Blessed be upon this night."

I nod at William.

"Blessed be upon this night," he says daubing his cheeks

with his handkerchief. "I will miss her more than I can say."

As the pentagram groans once more, each stone slab unfolds to allow the kaleidoscope of lights to swaddle Mary. William falls to his knees, overcome as her body descends to take its place next to Caroline's.

As the brightness fades, my eyes adjust to scan the darkness. Mary's body slows to a suspended state amongst the velvety shadows.

It's then, my heart plummets like a penny being tossed into a wishing well. That cannot be right.

Where's Caroline?

CHAPTER TWENTY-SIX

Gaian – Hunter's Moon: Hannah
Freya, Found

The sun filters through the network of trees as it rises and even though its autumn it's still comforting, like it is back home. Alpha pads the way as we string out in a line; Althea ordering us to stay within touching distance of each other.

The occasional twitter of birds breaks patches of silence that has settled all around us like dust. Gran says that the lack of rustling and natural 'chitter-chatter' alarms her somewhat. *It is strange.* I guess that could explain why Alpha's coat hasn't stopped flickering. Even the tips of her fur across her shoulder blades sometimes look like they've been dipped in ruby-coloured paint, adding an extra scoop of nerves to those already stirring in my stomach. *Is it Alpha reacting to me or am I reacting to her, though?*

"You look yooman to me?" asks Watton, his wiry rusty-coloured hair rising like the sun.

"I am human. At least some of me is. I'm Hannah."

"This is my granddaughter, Watton," calls Gran which halts him in his tracks. Alpha turns, "Yip, yip, yip," which is her way of saying get a move on.

"Oh. *Oh!* I see. Well, in that case..." he says flinging one arm back and immediately I know what that means.

Not again!

After Galtonia bowed, I did feel bad for being rude. I wouldn't feel bad now though. I could list a lot of things I could do to her and not feel bad about, but it's hate like that, that she wants me to feel according to the furies and that'll just get me in trouble. This time, I grab Watton's free hand and shake it. "It's very nice to meet you." I clutch it unwilling to let go. Watton tries to tug his hand away, but I hold tight, at least until Evelyn interrupts offering her own. I practically pass it to her. *I can't stand all that bowing.*

"And I am Evelyn, a Light Keeper from the Walsingham line and these are two of my children. Meet Constance, my eldest and her brother, Jack."

They both smile and nod politely. Jack looks Watton up and down as Watton nods in return. Jack's brow creases as he stares at the rags on Watton's feet, tied neatly into a bow with string around his ankles. *That can't be comfortable.*

I quietly step back to avoid any more attention or bowing that Watton seems to think necessary and rejoin Alpha now with Gran at the front of our line. I trail my hands through the bushes and against the leaves and flowers as we head for Ffenland. A black insect that sort of looks like a dragonfly lands on my outstretched arm like it's found a perch. Offering my palm instead, it hops across. Cool. Gran whispers that it's a rainfly, but spelt r-e-i-g-n because they live the longest and are like Queen Bees amongst their species. As I hold it up to my face it rubs its front legs then crosses them after sitting down. I think it wants to stay, but I put it back onto a leaf.

"Wait," begins Watton. "Did you just say two've 'em?"

Evelyn's heart flutters at Watton's question. *Why am I feeling her so much now?*

"My youngest, Harriet, has been taken. We were on our way to you and your kinfolk for help. I must find my youngest, Watton. Please tell me you can help us?"

"Well, I's imagine so. It ain't worth knowing if the Ffens 'ant 'eard on it. That's what our elders all say."

"Then I am not without hope," replies Evelyn taking Constance's hand as if she might vanish. Her nerves continue fluttering almost stealing my breath. She's fighting so hard to keep it together. *Will I ever get used to being an Empath?*

"Keep on," orders Althea from the rear. "And Alpha, quicken the pace. We aren't all that far now."

Watton runs ahead to join Alpha just in front of me and Gran and a vile smell wafts across. *Urgh.*

Has that come from Watton? Yuck!

****

I don't have a watch and daren't turn my phone on to check the time – that's if time is even the same here – so I've no idea how long we've walked for. Lilith said that we were getting closer to the border and it does look like the woodland is thinning.

Mingling amongst the last line of rowans, we stand staring out at the Ffenlands. That vile smell still lingers in the air but Watton is nowhere near me now. *Maybe it was Alpha. Gross!* But surely the smell would fade, wouldn't it? I can't be the only one smelling it, surely?

"Watton," begins Elric. "When you returned with the flocks, was there this stench lingering in the air as it is now?" *Not just me then.*

"Yes. I 'adn't really paid attention, but now you mention it. Smells like my uncle's bottom after he's bin at the brockroots."

Lovely.

"It isn't brockroot," says Lilith. "I'm reasonably certain the aroma is sea-stickle. It's an aroma found in many a sea-dweller or plant."

"What on earth is that vile stench?" asks Jack covering his mouth. "It's disgusting!" *Tell it like it is, Jack.*

"Sea-stickle? Are you certain?" asks Althea.

"Yes. I don't tend near water, but it's so distinct. I never forget an aroma once inhaled."

"Where have you come across the scent before, Lilith?" ask Elric, his chest feathers fanning his face as if to waft the smell away.

"Now that I am not sure of, but it feels like it's attached to a memory from when I was foundling."

"Gran, what's a foundling?"

"An infant who has lost their parents or been abandoned by them."

Lilith's an orphan! I didn't expect that, especially with Gran saying she's her godmother. I guess because she talks of Holt and him being her elder. I thought he was probably her dad.

"Is it safe to cross onto the lands now, Althea?" asks Evelyn eager to continue.

I'm desperate to find Mum, but having a child taken? That's worse, isn't it? But I am a kid with no parents, so maybe that's worse. Or maybe it isn't about what's worse because, let's face it, it is all totally and completely...I bite my tongue and just spell out a rude word in my head so if Gran does hear me, I only spelt a bad word and didn't say it. *She absolutely hates bad language of any sort.* I get it. I do. She says its 'unladylike'.

Jack continues with his shopping list of questions for Elric. How fast can he fly? Can Elric teach him? What's the heaviest thing he's ever lifted? Is he the king of the gryphons?

I wonder if we can fly. Jack, Constance and me. That would be beyond.

"It looks clear. And the Ffens need us. We cannot abandon them. We stand a chance of discovering more about what happened to Harriet if we stay a while and help," replies Althea.

Being hit by a boulder-sized sense of worry from Evelyn, I take her hand and together we march forward. A daughter without a mother and a mother without a daughter. A mismatched pair in some ways, but still a pair. *Still family.*

Watton runs to our side crying out, "Wait, wait! If we takes the northern pathway it'll be a lot safer 'cos it's furthest from the port and we can sees it more clearly. I reckon whatever attacked our village prob'ly come that way," he points.

Leading us down a steep embankment, Watton brings us to a narrow pathway cutting through a huge field of tall grasses and pond reeds, which look like violet-coloured lollipops. It reminds me of holidaying with Mum and Dad on the Norfolk Broads a bit and all the little canal routes we'd follow. In the distance, clusters of little wooden huts appear with thatched roofs and smokeless chimneys. It's so still. So quiet. Gran repeats that the absence of nature's hum is never a good sign.

Being closer now, the smell, like rotting broccoli, has grown stronger.

"I reckon Althea and Lilith is best tending on 'em," says

Watton.

"Yes, but we stay close. Jack don't leave Elric's side. Constance, you're with me and your mother. Eleanor and Alpha flank our young protégé."

Protégé?

I look at Gran blankly.

"A talented student with potential, shall we say," explains Gran.

But a student of what? Can't exactly stick this lesson in a timetable, can you?

Potential.

That's what they referred to me as before I was gifted with Mum's inheritance by the Hollow Tree. It really isn't just me though. Everyone's filled with bags of potential. Especially us kids. I mean, we're at the beginning of everything aren't we? But it's not right to say that adults are at the end of everything. Mum's still young. She's got ages left. I hope. At least, she has if me and Gran can find her.

As we approach what's left of the village, Watton whimpers and Althea offers her hand. *Not all warrior, then.*

"How do we find Freya? I be lost wi'out 'er. She's my bestest ever friend," sobs Watton wiping his nose across his sleeve. *Nice to know it's not just us humans that have gross habits.*

"Lilith and I will ascertain what's happened to your

kinfolk and treat them. The more information we have from witnesses, the better," Althea replies.

Only a few of the huts close by are left standing. Gran points to the largest with a sloping roof and at least ten walls that still stand. Other huts in the distance have been completely flattened. Benches, wooden pots, pans and clothes litter the village. It's not just household things though, I realise as up ahead Althea, trailed by Watton, approaches the nearest of dozens of bodies. She kneels at what looks like a child with cropped black hair and dressed in hemp-like sacks which have been made into trousers and t-shirts similar to Watton's.

"That's Thim. At least that's what everyone calls him cos he's so small like a thimble. He's Walt's youngest. Poor little fella. Din't stand a chance," says Watton before turning to Evelyn. "When you said your little 'un had been taken, you meant as in she's been 'napped?"

"I did. So if you can help me get my daughter back."

"Why haven't the 'nappers pinched all these little 'uns as well?"

Althea frowns, "Do you really not know who these children are?" and points to Jack and Constance.

"I's not have psychic powers like you lots do."

Above us, Elric's wings create a draught as he scans the village. Right now, I'm glad I can't see what he can.

Gran, who's been so quiet again, approaches Watton. "I find it somewhat hard to believe that you've heard nothing of what has been happening to Gaia, especially with all the extreme climate changes you've experienced as we have on Earth."

"Everyone's sayin' she's sick, an' I'd heard talk of some shade stalkers been 'ont move, but I just tend the flocks is all. I don't like fuss and worry so I keeps away. I don't reckon much'ta gossip either."

Watton hangs his head like a school boy being told off but with no clue why. He rubs his hands against the grass as if for comfort. I don't like seeing him like that.

"What if it wasn't gossip though, Watton?" I ask as Althea lifts Thim's frail body and cradles it.

"He's still damp and that stench hasn't gone anywhere," she says smelling his hair. "Have any of you ever smelt this before?"

Standing a little away from us all, Elric sniffs the air but shakes his head. Alpha, too. If they don't know what it is, and Lilith barely recognises it, how can we help?

"If Watton knows nothing and every one of the Ffens who might know something is out cold then how can they help?" Evelyn says, before turning to Watton. "I am so very sorry this has happened to you and your kinfolk. Truly, I am, but I have to find my daughter and we must have safe passage to Gaia. A great many lives depend upon this."

"Oh dear!" he exclaims. "Oh dear! This is very bad isn't it?"

"But every one of the Ffens isn't here," says Constance.

Of course! She means Freya, but before Constance can explain, the sky darkens like a swarm of bees has settled over the sun, blocking nearly all of the light.

"Ah! The cavalry's here!" announces Elric, his wings ruffling.

The swarm grows closer, creating an enormous eagle-shaped formation. *Are they…Gryphons?*

"Dive!" growls a voice so deep it echoes across the valley.

Gran has a huge smile across her face. *This must be good. Really good.*

Each of the gryphons land one after the other, bouncing forward, their bronzed wings flapping then folding. There must be at least a dozen of them and all kind of look like Elric. The largest of the gryphons steps forward, his wings tinged with silver and grey tips, not black like Elric's. Jack's mouth is wide open, his eyes bright, like he's just discovered a whole army of new best friends to play with.

Elric walks forward and they don't just shake hands, they shake entire arms, pulling themselves into each other's shoulders. "Now then lad," begins who I'm guessing is the leader.

"Father," replies Elric. "How did you know?"

Father?

"Watton sent a Finch Flyer."

That's probably their version of a text.

"Everyone, this is Eldred, my father. Commander of the Gryphon Battalions."

Clearly pleased, Eldred's chest puffs out. "Never tire of hearing that," he smirks. "So, what enormous pile of Shire dung have you lot been wading into now, then?"

"Eldred! Eldred! You came!" Watton jigs about, clearly the best news of the day.

"Of course I did. And, my little friend, we found something that you might be missing." Eldred signals to one of the other gryphons. They bend down letting someone slide down from their back.

"Freya!"

CHAPTER TWENTY-SEVEN
Vishlik

"Where've you bin?" shouts Watton flinging his arms around Freya's neck and pretty much flattening her against the glistening grass.

"Gerroff me you big fat turnip!" cries Freya shoving Watton – who could literally never be described as 'big' or 'fat' – off, then picking herself up. She brushes her sackcloth dress down then offers her hand to pull Watton up. He bounces puppy-like for a moment before Freya yanks his arm to calm down.

"Sorry. I knows I is a bit giddy, but you's my bestest ever friend and I thought I'd never sees you again. That's what I told that lot," Watton says pointing at us. "So, go on then. Where was ya?"

"Stuck up our bloomin' cook pine tree," replies Freya. "I didn't reckon they could get me up there."

"Who's 'they'?" asks Althea still cradling Thim. She bends down to allow Freya to reach up and stroke his cheek.

"Poor Thim," she sighs. "We were teaching him how to climb." She looks up at Althea. "It was the Vishliks I saw. They's wiped out the whole village. I seen it all from up there," she points. Everyone turns to look across the village to the last line of rowans before the valley dips where a cluster of cook pine trees juts out. One bends lower than the rest as if it's reaching out to touch us. *Their roots must be strong to hold their trunks like that.*

Searching the floor, Freya spots a dock leaf which she dabs against her cheeks like a handkerchief before wringing it out and returning it to where she found it.

"What exactly did you see?" asks Elric.

We've all now circled this little Ffen which makes me suddenly protective of her. "Everybody needs to give Freya some space, OK?" I say.

She freezes, her eyes glistening as fresh tears spill. I pick up the dock leaf and pass it to her. Her mouth smiles but her eyes are still filled with sadness. She walks away to a cluster of stumps by one of the huts that hasn't been flattened in the attack and sits down tugging at the frayed edges of the dress. Maybe she's not ready to talk about it.

"Give her a minute," I say moving in front of Elric as if not to let him pass. Not that I could actually stop him. He's a mammoth compared to me.

"Very well," he replies.

"We can't just leave the villagers like this." says Lilith looking at Gran almost like she's waiting for an order from her.

"Can't we move them?" begins Constance. "I mean, we moved Mary to protect her, didn't we? So, there must be something we can do."

Jack wanders between clusters of bodies nearby. Some looking like they've just fallen asleep against one another. He notices a body of another small Ffen, bends down and picks up what looks like a wooden toy. Jack sits, just like he did with Mary, his head sinks. Little sobs hiccup from his chest. He's colouring me in again but not with dark red crayons. This time they feel a deep shade of blue, which makes sense. His feelings aren't furious or fast. They're slow and careless like he's lost interest. That's not good.

"Gran, what are we going to do? I don't know how much I can take. We have to find Harriet for Evelyn's sake, but we can't leave the villagers like this. Can't you do something?"

She doesn't reply, just nods while continuing to stare out to the valley. *What is she looking at? The sea beyond the hills?* I try, just for a minute, to push my way into her thoughts, but can't find a way in. *She must know I'm trying.*

Clearing his throat to get our attention, Eldred removes part of the armour strapped to his arm and chest letting his plume of silver feathers ruffle as he strides over.

"Ah, that's better," he announces gruffly like his throat is paved with gravel. "Come here lovely lady," he begins taking Gran's hand to kiss. "It's been a long time old friend." Eldred's huge bear hug leaves Gran's feet dangling.

"Er, I know full well what category my advanced years fall into, Eldred, thank you! I am in no need of a reminder," she smiles softly. "Now, if you put me down you can tell me what the proposal is that you wish to make!"

"Always know what I'm thinking, don't you? I guess you know me all too well."

Is Eldred kidding? He doesn't know Gran can read minds?

Gran gives me a sharp look. *O-kay. Apparently not. Keep your mouth shut that means.*

"Let this lot," he gestures to his flock, "gather the bodies into one safe place. You can cast one of those protection spells of yours over it, or Evelyn can seeing as she's a Light Keeper. The hallow hall looks like it's borne little damage making it a far safer option. Not that we have many options left in the village. I can leave my lot here guarding the poor souls. I will join you all to locate the little one. I'm sure Elric won't mind me tagging along."

"All Gryphons are welcome. Especially dear friends. Even better when those friends are skilled. And, it would hasten our departure to Gaia. Thanks to Freya, I believe I know where she is," replies Gran.

Thanks to Freya?

"Then let us hear what the young Ffen has to say on the matter," replies Eldred, winking at me as he passes and instructs his, well, flock, I guess, to scour the village and return each fallen Ffen to the safety of the hallow hall not far from where we entered. Bounding over to Freya where she sits quietly, Watton at her side, Eldred scoops her up and sits her on his knee like it's a visit to Father Christmas.

"Now then little Freya the Ffen. Tell all these kind folk exactly what you saw and don't spare the horses," he says sounding just like Gran.

Watton whispers something in Freya's ear.

"Only if she holds my hand," replies Freya pointing at me. I smile through gritted teeth realising exactly what Watton has whispered.

Gran nudges me forward.

"I'm not sitting on Eldred's knee!" I scowl before sitting just close enough so Freya can take my hand.

As she begins, her voice trembles, "I's wanted t'look for Gaia. That's why I love cook pines. They all'us know where she be an' I'd heard she were real sick. I thought if I whispered to her she'd hear me and if I wished really really hard she'd get well. The Elders told Thim's father they thought Gaia was sickenin' for summat 'cos of all the strange weather we bin 'avin. I wasn't ear-wiggin' if that's what yous all thinkin'," Freya assures us. "I just over'eard when I was delivering last'at heggs."

"Heggs?"

I look across at Gran who smirks.

"Hawthorn eggs. Eggs from hawthorns. Heggs."

I bite my lips together, look down and try not to laugh. I

don't know why it's funny, but it is. Apparently, only to me and Gran though.

Freya continues, "Everyone were packin' up their stalls. An I's remember Watton bin sent t'round up last'at flocks because some 'ad strayed onta Rushan's lands so off he went. I'd delivered all my heggs for the day so I's left to go climb our cook pine to whisper to Gaia. I love tellin' her all my secrets."

Watton blushes. *Aw!*

"I'd nearly gotten tut top when I 'eard a strange noise as if the ground were breaking apart. My heart started fluttering as fast as a beebonnet. The tree was shaking so violently but I gripped its fur as tight as I could and wrapped my legs around its trunk. I still slipped and scraped my shinbone, right there," points Freya holding her leg out for everyone to look at it.

"I will tend to that shortly," says Lilith but doesn't leave to look for hazel leaves, clearly hanging on Freya's every word.

"I closed my eyes not wantin' to see. I was so scared as the wind howled and whooped. I thought it must be wallopin' everythin' in its path. It was only when I's peered through my lashes that I realised it wasn't the wind but the blummin' ocean crashin' through all'at trees, flattenin' everythin' in its path. Oh, I's never 'eard the ocean make noises like it. Was as if it were snarlin' and snappin.'"

"What do you mean snapping and snarling?" asks Gran.

"The ocean 'ad dark shadows inside. I di'n't know what they were at first, but then I remembered soma-the Elders' tales of vicious creatures that lived int deepest parts at'ocean. Little fishy bodies an' one giant glassy eye that stares out at ya from under the water. Theys 'ave mouths filled with razor rocks that sink into ya skin an' start drainin' your essence from ya."

"That would explain these marks," says Lilith rolling back Thim's trouser leg, revealing jagged puncture marks where the Vishliks had latched on.

Poor Thim. Poor Ffens. They must have been terrified.

"Continue, Freya please," Gran instructs.

"Rights when I's thought we was all done for, somethin' strange 'appened. Was like all the air in the world was about to set on fire. I could hear the Vishliks screaming and squawking. As the waves crashed against the trees, it knocked many of the Vishliks clean out. Their bodies was just bobblin' along ont top'at water. Even my skin started bubblin'! I gots red welts all over, I have. That's when I knew that everyone int' village either be drowned or be boiled alive! Finally, it got so hot that the Vishliks began bursting and popping right inside the water! Poof! Jus' like that!" she says clicking her fingers.

Everyone stares blankly at Freya.

"This making sense to any of you lot?" asks Eldred.

"Actually, yes. It would coincide with when we were all paralysed by the fever," explains Lilith. "The closer we got to the Ffens, the worse the heat became until we had to stop."

"All except Hannah!" exclaims Jack, to which Eldred's cheeks puff out a long sigh of air.

"You're a little mystery aren't you?" says Eldred after a moment.

"Wait! I haven't finished!" scowls Freya. "And you know what?" she asks but doesn't wait for a reply. "I think it was Gaia. I reckon she heard my whispers and saved us all from drowning. How else could that 'ave happened, aye? But when I looks out after-ta mist 'ad cleared, I couldn't believe what I saw! Everyone were dead. I cried and cried and just clung to the tree."

"Your family and friends aren't dead. They're all perfectly safe. The whole village, at least as far as we can tell so far, has survived," explains Althea. "But that doesn't mean there are no fatalities. This we need to ascertain."

"You saved them, Frey! Oh my goodness, yous the best!" cries Watton. "If yous 'adn't whispered to Gaia, she'd never 'ave known."

Maybe Watton has a point.

"Really? They ain't dead? I saved 'em?" she asks, turning to me.

"Yes, Freya. I think you did," I nod.

I mean, if I can talk to trees then maybe Gaia really did hear her. It is possible, isn't it?

CHAPTER TWENTY-EIGHT

Caroline
Elijah Moon

The wind's breath blankets my heat-pricked skin. I peel my eyelids back to be met with throbbing red welts where my skin bubbled against the searing heat. I'm not in the water anymore. No shady cool patches I can hide in. *How did I get out?*

A tightness, a soreness permeates my knees, my elbows and palms. *Did I crawl across a river bed?* The breeze adds to the evidence that I did. My fingertips explore the ground. Grass. Rocks. Sand.

In the distance, a skylark – at least that's what it sounds like – zips from my peripheral vision landing on a rock too close to my face to feel comfortable. Taking every ounce of strength I have, I push against the dusty ground and roll over feeling for the comfort of more greenery. A long shadow crosses the sunlight I wince against. It's pulsing heat eager to lull me to sleep, to rest.

A soft crack sharpens every sense I have, eyes widening. "Who's there?"

I try to push myself up again, aware that the shadow is tall not long and belonging to some *one* not some *thing.*

"Here, let me help you," someone says with a soft lilt, pulling me up under my arms.

I fight against the grip realising the voice is male.

"Get off me!"

"Listen now. You are badly hurt and I am an apothecary. Wouldn't it be wise to let me help you?"

But how do I trust a stranger?

"I will not hurt you. Let me heal these wounds before they become infected."

I try to focus, but their image blurs.

"I…need…to…" but words fail me.

As he lifts me up, I give in.

"Can you tell me your name?" He's too close. His breath kisses my cheeks.

I try to summon moisture to my mouth, lips, but my entire body feels parched despite being entombed in a watery casket for days…weeks…*I don't even know.*

"Caro…" I begin as my body is hoisted up but am overcome with dizziness from the motion and fight the nausea instead. My eyelids grow heavy.

"Well, Caro, I am sure when you're well once more, it will be a pleasure to meet you. My name is Elijah. Elijah Moon."

CHAPTER TWENTY-NINE

Hannah
Lessons

"Hannah, walk with me," says Lilith passing me a piece of bark she's picked from the ground.

We pass the Hallow Hall, its enormous thatched roof casting a shadow across our pathway to the edge of the woodland where we'd entered the village.

"How long does sunrise take here?" I ask.

"Depends upon the season. It's autumn, but the sun will be in ascension for another few hours," she replies picking up what looks like a dandelion, its fluffy head is bluish, not white like they are back home. "This is the cerulion."

"So it's literally a blue dandelion?"

"It is. I do know many of the flowers that reside on Earth. Usually they're a late spring flower, but with Gaia's fever rising and falling sharply and frequently their natural cycle has been disrupted." She blows the cerulion's head releasing its fluffy petals into the air. They soar upwards on the breeze. "Their reappearance is not only unusual, but dangerous."

"Dangerous? Why?"

"They should be well into their hibernation phase, but are still flowering and dispersing."

"And that's dangerous?"

215

"Perhaps 'dangerous' is the wrong word. Alarming would be more precise. You see, before I was bestowed with the guardianship by Gaia, I, like all dryads across all four kingdoms were working to understand what was happening to our environment. We are still trying to decipher what every unnatural occurrence means for our planet and Gaia herself. That is why I was raised."

"What do you mean 'raised'?"

Surely Lilith wasn't born because of climate change?

As we wander between two rowans, I look back to see Gran, Althea and Evelyn deep in discussion. *Nothing new there then.* I don't even attempt to listen in. Alpha pads her way across to where Lilith and me are examining the trunks of the rowans. Well, Lilith is. I'm not really sure what I'm doing other than admiring the bark. Alpha squats nearby, wees then scratches the grass to cover it. Very ladylike.

"I was raised earlier than normal as a Visionheir. I am the youngest to ever be called from Holt's lineage. With my vision being tampered with and our connection, it is imperative that I speak to him. But what is of equal importance, is that I teach you at least some of what I would have passed on to Harriet."

Lilith's head drops for a moment feeling the weight of the loss. *She must feel so guilty.* It really wasn't her fault, though.

"You were meant to teach as well as protect?"

"Yes. It is our duty."

"So, Althea is a mentor to Constance and Elric is a mentor to Jack?"

"Jack has bonded with Elric although Althea was meant to be his assigned Guardian. And I, Harriet's."

"So you're going to teach me about bark?" I smile holding up the rotted piece.

"Look at it. Tell me what you see."

Really?

"It's a sort of hazel-brown, lots of ridges. It feels rough. And, is covered in lots of tiny holes."

"Does it smell?"

I sniff the bark. It's not a strong scent, but there's something strange. It's a chemical smell, not natural like I expected.

"Remember that scent, Hannah. It is the scent of bark beetles. They are tiny creatures, almond in shape with long, thin comb-like antennas. Bark beetles also have minuscule holes across the shells with symmetrical patterns in browns, creams and blacks. If they ever bore into a tree, the tree's fate is set. The invaders will spread their larvae through its cambium, the layer beneath the bark, before consuming the tree from the inside weakening it until it can no longer stand. The tree will crumble within a few decades.

"Poor tree! I can't imagine that. Being eaten alive from the inside." The thought makes me shudder.

"It is a minute creature, but deadly. They bring slow death. The worst kind."

I stare at the hundreds of holes in the piece of bark no bigger than my hand imagining armies of bark beetles boring into the defenceless trees. The pain the tree must have felt makes my heart ache for a moment.

"Can't the trees stop them?"

"Depends upon the tree. Each species has a different defence mechanism."

"Hannah!" calls Gran, making me jump. "We need to leave. Now!"

"What's the matter?"

Escorted by Alpha, Lilith leads us past Eldred's platoon of gryphons carrying body after body into the Hallow Hall. My heart slumps to my stomach.

"Tell them what you told us, Freya," instructs Gran.

As we arrive, Freya is fretting. It's not that I can feel her, but see her. She flaps her arms against her body like she's trying to take off.

"Well, when I was up our cook pine, I saw summat. And I'd forgot' till now. It was a vessel. It left port an' travelled south."

"And that's bad?" I ask looking from face to face.

Elric's clearly agitated so Eldred places his hand on his son's shoulder to calm him.

"I dint see what was loaded onto it, but it were heavily guarded."

"Guarded by who?" Lilith asks, unable to hide her alarm.

"Not who, but what," adds Eldred.

"Volkhas. A dozen, I reckon," says Freya.

Althea places Thim into Watton's arms. He's very quiet. Too quiet. "They're higher-level shade stalkers," she begins. "Which means whatever and whoever was on that vessel requires protection. A lot of protection."

"Even just one Volkha would have been alarming. But a dozen?" says Elric exchanging a look with his father that sends a shudder right down my spine again.

"We think, my darling," begins Gran, "that whoever it was, it must be whichever Lord has betrayed Gaia because only a Lord could command that level of protection and…"

Gran pauses as if finishing her sentence will cause pain. I know what she's going to say, but Evelyn beats her to it.

"… *they've* got Harriet," she gasps.

❧ CHAPTER THIRTY ❧
Caroline
A Home from Home

I don't know what wakes me first, the sharp throbbing across my temples or the delicious aromas triggering my hunger clock. The motion sickness has faded enough for me to sit up and take in my surroundings.

I recognise the sprites immediately. The gentle resting hums and tinkle-tinkle of motions are sweet, despite their presence being an uncomfortable reminder of past mistakes. They cluster across the ceiling creating real-life fairy lights that emit a warm fire-like glow. Every wall is littered with either shelves full of old books or mismatched ceramics. Dried flowers hang between the pots and crockery. It is a small simple room, circular in shape. Unusual. I'd swear it was the inside of a tree, but that's ridiculous, right? *It's the exhaustion.* His home is comforting. But as I look around I can't help but feel there's something missing. Of course. There isn't a single photograph anywhere. No faces in frames to tell a story. *No family?*

"Ah, you've risen. Can't resist the spices, eh?"

"Oh, yes, I suppose," I reply pulling the sheet up to my neck line.

"Well, when you're ready to eat, let me know and I can assist you to the table."

Perching on the edge of the sofa, my innate stubborn streak kicks in as I wrap the sheet toga-like around me before attempting to stand. As if slapped by a sudden dizziness, I reach out for something to hold onto and immediately feel his hands take mine, then his arm slips around my waist and I am suddenly aware of his vanilla scent and warm cocoa skin against mine.

"Stubborn, I see," he chuckles.

"Yes. Probably too much for my own good."

"Well, Caro, you don't have to be so with me."

"It's Caroline," I correct.

"I thought it might be. Caro didn't sound quite right," he says pulling out a high backed chair with wooden spindles and filled with worn and weary cushions.

As he lowers me into it, I finally see his face. *My age?* Hard to tell. Silver eyes highlight the silver flecks running through his thick black hair. Freckles decorate his nose, just like Hannah's.

Hannah!

I clasp his forearm wanting to pull myself back up, but the sharpness of the pain feels like a surgeon's scalpel against my temples, minus the anaesthesia.

"Caroline. Un bel nome."

I sit and let him go.

"Thank you. That's very kind."

"You know Italian?"

"A little, yes. And…you're Elijah?"

"You remembered," he says crossing over to a small kitchenette and spooning soup into two wooden bowls. "There is bread on the table. Fresh today."

Diving in to grab one of the wedges, I wince as the rawness of the wounds across my hands remind me of what I've escaped. Despite the pain, I rip into the fresh bread, devouring chunks between swigs of cold crisp water straight from the bottle. The cool glass eases the sting of the cuts and welts on my palms. Placing the bottle back down, it's only then I notice the tankards, the folded napkins, the cutlery. Everything is set. Even a gleaming butter knife. For a split second, I am tempted to wrap it in my napkin and place it on my lap. *Stupid.* If he was going to hurt me, wouldn't he have done so by now? I shake the thought from my mind. He has shown me nothing but kindness. And, so far, all I have done is devour his food and mistrust him.

It is not easy to trust these days.

I butter two more wedges of bread despite the previous helpings already settling heavy on my food deprived stomach. As Elijah serves the soup, I realise how grateful I am to be free from the watery casket I've been trapped in for…I can't even begin to imagine how long.

"May I ask, how did you end up on the riverbank?"

Would he believe me if I explained?

I spoon the soup down, the turmeric and garam warming my insides, all the while hoping to avoid answering the series of questions he no doubt has. I would too if the situation was reversed, I guess. Elijah nods, pursing his lips, hopefully realising I don't want, or rather, I don't know how to answer his question.

Taking a side plate, he brushes the crumbs from the table onto it, then opens the window to balance the plate on its sill.

"For the birds," he says sitting back down.

"That's very thoughtful of you."

"It is important to think of more than just yourself."

My head falls and I drop the spoon back into the bowl.

"Did I say something to upset you?"

"I need to find my daughter."

I stand, searching the floor for my shoes, but the dizziness is relentless, overwhelming me again and I slump onto the chair close to the window. Dammit!

"It is clear you are not well enough. Whatever happened to you has taken a great toll on your body, and, if you'll forgive me, perhaps on your mind, too."

"I can't stay here. Thank you for your hospitality but I must go. I have to find my daughter!"

"Do you know where she is?"

I shake my head.

"Do you know how to find her?"

I sigh. "No."

"You will need to rest for a little while longer. A day or two. If you do so, then you'll be stronger and I will help you to find your daughter."

"How can I trust you?" I blurt, surprised by my own frankness not to mention rudeness.

"Have I given you any reason not to trust me?"

"No. Forgive me," I admit suddenly ashamed of myself. "I'm not used to…"

"I give you my word. You are safe here and we will find your daughter. I know Gaian like the back of my hand as we humans like to say."

"Gaian?" I fight to catch my breath.

"Yes. Did you think you were still on Earth, Caroline?"

CHAPTER THIRTY-ONE

Earth – November: Joyce
The Surgeon and the Officer

Escorted by Bea and Delta, their coats flickering between slate grey and canary yellow, William enters the long hall in the west wing of Windsor House ahead of me and begins, as requested, to light the candelabras adorning the mahogany walls. Bea and Delta remain tethered to him; a sign of their mistrust following our little fracas.

"I must say I feel somewhat relieved that Mary…that her body can be preserved and protected along with Caroline's. At least until such time that the whole family…" he pauses, steadying himself, knuckles pressed against the dresser, "… until we can all give her a proper burial. It is what she would have wanted."

"Yes, Mary will be safe with Caroline," I lie.

I cannot abide lying, but sometimes it is a necessary means. *And who knows what may trigger a further reaction in him?*

"Is there no way you can send me back to them?"

"No, William. I'm afraid that's impossible."

"But, Harriet is my daughter too. I should be out there looking for her! Joyce, please. I beg you. I am her father. Above all others, it is my duty to protect. To find her. It should be me!"

Without either of them even taking a step, William heeds Beattie and Delta's warning.

"I won't raise your hopes, but the sooner we do the autopsy, the sooner I will have some answers."

Defeated, William sighs and resumes lighting the last remaining candelabras. It pains me to see the father of the Elementals so forlorn.

Having stacked all the chairs neatly away I light my candle and arrange the bowls of lavender, camomile and the valerian tonic. With one eye on William, I remove a gilt-edged dagger from the glass cabinet, lock it and drop the key into the soil of the potted Norfolk Island pine.

As night draws in and the rain accelerates I close the thick mauve curtains aware of the light show about to commence.

"They're done."

"Thank you."

As William waits, a sense of awkwardness suspends itself between us. From his lack of eye-contact, it appears the shame of his earlier actions may have settled on his shoulders. I know full well it is not his true nature. Despite my many acceptances of his many apologies, he appears to bear the weight most heavily.

"Bea, Delta, you may settle."

As they remove themselves to the fireplace, Delta sniffs

in William's direction as if to remind him of their constant presence. I conjure a small orb and toss it onto the logs reigniting them to begin warming us all.

"It really is quite strange being here," he begins. "To think I roamed these corridors and sat in front of the very same fireplace two hundred years ago."

"I imagine it must be quite disconcerting for you."

"Yes. But, comforting, too. Knowing it's still a home. Still loved."

"Not to mention it survived both World Wars."

"The future sounds like a terrifying place."

"It was. Or rather, it can be. But doesn't every generation think that?"

"Yes, I imagine it does."

"We seem to be a nostalgic species, don't you think?"

Willliam nods, lost in thought.

"Well then, if you lie on the table and place your head on this cushion."

He glances around the room, "Are you sure you can see what you're doing?"

"You've pre-empted me. Lie down, take long deep breaths in and out of your nose," I say pinching William's wrist between my fingers. "We must steady that the racing heart of yours. Here, drink this," I add passing the first draft of the Valerian tonic for him to sip.

Leaving William briefly to open the rear window, I whistle just loud enough for it to carry on the wind without being lost amongst the deluge of rain. It doesn't take Ixy, Rubes and Licia long to leave their nests deep in the hollow tree's canopy. Within a second or two, they emerge, surrounded by dozens more sprites. Just like a murmuration of starlings at sunset, the sprites swoop and curl lighting each blade of rain they cut through creating a waterfall of light until finally the large flock zip through the window, tinkling as they pass. I latch it leaving a narrow gap should they require it.

Zipping and zagging around Bea and Delta's heads, neither of which raise more than an ear to our visitors, finally the sprites settle into a hum above the table forming an all-encompassing halo above us both.

"What in the Lord's name are they?" asks William pushing himself up onto his elbows.

"No, no. I think you mean, what in Gaia's name are they? Sprites. They're here to assist with the procedure."

"What?"

"Don't be alarmed. Rubes and Licia are accomplished sprites. Ixy, too. Have some faith, William. Now, lie back down."

I mix the remainder of the Valerian tonic with the lavender and camomile then pass it to William who gives me a look of trepidation before throwing it back like a shot of bourbon. I grab his arm taking some fraction of his weight as the effects take hold all too quickly.

"Harriet. My...Harri..." he slurs as slumber beckons.

"Right, my little rays. I need every ounce of your light cast here," I say pointing to the centre of William's chest. Each cluster of sprites guides their light to settle where directed.

Taking the dagger, I cross it through Ixy's stream of light, his being closest. Their combined light streams fan out filling the room.

"This night, I seek the blessing and light of all Keepers.
Those past and those present in this and all realms.
I beseech you!
Awaken and bestow your light upon this
elemental father.
Let his astral self project out of this corporeal home.
Where there is righteousness let it be known.
Where there is conflict, let it be overthrown.
Where there is dishonour let it atone.
And if this soul should harbour darkness,
let it be shown.
Take up this man of blood and bone.
Encompass him in the sanctity of your everlasting light.
To reveal a darkness that lingers out of sight."

Taking William's hand I draw the blade across his palm then place it onto his chest allowing streams of light, not blood, to trickle and pool like oil in water with the sprites' light.

Sparks of energy crackle, then...

Vrumph!

Bursting from his chest, William's soul fans out, glowing and gleaming, displaying the innermost constructs of his being. Taking the blade, once more, I pass it through Ixy's light, re-cleansing it. Ixy tinkles and giggles. Licia purses her lips scowling at Ixy as she and Rubes direct their flocks streams. Beginning with as great a degree of precision as possible, I part each layer of William's astral self in order to seek out the darkness Evelyn had discovered. His soul spans out into every corner of the hall. Some streams are too bright to even look at. *Always a good sign.* After repositioning several layers, I lift and slide not one, but two layers of empathy, taking great care not to displace their roots. My instincts are right.

Where else do you hide something so dark but underneath something so light?

Rooted within the lower atrium is a small patch of darkness, like a shadow on an x-ray - a warning of a growing disease - that requires the skill of a surgeon. Cautiously, I immerse the blade into the shadow, then pause. After a moment, I press a little further. The structure of his soul responds calmly to each invasion of the blade. Picking up a glass jar, I slice a tiny part of the shadow off. Clinging to the blade, I transfer it into the jar then screw the lid back on tightly. Instantly, the wound stitches itself back together, more cells producing an enlarged shadow.

Dammit!

After re-layering William's soul, Delta awakens, his low rumble alerting me to something approaching. I listen. The sound of tyres crunching against the gravel. After a moment or two footsteps cross the courtyard. I place the dagger down unable to finish the last stage of the autopsy. The brass knocker clacks.

"Bea, stay here with William. Delta, with me."

As I exit the hall, I peer around the curtains to see a police car bathed in the activated floodlights. The brass knocker clacks again, only louder.

"Who is it?" I call, pulling a shawl down from the rack and wrapping it around my shoulders.

"My name is Officer Griffiths from the Attleborough Constabulary. May I speak with you?"

I open the door, Delta positioned slightly back inside the dimly lit porch.

"Good evening officer. If you'll be so kind as to provide me with your identification."

He flips his ID badge which I take from his hand and inspect comparing the rather unflattering photograph with the real thing.

"Would you mind if I came in? Horrible out here this evening," he says stepping forward. But being uninvited is something Delta takes exception to and steps into view.

"Goodness!" Officer Griffiths gasps and takes a step back. "Funny-looking dog."

"That might be to do with the fact that he isn't a dog at all. This is Delta. A Scandinavian fox. He's a rare breed. The largest of their kind."

"Well, would you and your rare breed mind if I came in and ask some you questions?"

"What is this regarding? Little late for house calls, isn't it?"

"It's on my way home. Thought I would see if there was a chance we could chat. It's about Willow's. You see the duty rota identifies you as being on shift the night the nursing home was practically demolished. We're just trying to understand what happened."

"I will happily answer questions, but if you could return tomorrow at a more civilised hour, it would be greatly appreciated. I'm very tired."

The officer peers over my shoulder as if searching for something.

"It won't take long," he presses.

"Like I said, this isn't exactly a civilised hour."

"Right, well. Here, I'll leave you my card. If you can ring me in the morning to make an appointment that would be appreciated," he says holding his card out which I take and glance at.

"Thank you. Now, if you'll excuse me. I really must get to bed."

I inch the door forcing Officer Griffiths to step back out into the torrential rain, then slide each bolt across and remove the key placing it under the umbrella stand. From the hall window I watch him leave, before returning to the hall.

What on Earth!

William, his body trembling, perspiration running down his temples, stands with fists balled. Dead eyes lock upon me. Bea stalks the space between patient and surgeon. Surprisingly, William charges down the long hall heading for the east door rather than me. Delta reacts throwing the full force of her weight at him catapulting them back. They slam into the bookcase.

William pushes himself up and turns to me. Conjuring an orb, I launch it straight into the partially open wound across his chest. Delta shakes his dazed head from the impact and prowls towards where William, now pinned to the half demolished bookcase, struggles against its hold.

"What have you done to me old woman?"

"That really is most impolite. Nothing more than was necessary."

"You'll pay for this," he sneers. "Just you wait! Witch!"

I shudder.

I approach William cautiously now unable to shake the feeling that…*Galtonia? Is it possible?*

"Maybe you will ensure I pay for this," I begin. "But until such time…"

And with that I slam the orb into his chest cavity expunging in the darkness coursing through him. *I'm in no doubt the shadow will rise again.*

How long the orb's affects will hold, I have no idea, but for now his encasement in light is both welcome as much as it is necessary.

Delta and Bea sidle up to me, panting heavily. And just like Hannah does, I push my fingers into their hair, understanding now exactly why she does. Both foxes lean against my legs, they too seeking comfort.

"Eleanor, old friend. If you can hear me, we need to talk."

And although I do not relish keeping the truth from Evelyn and Hannah, they cannot find out what has happened. Not yet, anyway.

CHAPTER THIRTY-TWO

Gaian – Hunter's Moon: Hannah
Trees Don't Lie

I can't believe Harriet was here. At least that's what everyone thinks. We were so close.

Evelyn, arms folded tightly across her chest, hovers nearby as we all cluster round Eldred. With most of the Ffens bodies now inside the Hallow Hall, Eldred summons three of his gryphons across, leaving the rest to watch over Watton's 'kinfolk' as Gran had called them.

"Benedict, I am entrusting you to return home and march the armies West. I'll send word of precise locations when I have them," Eldred says taking each of the gryphon's arms and not exactly shaking them, more like holding them for a moment. Elric does the same, placing one hand on Benedict's shoulder, ruffling his prune-coloured feathers. Like Elric's, each feather looks as if it's been dipped in ink, but Benedict's is the brightest blue I've ever seen.

"Swiftly and safely little brother," he says.

That's Elric's brother?

"Not in a blood sense," Gran interrupts. *"More in the sense of a brotherhood."*

"Okay. I get it. Like all us lot in a way."

"Yes, I suppose."

Benedict and the other two gryphons, bend down

slightly, then push off the ground. Their wings spread creating a backdraft over us. *Whomp. Whomp. Whomp.* Swooping clear of the rowans' canopies within seconds they vanish. Alpha's coat flickers like a wind-kissed candle from emerald to jade. *Yes, girl. I am jealous. I so want to fly.*

Gathering us all round, Eldred kneels over a map of stones and sand, clearing his throat to ensure we're all listening. He replaces the leaves back to where they'd been positioned before the gryphons' breeze sent them flying.

"Right, then. If whoever Freya saw is indeed travelling south then I reckon it will take at least two days to circumnavigate the Rushan's lands. I'm working on the assumption that our traitor isn't Lord East. These are his lands, see and even his alliance with our Cossack friends is tepid."

"I'd hardly call them friends. Friends you can trust," adds Elric crouching down and rubbing the tuft of tiny ebony and fawn-coloured feathers under his chin.

"That's not always true," I snap. "Galtonia was Gran's friend once and look how that turned out." I slowly raise my gaze to meet Gran's.

"I didn't mean that to sound like I blame you. I don't."

Gran smiles as if to say it's okay, but her eyes tell me something different. Alpha's coat flickers to a sort of mauve colour. Is that her way of letting Gran know how I feel? That

I'm sorry I blurted out what sounded like an accusation. I never understood what that meant until Mum explained, her being a solicitor an' all. *Should Gran have realised Galtonia would betray us? Does anyone see betrayal before it happens?* I join Gran and take her hand. She squeezes mine with that vice-like grip.

"You've been blocking me a lot, haven't you?"

"Necessary. For now. Trust me?"

I nod. I do trust her. More than anyone, probably.

"Look, how the Rushans run their trades is up to them. For now, they're neutral. I'd prefer it if we kept it that way. The Lords won't cross their lands if they don't have to. They don't welcome strangers there. Young Watton needs to be very careful with that flock of his. The next time they stray..." Eldred pauses turning to eyeball Watton amongst our circle, "... leave them. Right?"

"I will. I promise!" Watton's lip quivers.

"The Volkhas are already half a day ahead of us. If we stand any chance of retrieving Harriet we have to make up some ground somehow," says Evelyn.

"Mother is right. We have to get my sister back. Can't we all just piggyback on you and Elric?" asks Jack.

"There aren't enough of us to protect the Ffens and return to Valeria to raise the armies. And if we take to the skies, then we lose all means of protection. We can't hide in the clouds, young man. There is a limit to how high even gryphons can soar," says Eldred.

Jack looks disappointed. Even Constance does a little. She seems to be bonding with Althea and is staying as close to her as Jack is to Elric.

"Eleanor, it may have been a great many years since you lived here but Gaian hasn't changed all that much. What is your counsel?" asks Elric, standing to address Gran. *Her opinion really matters here.*

Gran's calculation face fades as she glances from Freya to me and back again.

"Eleanor? I know that face. What is it?" asks Evelyn recognising the family trait like I do in Mum and she does in me.

"I may know where Gaia is. At least I hope. You see, Eldred found our little Ffen here up a cook pine tree," explains Gran smiling down at Freya whilst Watton adds little stones all over Eldred's map. "And cook pines are universally acknowledged to be a living breathing weathervane for Gaia. Wherever she is, the cook pines will show you."

"So, shouldn't we just proceed in that direction?" asks Constance.

"If only it were that easy," replies Althea.

Constance for a moment looks as disappointed at Althea's reply as Jack did to Eldred's. It is then that a faint shading sensation begins colouring me in. The warm lilac and peach tones are coming from Constance. Her cheeks are glowing, too. She stares at Althea, admiring the tribal markings adorning her warrior witch protector's ebony skin.

"Constance is not wrong though. That must, at the very least, be our direction of travel. I'm sorry, but all this posturing and strategising isn't getting me any closer to saving my other daughter!"

Evelyn can't hide her anger. *Why should she?*

"Well, if you'll forgive me, all this posturing and strategizing might just be the reason we avoid a bloodbath with that not exactly insignificant set of Volkhas guarding said daughter," barks Elric standing to stretch, puffing his chest out.

Lilith immediately steps to his side and cups his face in her hands. They stare at each other for only a moment before she lets him go. Elric's body relaxes, wings swaying; his shoulders drop as if Lilith has drawn out all the tension trapped inside him.

"I do believe she has a point. If the cook pines are telling us Gaia is that way," points Lilith, "... then that is where we should head towards. Trees don't lie. It is impossible. Evelyn wants her daughter back and Hannah wants her mother back. Not to mention we've the Mother of all mothers to save." Lilith smiles, but her tone is anything but light.

"Thank you, Lilith. Your temperament will be a most welcome enhancement to our family when that son of mine…" sighs Eldred casting a glance at his son who looks as if he's pretending not to have heard. "Right! Listen up!"

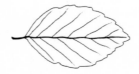

CHAPTER THIRTY-THREE

Roots

I didn't expect Watton to cry as we left him and Freya with Eldred's gryphons protecting his kin. He really is button-cute. Before leaving on our trek into the Valerian Mountains they'd both dashed off into the Hallow Hall, returning with three long hook-handled wicker baskets hanging from their shoulders full of lemon parsley, betel berries, mawberries and carissa fruits. Freya, showing me how to crack the betel berry, pressed the top of it with her thumb until it released a 'shh' sound like fizzy pop. After peeling back the thick skin and devouring the ruby red flesh, she tossed one over to me. I couldn't help but look at Gran, 'You'll love the flavour despite the fruit's most unfortunate name,' she had said. She was right, of course. Watton explained that because their shell-like skin is shiny, they're easy to spot in the sunlight, so we can continue filling the baskets when we find them.

Padding over, Alpha had sniffed and licked the betel berry juice sticking to my fingers.

"Are you okay to eat these?"

She'd nodded.

"Good. Can't have you getting food poisoning."

Alpha wrinkled her nose but then took the other half and wolfed it down.

"Yous will come back won't ya. Promise?" Watton had asked as I dabbed his tears with a dock leaf like Freya had.

"I promise, Watton," I replied as he wrapped his arms around my legs and pressed his head into my stomach.

****

We've only been walking a few hours and I can't believe how much I'm missing them. It's so much quieter without them, too. The higher we climb up out of Ffenland towards the first slopes of the Valerian Mountains the crisper the air gets so I untie my jumper from around my waist and pull it back on.

Gran's still keeping her distance, which means she knows something. But I promised that I'd trust her, so I will. I can't plague Gran for answers like I did with Mum. Besides, Gran isn't exactly afraid to tell me the truth, is she?

Elric picks up a betel berry and tosses it up to Jack who, bouncing on Elric's shoulders like a five-year-old, catches each one in his basket. Evelyn keeps a tight grip on Constance, and I'm sandwiched between Althea and Lilith. I am dying to ask if we're nearly there yet, but keep my trap shut not wanting to whinge like a brat. Instead, much to my embarrassment, Lilith delights in telling Althea all about my little run-in with the furies.

"Hmm, there's always room with us should you wish to join a coven of warrior witches you know," offers Althea.

"Thanks, but I think this Potential stuff is enough for the moment. I still haven't really figured out what it means or what I even have to do. I reckon Constance would though."

"What makes you say that?"

"She watches you a lot."

"Interesting."

"Well," begins Lilith pausing to smell the air again. "Start with harnessing nature's forces."

"All of them?" I ask.

"Eleanor, have you not explained the basics yet?" asks Althea clearly unimpressed with Gran's teaching style.

"Not in as much detail as either of you would. And we have been a tad busy," she replies arching that brow of hers impossibly high. I smirk. She's not wrong.

"Just keep listening, absorbing and feeling. That is where you truly learn," adds Lilith stroking straggles of hair from my shoulders triggering my 'Mum response'. Their kindness. Their looks. Their advice. They don't even know how they make me feel. Sad, but loved all in one go. *I've just gotta focus on the love part.*

"I suddenly seem to know a load of random nature facts. Is that normal?"

"What is 'normal'?" asks Lilith.

"That's just it. I don't know."

"You have inherited Gaia's gifts as her Potential, but you

are different beings completely and how you wield and nurture those gifts will be different to how Gaia does. You see, being of a tender age still, you only know what you have been taught, how you've been raised and those parameters put on you by your significant society – those close to you – and as you grow, you experience the peripheral one and develop your beliefs and morals accordingly, but staying true to who you are," explains Althea.

I think I get what she means.

"How do I harness nature though?"

"Instinct. Like when you dived to save the Cresta. You knew what the bird needed in that moment and responded." Althea stops for a second, her eyes burn into mine. "Remember this: Gaia is a provider. All that we have is because of her benevolence. Contemplate that."

"That's the problem on Earth, though. Too many people are asking too much of her," I reply.

"You have a fast mind like your Grandmother, Hannah," says Althea a small smile curling at the side of her mouth, as we set off again. "Life must have an equilibrium. If not, there are consequences."

"Stop!" Lilith shouts suddenly raising her hand and sniffing the air again.

"What is it?" barks Elric, his wings flexing.

"The forest scent...I've registered little change."

I guess that's a dryad skill.

"Lilith?" asks Gran. "What are you sensing?"

"It's more a case of what I'm not sensing. We've been trekking more than half a day now and making good time, so at this altitude, I would expect aromas of fir, spruce and, at the very least, elderwood." Lilith inhales several times, closing her eyes. "Nothing."

"What does that mean?" asks Evelyn pulling Constance with her.

"The alpine forest should have begun by now. Look," she points further up the gravelled pathway stretching out in front of us. Dozens of hillsides littered with greenery. "Not a spruce insight and no frost on the ground. It's as if winter has receded."

"A consequence of Gaia's fevers, perhaps?" asks Elric.

"Should I get down?" asks Jack.

"No! Everyone stay still," orders Lilith. She scans the bushes and surrounding grounds before glancing back to the trees we've passed. She takes the edge of her delicate robes, wafting them so gently but enough to create a breeze, which lifts her four or five feet from the ground. As if skating slowly through the air, Lilith approaches a small tree, no taller than Jack, shaking her head as if she can't believe what she's seeing, then floats down to pick a leaf from the foot of what she calls 'the sapling'.

Turning first to Elric, then the rest of us, her face drains of colour.

"Slowly, very slowly, move back!" she mouths before flattening her hand instructing every move we make. Eldred lets his wings unfurl and blanket us like Galtonia's cloak once did to protect me as we lower ourselves onto hands and knees.

Elric hesitates as Jack clings to his back, clearly not keen on leaving Lilith's side as she assesses the danger. I breathe deeply and push Jack's fears back down. His brow furrows as he mouths 'Mother' at Evelyn.

Gran broadcasts, *"What have you found?"*

"Sandbox saplings," Lilith whispers. "I wasn't sure until I read the leaf. They shouldn't be here."

Read the leaf? Like a fortune teller?

"Can you retrace your steps?" Gran asks.

Lilith shakes her head. Too late!

"They know I'm here," she mouths. "I touched the leaf to read it and they felt me. A message is running through every fibre in their root systems, awakening them all. I don't trust them and they certainly don't trust me."

What? The saplings know?

"Let me get you!" Elric hisses. "I can make it."

Lilith just points to Jack and Elric's head drops. He knows he can't risk the life of an Elemental.

"Please don't let me fall!" Jack sobs into Elric's feathered collar.

"Any loud noises or sudden moves and all the saplings will explode. Even at this young age, those pods can do an immense amount of damage."

"What?" gasps Constance. She turns to me, eyes pleading. "Can't you do something?"

I don't know, but I can try.

I look at Gran partly for permission, partly for courage. She nods. From underneath Eldred's feathers, Alpha whimpers but begins moving.

"No, girl. Stay!" I warn. *I can't lose her, too.*

Eldred's feathery blanket tickles my face as I push out from underneath, but as I do, I close my eyes for a moment and whisper, "Hollow Tree, can you help me?"

Instantly, the Hollow Tree shows me a picture of itself reminding me of the gift retrieval. Bright emerald light bleeds out of it, unearthed fluorescent roots reaching and stretching. For only a few seconds, Harriet's face appears, golden fire gleaming in her eyes.

Of course!

I push myself up, covering my eyes with my palms and concentrate on Harriet's image until the white fire ignites.

"I take her place, same element, different face!"

"She's on fire!" Jack whispers, but I hear every syllable.

I press my finger to my lips to silence him. He nods, mouth open wide. This time the fire is a river of gold trickling down my arms to my fingertips.

In the silence, I hear the urgent chatter of roots; Lilith was right! I inch closer to her then lower myself to the ground, forcing my hands into the soft soil letting the fire spread. It seeks out the network of sandbox roots. As the ground begins to tremble, huge families of trees sway all around. I push the fire further down. Roots burst to the surface, sizzling before they crumble.

The saplings are fast! Exploding suddenly at the threat. Lilith runs…

"Argh!"

Hit, she falls.

Elric encloses his wings trapping Jack inside, then lowers himself down to reach out for Lilith as I push Harriet's elemental fire through a billion root systems. The fire rushes up dozens of stems scattered around us, each sapling bursts into flames. Crackles and snaps fill the air leaving nothing but their charred snowflake remains fluttering up into the canopies above us. I wince against the stinging sharpness of the fizz and hiss each explosion releases.

Elric scrambles across the floor to pull Lilith to safety.

Crack!

From high up, the splintered trunk of an enormous elm

snaps sending it plummeting down on top of me. I yank my hands free from the ground to cover my head, but it doesn't hit! Flying across into a nearby clearing, the elm's trunk strikes a cluster of firs then rebounds rolling back towards us before settling close by.

Gran?

But as I turn, I realise it isn't her.

Constance kneels, trembling, arms outstretched. Her nerves hit me as hard as the elm hit the fir trees, making me gasp for breath.

"Extraordinary!" exclaims Althea. "I think you could be right, Hannah."

Rushing across to me, Constance throws her arms around my neck, swamping me with waves of relief.

"You okay?"

"I cannot say," she replies panting heavily.

"I'm definitely not the only one who can do something," I grin.

"I think I just pushed the air. At least, oh, I don't really know." Constance hugs me again tightly and we share a smile.

Is this what having a sister feels like?

"Enough of that, you two. Lilith is injured," Gran reminds us.

As Constance joins the others, I keep at a distance to

practise reflecting everyone's pain and fear which stings as if my body is being dragged through a field of nettles.

Light streams in from the gap where the elm's crown had stood, probably for decades. Maybe centuries. I press my fingers into the sap bleeding from its splintered trunk. Both Lilith and the elm are wounded. I look around as the last remaining plumes of smoke and ash vanish. If the sandbox trees aren't meant to be here then this was a trap. Someone weaponised the trees against us and I destroyed them because of it. A familiar dark feeling snakes inside my stomach, telling me I already know who...

CHAPTER THIRTY-FOUR

Letting Go

Elric cradles Lilith's body, teeth clenched, tears streaming down his face.

"One of us has to take her to Holt," Eldred repeats.

I'd got used to having Watton and Freya with us, but our numbers are dwindling again. It doesn't feel right.

"I have said I will do it," snaps Elric. "She's my…"

"We all know what Lilith means to you," Eldred replies placing his hand on his son's shoulder.

"You would leave the Elementals with only one Guardian?" says Althea flatly. So much for sympathy. *Maybe I should dose her up with a drop of my empathy?*

"Elric, you are needed now more than ever. I don't need to remind you of the duty you've been assigned."

"I think you just did, Gran," I say.

Evelyn kneels at Elric's side. *Maybe she can get through to him.* He looks so lost, just combing Lilith's hair with his fingers. He leans in and whispers something into her ear so I decide to give them some privacy, whilst everyone else just stands and stares.

Sitting down under a silver birch, just like the few in our garden back home which Gran planted, Jack and Constance decide to join me and leave the adults to it.

"Is it my fault?" whispers Jack, plucking at a blade of grass.

I place my hand on top of his. "Trees feel pain, so I'm guessing other plants might. And no, it's not your fault."

"Why on Earth should you think that?" asks Constance re-lacing her boots.

"Well, if I hadn't insisted on riding on his back he could have saved her."

"No, I don't think even Elric was fast enough to reach her. Lilith told us not to move. She was protecting us," I say hoping guilt doesn't swamp him completely. It's getting easier to reflect Jack's emotions. Perhaps because I'm doing it quite a lot at the moment, or that's what it seems like."

As Evelyn speaks, we all fall silent.

"Listen to me, Elric. I know how you're feeling. I know what this feels like. Truly I do because I had to leave my husband behind in order to save my children."

Elric turns to Evelyn. Clearly she's caught his attention.

She continues, "It's heart breaking. Being forced to choose in such a way. And only those who have been forced into such a choice can truly understand."

Evelyn looks straight at Althea, who crosses her arms and turns away. *That's harsh.*

"And despite the pain, if the situation was reversed you know she would do her duty. But, Elric, I am asking you, not because you have a duty to, but because I need you. *All of you.* Please help me save my daughter. She isn't just an

Elemental to be protected. She is my own flesh and blood to be cherished." Evelyn brushes away a tear tumbling down Elric's cheek with the back of her hand as Eldred bends down and pulls his son's face to his.

"I will protect her just as I would you."

All three stand.

Cradling Lilith, Elric kisses her again before passing her into Eldred's arms.

"Father!" Elric's voice quivers as he presses one final kiss onto the back of Lilith's hand.

"With my life, Son."

Eldred holds her tightly allowing each one of us to, in our own way, say goodbye, for now, to Lilith.

Maybe I could check on her... I don't know how... silly idea.

Twirling strands of Lilith's silky auburn hair between my fingers, I feel several snap.

Er...

Gently, I pull my hand away, clench my fist and fold my arms into my chest trying to hide the strands from sight. I move away whilst everyone else kisses their goodbyes. *Where do I hide hair?* I just can't throw it away. Then I realise and begin plaiting into my own. At least I'll always have a tiny token of her with me.

As Eldred lifts from the ground and soars into the sky, Lilith cradled in his arms, Elric's cry pierces the sombre silence. He falls to his knees. Tears bleed from almost everyone's eyes. Even Althea, who seems to have a hard heart sighs but doesn't cry. Evelyn wraps her arms around Constance and Jack, who continues to sob. I feel the drip, drip, drip of his guilt. *He really thinks it's all his fault.*

Totally overwhelmed, I kneel and steady myself against the softness of the grass suddenly filled with enough emotions to fill a stadium. One of them rises sharply overpowering all the others...

I'm only thirteen but I have had enough loss to last ten lifetimes.

It ends now.

And I know who's ending it begins with.

CHAPTER THIRTY-FIVE

On the Rise

It's meant to be colder the higher up a mountain you get, isn't it? It was like that when me, Mum and her walker friends decided to tackle Snowden, the spring after Dad left. Mum said she needed some 'headspace' and that 'only a mountain would do'.

We had stood at the top, holding hands. I couldn't believe how beautiful it was. Giant patchworks in every shade of green you could think of. Jagged horizons and sweeping valleys. I remember looking at Mum and wondering why her eyes were closed, but then I thought maybe she's imprinting the view onto her memory.

But here, trekking up to what Althea says are the outlands of the Valerian Mountains, it's definitely not getting colder the higher we go. The air seems thicker, harder to swallow. Heat prickles sting my neck. *They really hurt.* Tied around my waist again, my jumper acts like a furnace against my skin, but I can't ditch it. Gaia's fevers change faster than our weather forecasts do.

Both Jack and Constance strip down as much as possible, shedding layers of 'Victorian propriety' Gran calls it. Constance unlaces her corset and flings it to the ground. *How did she breathe in that?*

"You can't do that on Earth now you know. You'd get fined

for it. No-one litters anymore. We just fill the oceans with plastic instead." *Now that makes me want to say bad words!*

"Oh goodness, I don't intend on leaving it. I just...really ..."

"Want to reject everything it stands for, dear?" Gran smirks then winks. Evelyn chuckles quietly to herself. It's good to see her smile a little.

"What do you mean?" asks Constance.

"Hannah's time is much more liberal minded and equal. Well, it's still a work-in-progress," Evelyn explains. "Women can..."

"Dress like men?" Constance asks staring at my jeans.

"Sometimes they dress like us."

"You mean for the theatre, like in Shakespeare's plays?"

"Not exactly."

Hmm, that's one for later.

"They wear whatever they choose to," Evelyn replies to which Constance's face lights up.

"Truly? That's ... wonderful. You're incredibly lucky, Hannah," she says as her envy and excitement bleed into one and bleed into me. *If only they both knew I can feel everything they experience.*

Even thirst. *Though that doesn't exactly fall into the empathy category.*

"I think Jack needs a drink."

"How did you know that?" he asks baffled.

"I do, too." *I could murder a brew.*

"Mother, is there nothing we can do about the heat?" he asks.

"You could make it rain," interrupts Constance. "But that didn't exactly work out well last time."

He could, though. He should.

Don't we all need to practise this elemental stuff?

Althea reaches up to a 'blood orange' tree. She taps the trunk as if she's tapping on a coffee counter waiting for service. A dozen bauble-like buds drop to the ground. Althea picks them all up, chucking them one after the other to us. Althea pulls at the stork like a ring pull and guzzles down the juice. Elric, tips his head back squeezing the bud and gulping it down, before eating its shrivelled remains.

As Althea leads us towards where Gaia awaits, Elric stays at the back to 'bring up the rear' Gran says.

The heat continues to throb so I roll up my jeans until they're over my knees. The fury-inflicted wound has vanished. Alpha weaves in and out of me, Constance and Jack, her tail tickling our legs.

"What if Elric hates me now?" whispers Jack still crestfallen.

I shake my head. "He doesn't. Absolutely not. He's just really upset at the situation. Not you. It'll be okay."

I turn to check on Elric as we carry on trudging up the rocky path. Mainly, he scans the surroundings, pausing occasionally, listening to every noise he doesn't like the sound of. Sometimes his wings unfurl and flicker pushing him up above us. I guess he just needs that 'headspace' too.

"There's a clearing a few miles ahead," he calls down. "A stream, too."

Elric turns to face the sun and from this angle I can see his expression. Like Mum, he closes his eyes. Both their losses are unfair. As I watch him, everything suddenly feels strange. Strange because even though we're all still guarded by him – a huge Gryphon – and a warrior witch, without Lilith here, it's like we've lost our navigator. Doesn't being a dryad mean she is more connected to the environment than any one of us?

"Sorry for ear-wigging, but, no, dearest," begins Gran. *"That would be you."*

Stomach-flip.

I stop.

Constance bumps into the back of me halting everyone else in their tracks. Elric lands close, "What are you sensing, Hannah?"

Lilith told me to pay attention. She meant to the environment. *It's quieter.* Is that because it's getting hotter? *Are the animals and birds dying?*

"What's the matter?" calls Evelyn. "Why have we…"

But Althea suddenly hisses, "Keep moving. Keep up! The butterbirds have stopped."

We rush after her, scrambling up the pathway.

"They're song is so distinct," Althea begins. "And when they stop, Gaia's fever will rise quickly. We don't have long. Elric saw water ahead. We must get to it before the fever hits. The closer we are to water, the better. Now, move!"

CHAPTER THIRTY-SIX

Caroline
Unexpected

I sip the greenish tea Elijah has brewed and for the first time in, I can't even remember, I feel calmer.

Sat near the latched door are two bags each with flasks attached, two large wooden staffs and a neatly folded pile of clothes.

"You look much … healthier," Elijah says taking the empty cup and refilling it.

"Thanks."

"There's food on the table. Eat and then we'll get this search party moving."

"Yes, we must move. How long have I slept?"

"Enough. Your eyes are brighter and your complexion is even."

My cheeks flush.

"Well, it was while you slept," he smiles.

I guess it's not easy to ignore someone sleeping when your home isn't much bigger than a matchbox.

"Do you know where we should look first?"

"No. But you do. Back to the riverbank. Isn't that where you said you saw your daughter? So, we start with what we know."

"Yes. That makes sense."

"From there, we look for tracks. If she wasn't alone, there'll be some we can decipher. That's why we leave tracks, so we can be followed."

"Or found."

"I like the way you think, Caroline."

My cheeks flush again. *What is the matter with me?*

"Have you done this sort of thing before?"

"Not really. I was a philosophy professor in my past life, but always loved walking. I walk anywhere and everywhere."

"Me, too! I mean, I love walking. It's not easy though working full-time and being a single mum."

"Oh, I am sorry to hear that."

"It's fine. I'm used to it, now. Damn hard, though."

"It pains me to hear that," he says then holds up his hand. "Don't feel obliged to explain. It is your business and no one else's."

"I can talk about it now. It doesn't hurt anymore. I'm over him. I don't think a shred of him exists in my heart any longer. In fact I don't think it, I know it."

"You sound like an incredibly strong woman, Caroline."

"Thank you. And what about you? I couldn't help but notice there are no photos. But, do they even have cameras or phones here?"

"No."

His answer is abrupt.

"Elijah, just exactly how did you get here?"

He glances at the door.

"Eat up. Let's get on our way."

"Oh, I'm sorry. I didn't mean to pry."

He busies himself tidying up and then perches on a buffet to pull his boots on, before placing a pair down for me. Each boot has a sock stuffed inside it. *He's so neat and tidy.* I guess he's not so willing to open up, which raises my suspicions and triggers my trust alarm.

But, just as my guard rises again, he says, "Mine is a long story so we may as well do something useful and enjoyable. If you *really* want to hear it, of course?"

I smile as that old guard of mine comes to a most unexpected halt.

CHAPTER THIRTY-SEVEN

Hannah
Haze

It happened so fast…we didn't stand a chance. Gaia's fever rose faster than Althea had predicted, flooring us all.

Next to me Alpha pants. Her eyes droop struggling to fix on mine.

"I'm here girl."

Even moving my hand to rest on Alpha's paw is hard work.

The scent of metallic blood – my blood – weeps from my knees from the fall …from the crawl…

Plumes of dust roll by. My fingertips find cracks in the arid ground. I squeeze my eyes forcing tears to wash the grit away. The heaviness against my chest lifts a little, but still it is hard to breathe.

Flashes of the lights bursting from the sun appear in front of me like a scene from one of those apocalyptic movies. We don't need those anymore…

The smallest of whimpers escapes Alpha's chest forcing me to face her.

"Are you injured?"

Her coat ripples from amber to green then back again. She is alert enough to show me that at least. But the return to amber is the usual warning. There is still a threat.

Closing my eyes, I focus on pushing the sound waves to broadcast.

"Answer me if you're okay. You don't have to speak. Just think."

I have no idea if Althea or Elric can hear me, if I can break into them or not but then Althea replies. *Does this mean I am growing stronger?*

"I am. Weak, but alive and unscathed."

Thank Gaia.

"You and Alpha are okay?"

"Yes."

"I can see you from where I am."

I repeat the broadcast only harder, louder. *Come on, Gran!*

"I'm fine," comes a voice, but it is not hers.

"Where are you?" I shout.

"Nearest to the edge of the clearing. Jack and Constance are here. They're okay," replies Evelyn. "Other than feeling like we've been hit by an avalanche."

"I'm all right. I'm going to try and get across to Evelyn and the children," Elric says, much to my relief. His voice is the clearest. Maybe he's the closest? I push myself up a little and turn to see where he is.

Huh!

Surrounding the clearing are the charred skeletons of trees, blacker than death. The dust begins to settle revealing hundreds more encircling us. Then I realise...the dream.

It was a warning.

"Can anyone see Gran? She hasn't replied. Please, Gran. Come on. Answer me!"

I feel Alpha move to press herself against me. I know, girl.

"She isn't with us, at least as far as I can tell," says Evelyn.

"Wait! In the distance behind Elric. Someone's there!" calls Althea.

My eyes narrow still fighting the dust creating a sandy haze which seems to throb against the sun's rays as they pierce their way through. Hope rises.

"Constance, can you push the dust away so I can see?"

"I will try," her voice trembles. I follow it straining to see her.

Constance, still kneeling, too weak to stand from the heat blast, raises her arms. Her energy pulses through her body. Her determination radiates out to me.

"Gran?" I bellow. "Can you hear me?"

"Push harder, Connie, please!"

I need to see her.

Constance pushes hard to clear the air just enough before slumping to the ground.

"She's okay, Hannah," calls Evelyn.

Like the sandbox trees exploding pods, rays of sun now burst through clearing the haze, but as they do Alpha growls as she crawls in front of me, teeth bared, her coat now a blaze of crimson...

No!

No!

NO!

Clutching her by her hair, Gran's body slumps against her captor's legs.

Flame red eyes, filled with delight, lock onto mine.

"The furies send their..." begins Galtonia. She pauses, raising her head slightly as she smirks, "... *warmest* regards."

CHAPTER THIRTY-EIGHT

The Return Of

Every atom of hate I hold towards Galtonia bubbles to the surface. With the haze from Gaia's fever easing, lightning rods of energy surge through me, the glow of the white fire ripples down my body. I glance down at my hands, the fire's glow is tinged emerald. Its pulsing rhythm darkens ever so slightly. I know this is exactly what Galtonia wants, but don't people just sometimes really need to get what they deserve?

"You...you...witch!"

"Careful, Hannah. You almost swore. Tut-tut. You know how much granny dear abhors swearing."

"In your case, she might make an exception!" I snap.

Galtonia's mouth curls delighted with my temper.

It's true. I want to spit out vile words like never before but, honestly, my swearing should be the least of her worries. She wants me filled with hate. That's how she wins. I check the white fire again half expecting it to have turned as black as Galtonia's soul.

'Be the Queen. Control the board.' Gran's little lesson had taught me. She's barely moving, but as long as her chest still rises, the game isn't over.

Recovered, Elric sweeps across to Evelyn, wings fully expanded blocking any attempt Galtonia might make to snatch Jack and Constance, or worse.

"Pathetic. Do you think you can protect them both? You're nothing but a blunt weapon. Like father, like son. Your time will come, Gryphon, as will his. I'll have you plucked and roasted before this day is done," snarls Galtonia.

"Unlikely. If you hadn't noticed, you're somewhat outnumbered. And that father of mine is leading his battalions here. Come on Galtonia, you can't be that thick to seriously think you can beat Althea and I, let alone her?" Elric gestures at me.

I glare at him. *Don't say stuff like that!*

Galtonia's eyes flash, that sly smirk of hers rises, "I'd forgotten. Do forgive my impoliteness. How is my dearest cousin?"

"She's not your cousin. Mention Lilith again and I swear I'll be the one doing the roasting."

Elric steps forward, but Jack screams and yanks hard on his wing, "Oh, I can beat you. And I'll enjoy every minute of it."

Galtonia flicks her cloak back, raises an arm then clicks her fingers.

I don't like this.

"Oh no, wait. My mistake. *We'll* be the ones enjoying every minute of this. Ladies!" Galtonia's voice crescendos as through the last wisps of the sun's haze, Alecta, Megaera and Tysaph emerge, looking even more bat-crazed than before. The hate that I fear so much rises into my throat. Visions of the black blade, of Mary's blood drenched body, of Constance's screams flash before me. I fall to my knees as their fears, their hate strikes me harder than ever before.

I don't know if I can control this.

For a second, I hold their pain, then reflect it back. *They need to face this.*

Galtonia parades like a peacock as Alecta prances past Gran, kicking her to see if she's alive.

"Ugh!" moans Gran to which Galtonia and the furies cackle, finding it hilarious to kick someone, *my someone*, when they're already down.

"Now, now, Alecta. Play nicely," Galtonia mocks.

Snarls rip from Alpha as her coat flickers furiously from silver to red to black to white. She's as hungry for revenge as I am. *Or...is that me? My revenge?*

Alpha stalks the space in front of me, protectively. I grit my teeth forcing myself to swallow hatred. I'll choke on it if I have to.

"Evelyn, help me!"

Behind Althea, inside the skeletal shadows of the trees, Evelyn stays hidden.

Alecta screeches, her tone like knives being sharpened, "Kill, kill, kill!"

She claps her hands with glee. Tysaph reaches out and belts her across the face. Stunned for a second, Alecta shields her head from further strikes but then sniggers to herself. Megaera, ignoring her sisters' fuss, remains the quietest of all. Like the saying goes, 'it is the quiet ones you've got to watch out for.'

Galtonia bends down at Gran's side, "Oh, how the mighty have fallen," she sneers. "The odds are now most definitely tipped in our favour. But at least your precious granddaughter has a little longer than perhaps you do."

Alpha howls, the only natural nocturnal noise of a once busy woodland.

Gran gasps, her hands skirting across the dry, dusty ground. Galtonia, turning to look at me, doesn't see it coming as Gran smashes a rock into her face. She falls back, stunned, holding her eye, before revealing what looks like olive-coloured blood pumping from it. As Gran flops back to the ground, her eyes fix on me before she closes them.

"Stay with me, Gran!"

Galtonia searches the floor maybe looking for leaves just as Lilith had for to mend my wound, but the ground is still too dry. Instead, she tears a piece from her skirt and presses it against the cut.

"Is that the best the once great Eleanor Walsingham can do? You're pathetic! Look at you! To think how we all admired you. Now, just a decaying wreck. Even your own daughter rejected you, your legacy, everything you stood for," Galtonia snaps.

I push myself up, fists balled. "I swear, if you mention my mother again or touch Gran once more, I'll beat you down...so...damn...hard!"

"Ah, there's my little protégé. Remind me, where exactly is Caroline? Still dead?"

Just as I'm about to unleash the white fire, dozens of roots, prick and stab my ankles. They sting, but I don't care. *"Thank you, Evelyn!"*

Like fibre optic cables, her light pulsates through the network of roots between us straight into my body. Total sugar rush.

"I pity you, Galtonia. A heart so filled with rage can never have known love. Not the love that Elric has for Lilith. Or the love that Gran and Mum have for me and me for them. I don't even think you've experienced the love Alpha and I share. None of it."

Alpha lets out a gleeful howl, as a wave of gold crests along her spine. Knowing how much Galtonia hates foxes, I think that's what Mum would say, adds insult to injury.

Galtonia's face drops, lip curling. *Definitely hit a nerve.*

"How else do you rid the world of darkness but by filling it with light?" I say, holding my hand out conjuring an orb.

I rub it against my leg like cricket players do before bowling then launch it at Galtonia, but she bats it away. *Test run*, Dad would have said.

"You'll need more than that, little girl" Galtonia scowls as the furies dance around behind her clearly excited.

Watching it all play out, Althea then steps forward, glancing across at me. I nod.

"What is it you've come here for exactly? Another Elemental? To kill us all? What does a dryad," Althea pauses and looks Galtonia up and down as if she's looking like something she's scraped from her shoe, "like you really want?"

"Let me have her!" screams Tysaph all of a sudden, bouncing her weight from left to right, her eyes fixed firmly on Althea. "I want to be the one who annihilates that pathetic excuse for a witch."

Looks like they've a score to settle.

Just as Galtonia is about to speak, I notice Alpha looking over her shoulder at me, her cheeks flushing golds and greys. *What is she trying to tell me?* I kneel at her side and whisper, "Is Gran okay?"

Alpha's eyes flash bronze to silver and gold. *So pretty.* I'll take that as a 'yes' then.

Galtonia ignoring Tysaph, cocks her head slightly, "Do you know why you were chosen, Althea? To be an Elemental Guardian?"

"Enlighten me," replies Althea, throwing her arms open as if to welcome Galtonia's wisdom.

"You think you're so special. Do you have any idea who persuaded the High Council in their final choices? Who do you think counselled Gaia on who would be the ideal recipients of such a prestigious honour? Goodness knows, anyone in the Kingdom could have been assigned to the Elementals but you were all chosen for specific reasons. Let me see. Elric. His loyalty is his frailty – torn between protecting his true love and doing his duty. One always distracting him from the other. And dear Lilith. Oh, poor, delicate little thing. So trusting and gentile but just because she is a dryad means she's tarred with the same brush as me. Never quite fully trusted, despite the purest of hearts. I believe that is guilt by association, in the human world."

Galtonia sighs, holding Althea's gaze for a moment. "And, you. Lauded as the greatest warrior witch of the four realms. Althea. So stubborn, so cold, so lacking of any real emotion. An empty shell with a heart of stone. All weaknesses to be exploited."

"You really love the sound of your own voice don't you." says Althea.

"Full of her own self-importance," calls Elric.

I can think of something else she is full of, too.

I've heard enough. This ends. Now.

"Constance, I need you!" I call trying to channel my voice to only her, but Althea must have heard, too, and flanks Constance as she darts across the distance between us to take my hand.

Constance channels her breath into me as fast as she can. As she does, I call to the tiny, untouched sandbox saplings littered around the clearing. They begin exploding as I launch dozens upon dozens of white fire orbs straight at Galtonia, who dives landing at the side of Gran, pulling her frail body up as a shield. I struggle to control the speed and strength of Constance's air surging through me, desperately pulling back as if the air streams are horse's reigns. My reactions aren't fast enough. Several of my own orbs strike Gran's chest as Galtonia cowers behind her. For a moment, Gran gasps, her eyes widen and lock on mine as a flash of light rushes through them then fades.

What have I done?

Gran's body crumbles to ash like all those plants she devoured for energy, for strength.

"NO!"

"Oh my God!" cries Evelyn.

To the sound of Galtonia's laughter filling the sky, Elric seizes Jack and traps him in his wings once more. Althea grabs Constance and drags her back to Evelyn, then pulling her swords from their sheaths repositions herself in front of them.

"Gran!"

But she's gone.

Alpha's howl is deafening. I fall to the ground...gripping her fur...holding onto the only thing I can...

CHAPTER THIRTY-NINE

Phoenix Rising

Have I just killed Gran?

I turn and throw up. This time, I miss Alpha. I wipe my sleeves across my mouth, listening to Galtonia laughing hysterically, sounding more and more like a fury.

"Oh, Hannah. You're fast becoming something of a legend!" she laughs, doubled over.

"Shut up! Shut up!"

Why did I listen to Gran? What was she thinking?

"Really, child. I *am* impressed. Very much so. Oh, I do wish you join us. And we do have a vacancy now," she says looking at a pile of ashes close to Gran's. "Poor, poor Alecta. Silly of her to pirouette around your grandmother mocking her like that. Totally oblivious to your little flurry of fireballs. Careless wench. Oh well," she shrugs.

"You're sick. Do you know that?"

"Yes, I have been told."

"You'd have killed Gran anyway. She'd much rather have died by my hand than yours!"

I can't believe what I'm saying!

"Yes, but I'm sure she'd much rather be alive than dead like her daughter. Stupid girl." Galtonia shakes her head from side to side slowly. "Tut tut tut. You've robbed me of the glory of killing the one and only Eleanor Walsingham."

Galtonia turns slightly then and from nowhere launches her own ruby-coloured orb straight at me. It strikes me in the gut, knocking me off my feet, but dissolves into the emerald tinged fire still pulsating across my body. Winded, I push myself up.

"Hmm, quite the little heiress now, aren't we? Shame you'll never actually inherit the full extent of Gaia's powers. And it looks like I'll need more myself if I'm to annihilate that bloodline of yours."

"Galtonia?"

"Yes, Hannah?"

"Shut up."

"That's rude. I've always been courteous to you, young lady. I use my manners…"

"But dead people don't actually need to."

"True."

My turn to smirk…

From the small pile of ashes, Gran rises so quickly, her body forming, taking shape. Shadows of wings stretch out then fill with flesh and bone. She is glorious. Like a sunrise.

Galtonia, her brow wrinkling, turns. Gran grabs her by the throat squeezing tightly.

"How?" she splutters.

Gran ignores her and flicks her enormous wings lifting them high into the air, swaying just enough to keep them both suspended. Every golden feather gleams and glimmers against the setting sun. Little crackles of fire from the movement of the feathers burst and fizz sending tiny firework streaks of light which linger against the navy and violet sky.

Thud! Thud! Thud!

The force of Elric's impact into Megaera makes the ground tremble as they tumble head over tail. Elric digs his claws in, but Megaera retaliates furiously ripping into his wing. Feathers fly. Elric cries in pain, taking blow after blow, but wrapping his huge hands around Megaera's leg, he launches her out towards the skeletal remains of the trees. She smashes through the weaker ones, obliterating them, sending their charred remains flying.

Reacting, Evelyn clasps her hands back around Jack's wrist, yanking him back as he attempts to charge at Megaera unable to hide his desperation to help Elric.

"Roots!" commands Evelyn, holding her arm summoning them from the earth. The trees might be scorched but the root systems are very much alive. Springing up to bind Megaera, one root coils around her mouth as she tries to scream out. She writhes as dozens more thick as steel cables bind her body. For a second I close my eyes feeling the network of roots pump nutrients into the remains of the wounded trees. *Incredible!*

With Alpha flanking me, I rush across to Elric as he kneels alongside Megaera's tightly bound body.

"Shall I dispose of her?" he asks.

Dispose?

I stare at him blankly not daring to confirm what I know he means.

"In Gaian, we often leave matters like this to Gaia and let nature judge whether to condemn or not."

I look around at all the scorched skeletons of trees I can barely recognise and my heart sinks at the thought that it's our fault. Humans. *Will nature condemn us?*

Alpha scratches through the remains of the burnt forest floor then picks up something. I hold out my hand and Alpha drops a piece of bark, wet with saliva onto my palm. She nods.

"I know, girl. It's so sad."

Her coat flickers a dirty yellow colour then back to its natural silver. Alpha nudges my hand closer to my face, wanting me to inspect her gift. Part of the bark crumbles, but as I turn it over I glance up to Alpha, shocked. She then looks at Megaera, lying bound and gagged.

"Elric, if Megaera can't escape then we should just leave her here. She can't escape, can she? Like just vanish."

"No, the roots have her bound to this place."

"I'll leave it to nature then."

Confusion crosses his face.

"But...you *are* nature, Hannah. You're the heiress. The Potential. You are not a separate entity. You are one part of the whole."

His words press their weight onto my shoulders.

Breathe. In and out. Come on, drama queen, keep it together.

"The elements will erode her eventually," Elric suggests. There's no malice in it. Just a statement of fact.

I can't speak. What would I even say?

Without words, I kneel at Megaera's side and press the piece of bark, riddled with thousands of tiny holes into her hand. She glances down and instantly begins screaming and thrashing against her restraints as Lilith's lesson rings in my ears like hot blood rushing through them. Another fury defeated, but it's nothing to feel good about.

As I walk away and head towards Evelyn, I glance up at Gran who, still clutching Galtonia by the neck gestures to where Althea and Tysaph are locked in a battle.

"I don't think Althea needs my help." I say.

"Watch. Learn." comes Gran's reply. *"You must learn as much as possible from those around you, Hannah. You never know when their time or yours will pass."*

I shudder.

What does Gran mean by that?

Before I can speak, Tysaph's cry sends a shiver streaking

down my spine. She vanishes. Althea, crouches slightly, flicking and rotating her swords, her eyes scanning the graveyard of trees.

"Hannah," hisses Evelyn just loud enough for me to hear. She beckons me back. Elric, heeding Evelyn's warning sweeps above me, hooking my arms and lifting me up. *Wow!* We soar across the ground as Alpha gallops beneath us like a thoroughbred. *She's so fast!*

Dropping me, Elric soars up and circles back above our heads. Evelyn opens her arms as if to welcome me home. We're careful to keep within the shadows of the trees as Elric hovers overhead, flinching at every sound. His eyes narrow and dart from place to place searching for the fury hidden amongst us.

"Kill the witch, Tysaph!" croaks Galtonia with what little breath she has left.

Gran ruffles her feathers showering Galtonia in a waterfall of fire. Her screams tear the silence as Gran's fire burns so brightly against the fading light.

Tysaph bursts suddenly from behind a row of charred firs throwing herself at Althea but rather than knocking her to the ground, Althea digs her heels in as they slide across the ground creating deep tracks. With swords in both Althea's hand, Tysaph takes advantage clutching Althea's arms driving her back before throwing her down.

Althea never once drops the swords. It's like they're part of her. An extension of her arms, her hands. Althea raises her legs then flips upright as the fury dances around her, taunting her.

"You're not witch enough or warrior enough to match me," cries Tysaph. Althea scowls.

"Pick one. And I'll soon prove that theory wrong."

"She's so confident," whispers Constance.

"I wish I could fight like her," adds Jack.

"Woman are warriors in Hannah's time," says Evelyn exchanging a look with me.

"You are so lucky, Hannah. The future sounds incredible," Constance says with a complete look of awe and envy on her face.

"Let's hope we can save that future," I say.

It'll take more than hope, I reckon.

"Very well, let's see how much of a warrior you really are!" challenges Tysaph.

Like a match hitting lighter fuel, Althea throws down her swords and charges straight at Tysaph, who dances from foot to foot. She launches herself up as Tysaph leaps to greet her. A hail of fists pound down on the fury like I've never seen before pushing Althea's buttons just like they did to me.

Is that what Tysaph wants?

The fury strikes back by sinking her claws into Althea's thigh and begins stabbing into her side. Clutching her fists together, Althea smashes them down onto Tysaph's neck. She hits the ground, completely dazed. For a second, Althea stumbles around, clutching her side. She's badly injured.

I have to do something!

Think!

"No, Hannah. Just watch!" echoes Gran's voice.

Althea straightens up and inhales deeply, stretching her arms out before towering over Tysaph and grabbing her by the hair. She clutches Tysaph's ragged clothes around the waist and flings her up, lifting her high above her head and throwing the fury across the forest. Like a bowling ball, Tysaph smashes through several trees, before slamming into one just like Megaera did. Glinting in the moon's light, Tysaph's attention is caught by Althea's swords. She darts across to them, too fast for Althea.

"Now warrior, you'll die by your own swords."

Althea doesn't speak, she just charges straight at Tysaph.

What is she doing?

Tysaph swings each sword back, ready to strike as Althea launches herself up. The swords cross...

Boom!

Tysaph is sent hurtling into the air before slamming back down on the ground, gasping for breath. Althea strides up to her.

"I am warrior and I am witch," cries Althea. She picks up her swords and drives them straight into Tysaph's chest.

"Althea bewitched her swords!"

"You're learning faster than I ever imagined, Hannah. Now, just one more dead end to deal with."

Elric lowers himself as Althea passes us. They take each other's arm, pulling each other into their shoulders, just like Elric did with his gryphon brothers.

"This...isn't...over!" Galtonia hisses.

"But they are," replies Althea.

"Still unwilling to remember what you were and who you were? Still unwilling to atone? You know, I never imagined our friendship would end like this," sighs Gran and I wonder how hurt she is by Galtonia's betrayal.

"Are you going to tell me how you survived Hannah's fire?"

"Forgotten who I am so soon? At the core of my soul is a Firebird and we devour fire, especially the white sort. And Hannah's was the ideal accelerant, it being so pure."

"You've taught her well, you know," gasps Galtonia clutching at Gran's claws.

"I have, but she is so much more than that. You cannot begin to fathom what or who she is. And, thankfully, Gaia will be safer because of her. We will find the antidote to whatever you and your Lord have poisoned her with."

"I suppose I could tell you, but where's the fun in that?"

"At least tell me which Lord tempted you?" asks Gran.

Galtonia's head begins to loll from side to side as Gran deprives her of air.

"That's the least of your worries," she hisses between what little breath she has left. "Harriet will be dead before nightfall and Gaia has only you to blame."

I'm suddenly hit by a wall of fear from Evelyn and struggle to breathe.

"Where is my daughter?" she screams, as Althea tries to restrain her, but Evelyn pushes her off. Althea holds her hands up and winces as she does so. *Maybe I can treat her wounds like Lilith treated mine?*

Elric steps in and pins Evelyn's arms to her sides pulling her back against his chest.

"Please Galtonia, for pity's sake, tell me where she is!" cries Evelyn.

"You survived our little trip through the hollow, too, I see. Shame. And, don't beg Evelyn. It really is…most unbecoming…from a woman like you."

"Tell me where Harriet is!" Evelyn rages as Constance and Jack cling to each other.

"You'll never find her. The sand timer has already turned."

"And your sand timer has run out," says Gran.

I can't watch.

The heat from Gran's fire prickles against my skin as I walk over to comfort Jack and Constance. It spits and crackles as it reduces Galtonia to dust.

CHAPTER FORTY

What the Water Left

The sound of the slap takes us all by surprise. Evelyn stands, her palm pressed to her cheek, as everyone stares at Althea who often seems more warrior than witch. In fact I haven't really see her do anything witchy at all. Not like I expect brooms and cauldrons exactly.

As the shock fades, Evelyn squares up to Althea.

"Never do that again!" she grimaces, removing her hand to reveal a deep red flush to her cheek.

"You were hysterical. Now you're not," Althea replies flatly.

"It seems to be a common trait amongst warrior witches. An absence of the heart. You have no idea what this is like."

"Mother! That's unfair!" snaps Constance. "Althea is not deserving of that."

Evelyn sighs, pausing for a second. "Forgive me. Constance is right. I'm just…I apologise."

"The thing is, you know *of* me, Evelyn, but you do not know me. So, please don't make assumptions."

Althea's right. None of us should.

While the drama settles, Gran pulls me to one side. I squeeze Constance's hand as I let her go.

"You were brave to stand up to your mother, you know," I say.

"It was very rude of me to speak in such a manner to my elder," Constance replies.

"You challenged someone because you felt they were wrong. Even if it's your own mother, it was still the right thing to do."

I smile and leave Constance to sit with Evelyn and Jack both still lost in sorrow.

"Looks like you could use a hug," Gran says pulling me in. Her honeysuckle scent and the da-dum, da-dum of her heart are always soothing. I love the feel of her phoenix feathers. So soft.

"That was some crazy plan, Gran. What if I'd really killed you or she had?"

The thought turns my stomach over and over.

"It was a risk. I won't lie. But I trusted our collective instincts and the fact that she was so desperate to turn you, blacken your heart and that if you blamed her for killing me then it would be enough to turn you. But what Galtonia failed to anticipate was the depth of your light, my dear. Now, walk with me," Gran says before taking my hand. For a second, a flutter of nerves rise like a kaleidoscope of butterflies. Not in my chest, but Gran's. *She's lowered her guard it seems.*

"I need to show you something and I also need to tell you something."

Okay, now the butterflies have a new home.

We approach a small embankment, just to the east of the clearing. What was a river is now completely bone dry.

"Did Gaia's fever do that?"

"Yes. They are becoming ever more dangerous. The threat to life is the highest I've ever known."

"Can Jack refill the rivers? Water *is* his element."

"Either of you can do it."

I can?

"Hannah, do you remember when you thought you'd seen your mother in the river?"

"Y-Yes."

The butterflies multiply creating a swarm of nerves in my chest.

"You were right. She was trapped in the water."

"What?" How do you know that?"

"I received a message from Joyce."

Joyce?

"Is that why you've been blocking me? Keeping your distance?"

"It is. You see, when Joyce and William interred Mary's body, Caroline's...your mother's...wasn't there. And Evelyn worked out that..."

"Evelyn knows? You both knew and didn't tell me?"

"You're just going to have to forgive me. It was absolutely

necessary, but you know me, if I can tell you the truth then I always will. This time there was a delay in the receipt of that truth."

Gran's feathers ruffle and I don't know if it's because of me or just because.

"Are you sure Mum's in the water?"

"Listen, Evelyn worked out that Caroline's element is water. It's her astrological sign. I never gave it a second thought. When the draconite knocked your mother out her conscience projected to safety; her element took over. It plunged her into her natural, and therefore, safest environment. She'd been trapped there ever since."

Trapped! Poor Mum!

I was so close to her! Now I get why Evelyn has been so fraught. Both of us, so close…

"Wait! That doesn't make sense though because we still had Mum's body."

"Now that part we are not sure of. But, Hannah, there's something else."

Wait. Gran said 'She'd been trapped'. Past tense.

"Gaia's fevers have been too numerous to count here. Never mind the havoc they've been wreaking back on Earth. They've worsened, considerably." Gran pauses and looks down into the river bed. "Hannah, all the rivers in the Northern realm may well have dried out like this one has. I don't…I don't know if..."

Fear grabs me by the throat.

"My mother isn't dead!" I gasp. "You promised me! You told me we'd find her!"

"I think you did find her."

"Stop speaking about her in the past tense!"

"But, if your mother was in the water then Gaia's fever may have…"

Gran stops, clutching her hand to her mouth. Tears streak down her face.

She's crying.

I've never seen her cry.

"No! You're wrong!"

"I wish I was, sweetheart, but I don't think I am."

My body fills with adrenalin. I run. I run and breathe because I don't know what else to do. I drop down into the dusty river bed, trip and smack hard into the ground. Sobbing, I pound my fists against the sandy seabed sending clouds of grit and dust into the air.

"MUM!"

I could have saved her.

Why didn't I save her?

What's wrong with me?

I smack my fists into the ground until they bleed and sting. After a moment, Gran kneels at my side, pulls me up and wraps her arms around me.

"I wish the furies had killed me. I wish the draconite had. I wish…"

Hearing that, Gran grabs my shoulders and shakes me, but doesn't slap me like Althea slapped Evelyn. Sparks of firelight ignite across her chest and shoulders making me flinch.

"Don't ever speak like that again."

"I hate it here! I want to go home."

"Now you listen to me. If we don't find Harriet and get you to Gaia, there'll be no home to return to. Do you understand?"

The heiress in me gets it.

But the thirteen-year-old-me just wants to go home.

****

Curled up, resting against Gran's legs, she strokes my hair as the sobs begin to fade. Alpha brushes my arm with her soft tail in a soothing motion, her coat a shade of olive.

I'm so lucky to have them both, but…

The sand and grit in the air against the dying haze of sun has settled heavily on my chest. I need water. *How ridiculous is that?* We're sat in a dry river bed, probably one of a thousand all dried from Gaia's searing heat. I wet my lips and squeeze my eyes against the grit as I push myself up.

"I need proof, Gran. I won't accept Mum's gone until I see her. I just can't."

Gran's reply isn't what I expected, "Neither can I, dearest."

"Really?"

"You see, neither Evelyn nor I can work out what happened between your mother being interred and Joyce discovering her body was missing. And your mother may have well chosen to or should I say demanded to, abdicate from her duty, but whether she likes it or not, she is and will remain a bloodline heiress. At least until..."

I don't know if Gran realises just how much hope she's poured into me.

"Okay, so let's just say that no-one else outside our circle knew what had happened to Mum because we'd hidden the evidence. Then, if no-one knew, no-one could have just taken her body."

"Carry on."

"Mum's body didn't just vanish. Isn't there a massive, or at least more of a chance that it's been reunited with her soul somehow? Because, like, how did she get here, otherwise? Couldn't something from this end have triggered it?"

"Be precise. What are you getting at?"

"What if something or someone has dragged Mum's body back to her soul? Maybe Gaia's fevers threatened the human part of Mum's life. That's possible, isn't it?"

"Yes, it could be."

Gran's calculation face appears.

"Then isn't it possible that if Mum's body and soul were reunited, and something has been keeping her trapped in the water, then after Gaia's fevers dried all the rivers, couldn't Mum have just crawled out from the river bed?"

Gran's face drops.

I think I'm on to something...

"Oh my goodness! Hannah, your river dream. I think Gaia might still want your mother after all."

...and so, it would seem, is Gran.

❧ CHAPTER FORTY-ONE ❧
Howl

The howl slices through the air like a blade.

Alpha!

Leaving Gran, my feet pound against the dusty riverbed, as I head towards the embankment and scramble up it. As my mind travels faster than my legs, questions strike me like a shower of spears falling from high.

Alpha's sorrowful howl cries out like it's on replay.

"What is it, girl?" I shout, unable to hide the panic in my voice.

I wish I could hear her thoughts, read her like Gran does.

As I grow closer to where the others are, Elric points, "There. She just suddenly ran."

Althea, swords drawn, positions herself, eyes flitting to every corner of the clearing.

I scan the grounds, tracking the rising hills. Now visible through the trees' skeletal limbs and no longer hidden by thick green canopies, the rocky hillside rises, a waterfall of clouds trailing down its face. Alpha stands on a ridge halfway up crying out in pain.

I continue running, yelling out, "Alpha, what's wrong? What's happened?"

Against the glow of the rising moon, her coat flickers from a sickly yellow to a deep dark burgundy.

"Please, Alpha!"

She scrapes at the rocks barking and howling furiously then as if she's seen something, suddenly throws herself forward.

"Alpha!" I scream, my heart leaping from my chest.

From behind me, Gran streaks across the sky, wings ablaze. She's so fast. Dipping down, she vanishes out of sight for a moment before soaring upwards from behind the top of the hill clutching the scruff of Alpha's neck in her claws. I track them as Gran circles back into the clearing, her fire fading to an afterglow as she drops Alpha to the ground right before landing herself.

"Thank you, Gran! I don't know what I'd have done…"

I run desperate to hold her, to comfort her, but Alpha suddenly rears up, barking and snarling which stops me dead in my tracks.

"What's the matter, girl?"

Did the furies get to her somehow?

But Alpha isn't staring at me. Her eyes are fixed on Gran. The second Gran turns, Alpha charges, but Gran doesn't move. Leaping high, Alpha's pads strike Gran's chest knocking her backwards. She barks and snarls directly into Gran's face.

Oh my god!

She's going to kill Gran!

My legs take over as I belt towards them, my lungs burning as I scream, "Alpha, stop! Don't!"

But she doesn't.

Alpha doesn't stop.

It's then I realise I never had any real control over her at all. *Why do we always think we should control other creatures? Hate that!*

Gran grabs Alpha's head as the howls fade to whimpers.

"No! Gran don't hurt her!"

I don't know who's more dangerous. A firebird or a giant silver fox.

As I arrive, Gran shoots me a look and says, "Hold Alpha's head, there and there," she points. "And listen. Listen to her. Listen for her. Every single thought you have must be pushed away. Nothing can invade the space."

Kneeling down, I shuffle as close as possible and place my hands on the side of Alpha's temples lifting her sunken head revealing eyes frosted like glass.

"Alpha, it's me. What's the matter, girl? Can you show me what happened?"

"She doesn't need to," comes a voice.

I turn.

"Joyce?"

CHAPTER FORTY-TWO
Attacks and Silverbacks

"I can't be away along. Beattie and Delta are injured. With Delta it's mainly superficial, but Beattie's injuries are internal. I may have to operate."

Alpha whimpers, but doesn't move.

"She's just been absolutely hysterical. That's why, isn't it?"

"I would imagine so. Alpha will have sensed it all. The pack are a collective after all. Being physically apart from each other doesn't matter to foxes."

"What happened?" I ask as my stomach somersaults.

Gran and I lock eyes as I realise she already knows and will have, by now, read Joyce's mind.

"How did they get injured? Are you okay?"

"Just about," she replies then turns to Gran. "Hannah can dip into my mind now just like you can. But I imagine you would prefer me to tell the tale."

"Couldn't one of us just broadcast this?" I ask Joyce.

"We are all here, so there's no point to a broadcast," says Gran.

"No, I mean like a movie. You've sent me those memory postcards before. Can't we replay what happened for all of us, but in a movie-mode kind of way?"

"I think we would all prefer to see exactly what happened

for ourselves," suggests Althea.

"Hannah, do you wish to try? It's more simple than one might imagine. And, you're the one who needs to do this more than any of us," asks Joyce. "So I don't mind you rummaging around in my head."

I remember how strange it felt. I hated it at first. Like I had absolutely no privacy any more. Like Gran had become the thought police. It still doesn't feel right at all, but I guess I have to try. And if it helps everyone...

Jack steps forward, "Shouldn't you," he points at Joyce's chest, "be protecting my Father and Mary?"

"That's why I'm here," replies Joyce.

Evelyn steps forward, but she seems to have left behind that powerful woman she once was.

"Believe me, Hannah. Evelyn may be distraught from the losses, but her resolve is very much intact." Gran says as her voice slips into my mind.

Gran doesn't have to say any more. I know what's coming...

"It's William, isn't it?"

"Yes. Hannah will show you," she replies, taking Evelyn's hand briefly before sitting down on the floor next to Alpha and me.

"Eleanor," Now, Joyce's voice trickles into mine and Gran's minds. *"I've brought a highly potent dose of lavender. We may*

need it."

Joyce doesn't make any further eye contact with Evelyn. She doesn't have to.

Nerves circle in my stomach.

"I can help you navigate," says Gran.

I glance down to Alpha, her eyes now clear.

"You don't have to watch this, Alph. Not if you don't want to."

Maybe somehow she's already seen it. From the intensity of feelings she radiated and the changes to her fur, I know she felt it. Alpha nestles her head onto my lap placing her paws into a V before burying her face between them.

I press a kiss onto her head and inhale her foxy scent.

"What do I do?"

****

From within an ice-blue orb, Gran conjures a crystal. Its edges are jagged and its surface is probably the deepest blue I've ever seen, making it look like a piece of frozen ocean.

"This is azurite. Through this you will channel what you read from Joyce," Gran begins. "Keep all focus upon the crystal and keep your mind as clear, ready to receive Joyce's memories."

So not to disturb Alpha, Joyce nudges as close as possible so we can both hold hands. To the side, I hear Jack and Constance gasp as Gran floats the crystal between us.

"How can I feel you when you're an astral projection?"

"Energy. I made the projection of myself as solid as possible, filled with as much energy as I could just like you've seen your Gran do. I pretty much ate a tree."

Joyce's eyes roll and we both smirk.

"Concentrate!" barks Gran. "I suspect we have very little time. Whoever controlled Galtonia will now be fully aware of exactly what has happened."

Joyce and I both focus upon the crystal and immediately I feel a pulling sensation as if it was Lilith pulling me into one of her visions. I guess this isn't so different.

The blues and silvers deep inside the crystal begin to swirl and intertwine.

Crack!

A blast of air splinters the crystal into two pieces, projecting out a fan of bright blue light.

"Now through the projection, Hannah, I want you to focus going into Joyce's thoughts. Focus on her third eye. The inner sight."

"Walk into her open mind. Show us exactly what happened."

Within the fan of light projected between us, the image of Windsor House appears. Like a virtual game, I imagine walking into the house, my hand turning the brass knob and entering through the reception. Everything is discoloured, like an old photograph. Looking left, I move towards the corridor. The vision whizzes forward making my stomach flip from the speed.

"Steady, Han. Not too fast."

Gran skirts around Joyce, pressing her hand onto her shoulder as if to steady her. I feel a hand upon mine and realise it must be Althea.

"Ease back a little, like you're pulling the reigns of a horse ever so gently," she says.

Cast into the vision, the image of the long hall appears. Inside, lights are dimmed and flitting up and down into the high church-like ceiling are dozens of sprites creating spirals of rainbow lights as they zip about. The pulling sensation returns as if Joyce is guiding me forwards towards the back wall. As the image grows clearer, I see William curled in a ball of light suspended above the remains of a broken dresser. In the corner next to a long-handled brush is a pile of glass and broken plates.

Once more the image whirrs and propels me forward, but I feel Althea's hand press down helping me control the speed of the vision. Joyce is now asleep in an armchair next to the fireplace, with Beattie and Delta at her feet. Beattie's ears twitch, then she lifts her head. Delta does the same and together they begin tracking sounds across the ceiling. Delta nudges Joyce to wake. She clutches the chair arms before darting up and running to a cabinet where she removes three small glass bottles. Ordered to leave, the sprites scatter locating an open window. They whip through the gap and vanish. Joyce, flanked by Beattie and Delta surround William and wait. Both silverbacks, teeth bared breathe heavily, waiting, listening.

Crash!

The creature bursts through the huge window, ripping the thick velvety curtain and sending glass and wooden beams flying. Joyce ducks. Beattie and Delta flatten their bodies for a second, as the shower of debris hits. Snapping the long oak table in half as it lands, the creature scours the room for a moment. It stalks towards Joyce who lobs all three bottles at it. *A sleeping potion?*

Each bottle smashes against the creature's mottled scales, their contents doing absolutely nothing at all. Joyce then conjures one orb after another striking it in its chest, but still the creature stomps towards them, steam pouring from its nostrils.

Beattie and Delta both launch at the creature, but it swings its thick arm striking each of them to send them hurtling down the hall. Beattie takes the brunt of the impact, slamming so hard into the wall, followed by Delta who rebounds off Beattie. Both smack into the ground out cold.

Oh my god! No wonder Alpha freaked out!

Finally the creature stops in front of Joyce, her orbs having had no impact at all. It glowers down at her, slaver trickles down its jaws. Joyce shouts something, but the creature just grunts. *She didn't stand a chance, even with two silverbacks.*

As the creature pulls its arm back ready to strike, Joyce clicks her fingers and disappears plunging the vision into blackness.

I blink and pull back snapping the connection. The projected light vanishes.

"What was that thing?" cries Jack.

"That was a Volkha," says Elric.

"What? That's what Freya saw?"

"Wait! What happened? Where's William?" screams Evelyn launching herself at Joyce. "Get the vision back. Bring it back!" She shakes Joyce violently.

"I have no recollection of what happened next because I wasn't there. I used an old parlour trick to remove my body elsewhere, and then projected straight here. I'm sorry."

"Don't apologise," says Althea. "It's thanks to you that we know this much."

Alpha raises her head. "I'm so sorry girl. But I promise it will be alright. Joyce will heal them both. She won't let anything happen to either of them."

Gran stands and pulls Evelyn back.

"Do something! You and Hannah must be able to do something. She's Gaia's heiress for goodness sake! Please, Eleanor. Please, save my family. *Our* family. This is your bloodline, too!"

"Drink this," says Gran. "I need you thinking straight. And it's easier than being slapped again."

Evelyn scowls and knocks back the tiny bottle of what I guess is lavender juice.

"Mother, where's our father?" asks Jack. His words hang in the air.

"I don't know. I don't know anything anymore."

Pit-pat, pit-pat, pit-pat...

Splodges of water smack the dry dusty ground. I look straight at Jack, but his eyes are clear. It's not him.

I guess that means a storm's coming...

CHAPTER FORTY-THREE

Caroline
Caved

Listening to Elijah explain how he ended up in Gaian makes my story a little less outlandish. His long coat flaps around his ankles as he strides out in front, continuing to point out the parts of Gaian he has discovered since finding himself here just over three years ago. Like a chocolate box, questions sit waiting to be picked. I don't want to pry or seem nosey, but I'm curious to know more about him. *Will his family be looking for him? Has he looked for a way home? Are there any other humans here? What makes him so particular and neat about everything he owns? Is he married?* I pick one.

"Elijah, what about your family? Aren't you worried about never seeing them again?"

Does he miss life on Earth?

Would I?

"My mother died giving birth to me. I spent my early years in Monserrat, a volcanic island close to Dominica. My father brought me to England when I was only young to study. He passed away before I graduated from Cambridge where I eventually became a professor."

"I am so sorry. I'm lucky enough to still have my mother, although we've only just reconnected."

"Why did you disconnect?" he asks pausing and pointing

at a cluster of stars emerging from behind a bank of grey cotton wool clouds.

"I made a choice she disagreed most vehemently with. In fact, I've made a few very questionable choices in my life. But we're talking. And there's Hannah, of course. She loves my mother so much. I love her. I've missed her."

"I hope you've told her that. I don't have that privilege to be able to say it to my father's face anymore."

I smile to hide the truth. I can't even remember when I last said it. Remaining lost in thought, we continue walking upward along a hilly pathway which overlooks a beautiful moonlit valley. Elijah seems to have a way of making me feel quite…something…*I don't know how he makes me feel, actually.*

"Down there is where I found you," he points. "Let us head there first."

"You carried me all the way up here? We've walked for over an hour."

I suddenly wish I weighed ten pounds less.

"You were a good work out!" he laughs, which carries out into the valley.

My cheeks flush. I. Am. Mortified!

"Relax, I'm strong and you don't weigh so much. You ladies, always worrying about your weight."

"It sounds as if you know."

"I was engaged to a lady a while ago, but we wanted different things in the end. The energy wasn't quite right. I knew that, but she was a good woman. I won't compromise now when it comes to how I feel about someone that's for sure."

"I get that. I feel quite the same."

As a cluster of thick dark clouds roll in, large raindrops fall smacking against the dry rocks arid from the heat wave giving rise to little puffs of dust.

"It will pass, I'm sure," says Elijah, but then he stops, looking back past me as something catches his eye. "Or maybe not."

Negotiating around a cluster of rocks in the middle of the pathway, Elijah turns me around and points. "Watch."

After a moment or two, half a dozen enormous lightning strikes hit land in the distance. One, so powerful, it creates an explosion of fire.

"Huh! What is that?"

"We must shelter. We may not have long. These storms have increased in ferocity these past three years."

The rain smacks down harder. Elijah grabs my hand as a deluge begins. Pulling me after him, he shouts, "At the bottom of this trail there's a cluster of small caves."

We bounce down the pathway, leaping over rocks as the rain lashes harder. In no time, the pathway has become a mudslide. I slip, but Elijah grabs my wrist to steady me.

"Stay on the edge where the rocks are," he says and lets my hand fall.

Rain runs thickly through my hair, matting it to my face. "How far is it?"

"We're close. We'll stay in the top one in case the land floods. We mustn't get trapped inside. We may have to move quickly."

"Are you sure it's safe?"

"Yes, much safer than out here for sure! Hurry!" he shouts yanking my arm over and over to keep me moving.

Argh!

My feet slip from beneath me and I'm propelled forwards smacking right into the back of him. We slide through the mud on knees and hands as we lose our grip on each other.

Ow!

Rocks and stones tear at my flesh, but I push myself up, fighting to draw breath through the torrential rain. Further down, Elijah rolls over and grips a rock to pull himself up.

"Where are we going?" I shout as thunder booms overhead.

"In there!" he points. I turn to see a small entrance a little way back up from where we fell. I slide down and lodge one foot against a rock, stretching out to him.

"Here, take my hand!" I cry.

Elijah reaches and grabs it and with every ounce of

strength I have I pull him up as he slips and slides against a river of mud. Navigating to the right, he manages to get a footing against a craggy path enabling us to then crawl back up to the cave's entrance, diving in just as the lightning strikes close in.

Gasping for breath, we lay for a moment as lightning pummels the ground only metres away. Elijah pulls me back.

"Stay back."

"What are we going to do?"

"Wait until it passes. Give me your bag. The matches are in there. We must make a fire and get dry."

I peel the bag from my shoulders and rummage through for the tin box Elijah says is filled with matches.

"I'll go further in and find some dry wood and leaves. Stay away from the edge. The lightning here in Gaian is not like that on Earth. It's much, much more powerful."

He turns to leave and begins hunting for material to burn, but I'm suddenly filled with panic, looking out to where trails of steam rise from the extinguished wounds littering the hillside.

"Wait!" I begin, but pause afraid of admitting my fears.

"I won't be long. I promise. I'll be just there," he points. "You're a strong woman, Caroline. Nothing to be afraid of."

I wish I could believe him.

CHAPTER FORTY-FOUR

Eleanor
Headlines

Images from the news coverage flash into my mind as I read Joyce's.

Flick, flick, flick.

BREAKING NEWS: Venice submerged and Mumbai on the brink.

Flick, flick, flick.

BREAKING NEWS: Pacific Hurricane – Final Death Toll Breached 100m UN Report Confirms.

Flick, flick, flick.

BREAKING NEWS: Canada closes its borders leaving millions of climate-migrants vulnerable. "We're full." says PM.

"Earth is a living hell," says Joyce as I break the connection. *"It's Gaia's fevers. It's accelerated everything."*

"But we've accelerated those. One of the Lords may well be taking advantage, but this is our fault. Make no mistake."

Joyce swallows the lump in her throat and turns away to avoid Hannah's eyeline.

"She is so powerful now, it's taking everything I have to block her and stop her reading both of us. Her empathy appears limitless. I'm worried it could overwhelm her."

"How did she take the news of Caroline?" Joyce asks

composing herself.

"*She's hopeful. As am I. Something happened to Caroline but I daren't imagine what for fear of Hannah latching on to it should she penetrate this firewall. It's exhausting blocking her continually.*"

"*But necessary. Do you suspect Gaia?*"

"*After the dream Hannah had, yes. Something tells me she's not forgiven Caroline for the abdication and will seek whatever revenge she can no matter the cost.*" I reply.

"*Can you not send someone to find her? Scour the lands, perhaps? There must be someone who can discover her whereabouts, surely?*" questions Joyce.

"*We cannot weaken our numbers here. We're more vulnerable than I would like, even with Galtonia and the furies extinguished.*"

Joyce claps her hand to her forehead as her projection flickers.

"I must return to Beattie and Delta. I don't have long. If I discover any more of what happened to William, I'll contact you. Stay safe, old friend."

"May the light protect you, always."

We squeeze each other tightly, before Joyce waves to Hannah and fades away. She darts over.

"I didn't get a chance to say goodbye!"

"She's tired and had to get back to the foxes. They need her now more than ever. And neither of us are spring chickens any more, as the saying goes."

"I wish I could astrally project," she says.

"You can. Something else to add to the list of things to learn."

Her face lights up.

"Let me guess. I've got to concentrate really hard?"

"Always."

A sudden clap of thunder triggers shivers down my spine as the storm rears up and gallops towards us.

CHAPTER FORTY-FIVE

Hannah
The Calm

Do storms always come from the west?

"We can't out run it. We must find shelter and fast," says Althea holding Jack's head in her hands, checking for any sign of influence.

Frustrated, he pulls her hands away. "It's not me!"

"Very well," she replies.

"There," Elric points, "is where the Valerian Mountains begin. Let's go."

"Are you okay? Have you enough energy for this?" I ask her.

"Yes. I followed Joyce's advice."

"You ate a tree, too?" My eyebrows practically leave my face.

"Well, consumed its energy. The root systems began reviving it the second I had consumed just enough."

How could we ever survive without trees?

Everyone begins moving as quickly as possible. I linger at the back of our pack and for a moment scan the graveyard filled with the remains of coniferous trees. Alpha waits at the edge of the clearing, still burdened by the weight of Beattie and Delta's suffering. I pause and walk to the closest tree, pressing my fingertips against the charred bark as rain splodges smack the dry ground sending dust balls into the air.

Evelyn's words echo back to me. *'She's Gaia's heiress for goodness sake.'*

Taking the deepest of breaths, I push hard against the bark desperate to find a way in, just as Lilith did.

Lilith.

After a moment, I feel the pulling sensation I'm becoming more and more used to. Closing my eyes, I try to channel anything I can into the tree, gratefulness, energy, sugar. I have no idea if I'm doing this right or not.

"Take what you need," I whisper.

A sudden ice-cold rush flows through my veins, so cold it stings a little. It lasts for just seconds. The tree pushes back releasing me. I remove my hand to reveal an exact imprint of it, but instead of the bark being charred, it just looks normal. Like it's been renewed. Regenerated. That's it. Between its crevices, its lime-coloured veins glow, as it starts spreading out from the print of my fingertips like blood being pumped through veins. *Amazing!*

A branch swings down and strokes my cheek. I hold it for a second.

Thank you.

That felt so good.

More and more rain splodges continue smacking the

ground, getting larger and larger.

"Yip, yip."

"I'm coming Alph."

I run towards her and realize the others must be some way ahead.

"Can you keep up?" I ask her. *My girl.* Her coat flashes bright blue. Challenge accepted, I think. We begin darting through trees, over stumps and ducking under low branches. The pathway is clearer than before even though we're climbing higher. I'd thought it would be rockier than this. Bounding upwards, I feel as light as air itself. Alpha, obviously faster, circles around me staying as close as possible. I listen for the others as feet and paws pad against the ground.

Where are they?

We climb higher, now clearing the tallest of the trees, up from the ridge and eventually come to an enormous ledge that seems to curve forever around the mountain.

Beautiful!

In the distance, the land looks so lush and colourful. I drink it all in suddenly wanting to drown in its beauty. But, then, considering what could have happened to Mum realise how stupid that is.

"I'll find you, Mum. I promise," I call out letting my voice sail away on the wind. Behind us the skies are darkening.

'Gran? Where are you all? We're on the ledge. Did you go higher?'

I wait for a moment.

A sudden heat rises, flushing my cheeks. Sweat beads pop up across my skin. Alpha begins panting heavily.

Gaia's fever must be rising again...

"Hannah. There you are, dearest."

...or maybe it's just Gaia...

CHAPTER FORTY-SIX
The Mother of All Nature

Oh. My. Goddess.

It's her.

Gaia stares at me then sways, before her knees buckle.

I dart forward through a wall of heat and a deluge of rain and pull Gaia up, bringing her face to face with me. The emerald eyes are just as they were in the dream, only her lashes are long and full like the finest branches of a bonsai tree. Her soft caramel complexion contrasts with flushed cheeks as she grapples at the carved golden collar around her neck.

"Shall I remove it? Can you breathe?" I begin trying to find a clasp, but Gaia smacks my hand away, startling me. She continues to loll from side to side just as Galtonia did right before she died. *Oh no!*

"Gaia! Gaia, it's me Hannah. I'm here. Don't die. Please."

Where is everyone?

"Gran!" I shout, listening to it echo out across the valley below.

"Who are you?" asks Gaia suddenly.

She's delirious.

Thunder rumbles ever closer as more and more bolts of lightning strike. I struggle to hold her up as the rain soaks us both to the bone.

Grabbing me by the throat, sounding just like Tysaph, Gaia screeches "Why are you trying to kill me?"

I can't breathe.

Behind us, Alpha growls and barks before launching herself at Gaia, but Gaia throws her arm out, her hand like a claw conducting Alpha like an instrument in the air, rotating her body. Alpha writhes in pain. Her howl slashes at my soul with the sharpness of a samurai sword.

Over. My. Dead. Body!

With every scrap of strength I have, I take a leaf out of Althea's book and slap Gaia across the face stunning her. As her grip loosens, I shove her hard in the chest and turn to dive under Alpha as she falls. My turn to catch her.

Ooph!

"I've got you girl."

Clutching Alpha tightly, she licks the rainwater from my face. We sit just panting, dripping and staring at the mother of all nature as she crawls across the ground, smacking it like she's lost her glasses or something.

"G-Gaia?" My voice quivers.

She stops. Emerald eyes bore into mine, but then a smile spreads across her face.

"Oh Hannah! You came. Forgive me. Forgive me."

But I daren't move. Alpha's coat flickers amber and her instincts never seem to be wrong.

"We came to help you. You asked me to, remember?" I hesitate. "Where's Gran?"

"They're all inside. I sent them inside."

As her fever seems to settle, so does the storm, the rain thinning to nothing more than a drizzle.

"Do you want me to help you up?"

"Yes."

Remaining cautious, Alpha gets up from my lap and approaches Gaia with me, her pink tongue lolling from her jaw. I pull the last water pod from my pocket and toss it up into the air. Incredibly, it hasn't burst. Alpha gulps it down.

"She's a loyal girl, isn't she? I've forgotten what loyalty is."

I bend down and taking Gaia's arm, hook it up over my shoulders. "Can you stand?"

She nods as reeds and thin straggly branches cloak my shoulders, slithering like grass snakes.

"You're a pretty little thing, aren't you?"

I smile, but as I do flashes from the dream snatch my attention away for a second. Mum vanishing under the water. Gaia's threat.

As the questions march like orderly foot soldiers, one steps out of line.

How on Earth do I trust the Mother of all Nature?

CHAPTER FORTY-SEVEN
Revenge – Part I

The sky darkens to a deep shade of indigo as we approach a large jagged fracture in the rock, the entrance to the first of dozens of mountains as far as I can see. A silence has blanketed us as if every creature on Gaian is holding its breath. The air is still muggy, humid not fresh or crisp as I thought it would be the higher we went.

Gaia stumbles a little, clearly weakened by the fever. Her scent is intoxicating. Waves of cinnamon, sea salt and frankincense, limes and rose, basil and rainwater –the only ones I recognise – swirl around me making my head light.

"So you're my little inheritor," she smiles as a kaleidoscope of cerise and jade fan out into her eyes. I look away still unable to shake the bad feeling that's curled up for the night in my stomach.

"I suppose I am."

"Suppose? I see there is need to instil a greater level of confidence in you."

She's Mother Nature for god's sake. She's actually real.

Maybe I'm just star struck. Isn't this, like, the ultimate celebrity sighting. I mean, what would the world say to her if she stood before us all? We're idiots. We don't learn. When do we go to Planet B? Can we have a selfie? *Someone would.*

I don't know what to say. This is beyond awkward. The march of the questions has come to a halt. Not one is volunteering to go first. *Typical.*

I daren't even attempt connecting to Gran because Gaia can probably hear every single word. She's probably listening to me right now. I pause, half expecting her to agree, like Gran does. But Gaia remains silent.

As we enter the mountain, our footsteps echo down the vast corridors. Gaia guides us into the centre one, with the smallest of all entrances.

"What would I do without you and Eleanor?" Gaia says as the cave opens out into an enormous space, lit by tiny little flames dotted all over the cave's walls, rising up high into the ceiling.

"I didn't expect you to be, well, awake. I thought the fevers would have kept you bed bound."

"Did you? Well, you caught me in a moment of wellness when neither the sweating sickness has, as you say, left me bed bound and delirious, nor have the Arctic chills infiltrated my skeletal structure leaving me paralysed."

"I'm so sorry this is happening to you."

We descend a set of stone stairs lined with ornately carved wooden handrails. It somehow looks familiar, which is rubbish, of course. I've never been anywhere like this before. *Wait! The chambers where we saw the High Council.*

That's it. It's very similar from what I can remember, only much, much larger. I look up at the ceiling and realise the little lights are moving.

"Fireflies and lighters," says Gaia seeing my face. "This is a hive."

Please don't let them be stingers!

"A hive?"

"Yes. A very large one," Gaia replies, arching one of her brows thick with leaves and minute branches.

Despite the glow, there are too many shadows, too many corners and a serious lack of family close by.

"Gaia, where's Gran?"

"I'd worry more about yourself, right now."

Gaia straightens up, but clings to my waist. Her breath is warm, the scent of butterscotch. "Your grandmother used you. You're a weapon against me, and I can't let that be," she says as threads of her hair curl and tighten around my neck. No! I claw at them as she lifts me from the ground.

I. Can't. Breathe.

Alpha doesn't charge. She knows Gaia is untouchable. Instead, she growls and barks with such ferocity as I gulp down little cups of air.

"Why...are...you...?" I gasp. "Gran!"

Gaia releases me. I hit the ground, coughing and spluttering as my lungs scream.

"Thought you'd usurp me, eh?"

What?

"Thought you could kill Galtonia without repercussions?"

WHAT?

"She was the one…who wanted…you dead!" I pant.

"Not true. You and the rest of humanity have poisoned me. Galtonia would never betray me so," Gaia barks, her eyes flashing ruby red, as strands of hair entwined with ivy and lemongrass, leaves from maples and ash trees and spindly branches flow out, petals dotted amongst them, dance above her shoulders in a breeze only she conducts.

She's right. We have poisoned her, but…

"That's true. We have. But one of the Lords of the High Council is out to usurp you."

"As if they could."

"They could and they are. If you don't believe me, read my mind. You can see everything that's happened. Watch it for yourself! Ask Lilith, even! She's a Visionheir."

"How do I know what you show me hasn't been tampered with?"

Lilith's were. At least we *think* they were. But still.

"Seriously? I'm not some dodgy corporate goon or self-serving politician."

That's why Mum fights them in the courtrooms.

"Ah, there's that confidence I was seeking."

"You kept calling me 'daughter of daughters' so why would I ever want to hurt you."

I can't believe this!

I want Gran to kill Galtonia all over again! I can feel a flicker of fury rising in me, but fight against it. This is exactly what Galtonia wanted!

"Where is my grandmother?"

Gaia raises her arm and the Fireflies and Lighters brighten instantly revealing what lies where the shadows once lived in every corner of the chamber.

They're all out cold.

At least, I hope they are.

Gran and Althea. Elric and Jack. Evelyn and Constance. Then I notice her. In the middle of the room, lying on a large stone slab...Harriet.

CHAPTER FORTY-EIGHT
Revenge – Part II

I leap down the stairs and slide on knees to where Gran's body lies. I press my hand to her chest. *Thump-thump. Thump-thump.*

"What have you done?" The hot scream burns my throat.

Gaia descends the stairs like a hunter out to slaughter its prey. *Me.*

"You summoned me, remember! You asked me to help you. You ordered the Elementals be brought here to save you."

Gaia rubs her temples for a second, swaying once more. I feel a tiny spike in the temperature. The fever…

"Please Gaia!" I run to her, taking her hands. "You're sick. You've been poisoned by one of the Lords. We need to find an antidote and soon! Your fever's destroying our worlds. Our homes."

Gaia crumbles in my arms as the fever rises way too fast. Her caramel skin glistens like morning dew. She claws at the golden collar. I press my fingers around the back of her neck, but there's no clasp. *Is it part of her?*

Her eyes roll, her body limp like a ragdoll. *What do I do?*

Galtonia planned this all along. She's a poisonous witch!

Oh. My. God.

She's the poison!

Is that even possible? She knew she was going to die. She wanted to. She was the antidote! *Dammit!* I sit clinging to Gaia lost in fever again, listening to the mountain grumble whilst Mother Nature's body trembles in my arms.

Across the chamber, Alpha pants desperate for air as she sniffs at Jack and Constance's bodies, then finally checks Althea's.

"Check Harriet."

Alpha leaps up onto the stone slab and sniffs Harriet's lifeless body.

"Is she alive?"

"Yip, yip," she replies licking Harriet's cheek.

"Oh thank god." *Why do I even say that! He's not here. If he ever was.*

Alpha jumps down and trots across to me, then paws my hand.

"You've got an idea, girl?"

She nods furiously as she lays at my side like a sphinx.

"Can you show me? Wait! Show!"

More furious nods.

I rest Gaia's head against my chest just like Gran has done for me so many times before. I place my hands either side of the Alpha's temples.

"Okay, girl. Let's do this."

I push every thought I have aside – easier said than done

as the saying goes.

"Show me," I whisper.

Alpha replays the scene of her nuzzling her face under her paws, but then peering out as Gran placed the azurite crystal between me and Joyce. The image fades.

"But I don't have a crystal," I say.

She shakes her head.

"I don't need one?"

One nod.

"Do you mean you want me to enter everyone else's minds?"

Head shake.

"Just Gran's?"

One nod.

Like she did with me at the nursing home.

"It's worth a try."

Just then, Gaia begins to stir as the fever fades a little.

"I'm so sorry, Hannah. Forgive me. I don't know what's real, anymore," Gaia says clasping my cheek. Her palm is soft, moist with sweat.

"We have to get you well again. *You* are the Mother of all Nature, not me. But I can't help you without Gran. There's so much more I have to learn. I need her."

A sudden red mist swirls in her eyes. Grabbing my wrist, she pulls us up as if we're puppets on ropes.

"You don't need her. She's the one trying to poison me. She's the one who wants her granddaughter to take my place. Caroline failed her so now everything has been spent on guiding you to this fate."

Ow!

"Gaia, you're hurting me!"

She shoves me back, hard. I stumble back, toppling over Alpha.

"Galtonia is the one who poisoned you, not Gran. You've been listening to what Galtonia has been dripping in your ear and for a long time I imagine."

"Liar!"

Gaia raises her arms.

Please! No!

I turn to run, but the force of the impact sends me hurtling across the chamber. *Ow!* Ribs snap as I hit the floor taking every breath I have. A dizziness hits me. Tears sting my eyes as a blackness engulfs me.

****

"Hannah. I'm here. Talk to me."

Gran's voice is so comforting.

"Are we dead?"

"Not yet."

"You're not exactly filling me with hope."

"Well, this I didn't expect. Our best shot is to tackle Gaia when

her fever hits. That, strangely, is when she's at her most rational."

"Can you please kill Galtonia again for me?"

"I'll haunt her when I'm dead. That do?"

"Yes. But not yet."

"Deal. Now, sorry but I've been poking around in that head of yours. You hung back to heal that tree and let it spread, yes?"

"I couldn't stop thinking about what Evelyn said. I had to do something. I'd remembered what Lilith had done so thought I'd try."

"Well, I want you to try again. Because I want every single one of us awake. If we have to incapacitate Gaia until we can figure out how to heal her, and yes, I think you're absolutely right about Galtonia's poison. It's a poison of the mind, not the body, then I'm going to need all the Wiccan power I can get."

"Will Evelyn hold it together when she sees Harriet?"

"I can only hope. I'll need you to channel the broadcast. Gaia might pick up on it, but if I can deflect our thoughts, she may never hear. But then again, she is Gaia, even if she's weakened."

"She scares me, Gran. She batted me away like I was a fly being squatted."

"You should be scared. We all should. If Gaia takes her revenge upon those she believed wrong her, there'll be no Earth left to return to and very little of Gaian either at this rate."

"So, what do I do?"

"Start self-healing. Mend your ribs. The 7th and 8th I think if *my Empath gift is accurate. Do exactly what you did to the tree, but internalise it. Then spread it out to each of us as if our roots were connected. The ground is soft enough in here. Use it."*

I imagine my hand pressing against my ribs where the pain radiates from and push what energy I have to that spot. Wincing as the ribs snap back into place, I pray that Gaia doesn't somehow realise what I'm doing. Is my body even moving?

"That's it. Now, that same energy, feel where Althea and Elric are, then Constance and Jack. Evelyn must be last of all."

Feeling the heat of the energy inside me weld the final splinters in my ribs back together, I then imagine pushing the energy out, feeling, listening for exactly where Althea and Elric are. I imagine them like lightning conductors reaching out to receive me just like plants do in a storm.

"Althea. Elric. Wake up."

The energy moves through my arms and down into my fingers. I press them against the ground and imagine pushing my fingers into the earth beneath them. It bleeds into the ground and shoots through channels of roots ready to heal.

"Ready to deflect?" I check.

"Yes."

"Everyone, listen to me. Gaia believes we're the ones out to usurp her. She's drunk every lie Galtonia ever told her. She truly

believes we're the traitors and she'll kill us. Only when her fever hits is such actually more..."

"...coherent," Gran interrupts.

"Thanks. We're going to distract Gaia so you can get the Elementals out of here. Keep your receptors open. Listen for instructions. We'll have to figure out how to heal Gaia when the Elementals are safe – they're the key to it, I think."

I have no idea if they've heard me. All I can do is hope.

I snap awake, inhaling the damp air. Energy pulses through my fingertips, channelling out to them. Althea's fingers twitch. Elric's feathery flanks begin to rise and fall. *It's working.*

"This gives me no pleasure in ending my own bloodline," Gaia announces, resting against one of dozens of large tree trunks jutting out from crevices in the mountain's wall.

Did she actually think that one through?

"That's like a turkey plucking its own feathers and settling down for the night in an oven on Christmas Eve!"

Her droning laugh fills the chamber and probably the rest too.

"Everyone get ready."

Right. Release the brat!

"Gaia!"

The laughter stops and she stands. Spreading my fingers, palms down, I press against air to push myself up in one swoop.

"Confidence growing. Too bad it's too late for you."

"Are you stupid?"

Oh my god, she's going to obliterate me!

"What did you say?"

"I'll just say it as I see it, if that's alright with you. You're stupid. Thick as a brick, we say up North. You've just said you want to end your own bloodline. Wipe out the future potential for life. You'll kill me to make yourself feel better, but if something does happen to you then everything you've spent billions of years building will die off and cease to exist until the whole universe goes back to black, to emptiness, to nothingness."

"I think one might have dipped one's toes in the confidence pool a little too much."

She throws her hand out, pushing a block of air straight at me. I throw myself down and roll away. From the corner of my eye, I see Alpha curled behind one of the pillars of the stone slab on which lies Harriet. *Clever girl.*

Taking a huge deep breath, I stand back up.

"Humanity is poisoning me. These parasites I created care for nothing but themselves. And your much lauded grandmother thought she'd take advantage and crown you in my place."

"We are parasites, but we're your parasites. And all my

grandmother has ever done is be loyal to you. I am being loyal to you. I came here to protect you, but you're too stupid to see the truth. And there are millions of humans loyal to you. I don't want to be Mother Nature!"

I said it.

I said it out loud.

"No, that burden was bestowed upon you by that treacherous mother of yours! She will die, just like you! You all will."

"She's only guilty of choosing me over you. But I'm telling you, that I choose to protect you, *if* you'll let me. And maybe you'll kill me for it, but then at least I've done my bit."

"Shut up! Shut up! Galtonia said you'd try to turn it. Persuade me with your poisonous words."

Gaia grabs her head, twitching and gasping for breath. The air is getting hotter.

I scan the room.

"Go!"

Elric and Althea both dart across the chamber and sweep Constance and Jack up. Evelyn, spotting Alpha dragging Harriet's dazed and weary body out towards the exit, dashes towards them and scoops Harriet into her arms, pressing kiss upon kiss over her little daughter's face. Alpha nudges Evelyn hard to move.

"Not so fast!"

Blasts of blinding silver lights pummel the chamber wall, sending huge splintering cracks racing up to the roof of the mountain's chamber. Rocks crumble and fall down, but Elric spreads his wings wide taking the brunt of each rock. Hundreds of fireflies and lighters spin into the air swirling, disorientated at the disruption to their hive. They flit from wall to wall. Several land upon my shoulders, little hums from their chests tingle against my skin as they try to settle.

Blast after blast strikes the wall until the exit is all but covered, leaving spears of light to pierce the chamber.

"Elric, can you get them out?"

"Yes. You focus on Gaia."

"Protect them at all costs."

He doesn't answer. He doesn't need to.

"Gran?"

"I'm ready when you are sweetheart."

"Gaia, stop! Please."

Weakened, she staggers around, before suddenly surging across the chamber towards me. She picks me up, digging nails into my arms as she lifts us up, high from the ground. *She's a fury.*

The fireflies and lighters scatter terrified.

"Let me join you," I say.

If it means saving my family…

Gaia's ruby-red eyes dull to a rosy amber.

"Well I never expected that," she says as a thin smile spreads across her face narrowing her eyes.

"If Galtonia was right, then I, I, ac-accept that. Her final wish was to convert me. Do it. It will prove my loyalty to you then you can be healed and there'll be no more suffering."

I have no idea if she believes me.

"I do know I am unwell. I am not stupid, despite your accusations. But there will be more suffering. Much more. The balance of our biosphere must be restored. There is much to reverse."

She lowers us to the ground, then removes the golden collar from her own neck, clasping it around mine.

"I see you have some flora already weaved into your hair."

"It belonged to Lilith."

Gaia pulls strands from her own hair then weaves them into mine. She cups my chin in her hand and with a motherly look kisses my cheek before whispering, "So beautiful."

She doesn't let my chin fall, despite my embarrassment.

"Thank you."

"Oh, Hannah. You tried."

No!

Instantly, Gaia's body begins pulsing with electric

currents. Bright blue, they crack and hiss as she holds my body out. I writhe against her grip, but it's useless.

"I LOVE YOU GRAN!"

The rush of fire passes between us, severing Gaia's grip as Gran blasts through the gap. I fall to the ground and as if in slow motion, watch Gran wrap her entire body and expanse of wings around Gaia entombing her in fire. But Gaia's sheer blue lightning rods strike hard, pummelling Gran's body hundreds of times like rounds of never-ending bullets.

I hit the ground, but feel nothing as I watch Gran's fire begin to fade. Gaia strikes Gran in the chest with a rod of lightning.

ARGH!!!

Every fibre in my body feels the charge striking Gran, extinguishing her fire.

No! Gran!

Gaia opens her grasp, letting Gran's feathery body plunge to the ground. Alpha appears and dives, taking the full force of the impact. She whimpers.

Shaking, I stand, feeling a charge pulse through me.

Don't hate her. Don't!

But I fly at Gaia, pushing every scrap of energy I can, turning her own electricity against her. We smack into each other and I begin pummelling my fists into her. She just takes them. She doesn't retaliate. I begin sobbing uncontrollably, weakening.

DO IT!

I grab Gaia's throat and push hard. We smack into the chamber wall.

"Hollow Tree! Help me!"

I punch a tree trunk creating a giant gaping hole. Oozing from it, glistening against the glow of the fireflies and lighters, lime liquid begins covering Gaia's body as another fever begins to take hold of her. I fall back. It dries quickly cocooning her inside it. She falls silent. It won't hold her for long, but maybe long enough.

As I float in the air, thousands of fireflies and lighters encompass me in an orb of light.

"Thank you. Forgive us for wreaking havoc in your hive. Please cocoon Gaia until she wakes. And when she wakes, leave and don't come back."

Every single light bug flickers and flutters, then together form a cocoon and wrap themselves around Gaia.

I fall to Gran's side, tears streaming, making it difficult to see. Alpha lies down Gran's side, nudging her arm, licking her fingers.

A little puff of air expels from Gran's mouth.

"Gran?"

Nothing.

She's gone.

Gran is dead.

Taking her hand, I press one final kiss onto the back of it before it crumbles into ash. I know deep down, she won't rise again. Not even a Firebird could rise from that.

But just as my head hangs, the tiniest wisp of air begins swirling around Gran's ashes.

Really? She's alive!

The air whips faster and faster, creating a miniature tornado.

I reach out to touch it.

"Gran?"

It lifts from the ground and turns, creating a spearhead which strikes into my chest knocking me flat.

I smack my head against the ground.

"I will always be with you now my darling, Hannah. Always inside. Our power comes from within. It is where our true strength lies."

"Gran!"

I sob.

I can't stop.

"Please! Come back! I can't live without you."

"I'm right here, my greatest love."

"I need you. I want you here."

"Trust me. I'm just inside, out of sight."

"I don't want to live any more. Take me with you."

"No, my sweetest treasure. Your mother needs you."

What?

"But I don't know if she's even alive."

"She is. I can feel her now. She's in Gaian. And the reason I know, is because she's not with me. Find her, darling. Save my daughter."

Every single shattered piece of my heart glows with hope, but each piece is so sharp and broken, I know it will never fit back together like before.

"Trust yourself. And trust Alpha. She will soothe your hurt more than you can ever imagine."

"I will. Gran?"

"I must leave now. I'm tired."

"I love you."

"I know. And I you."

CHAPTER FORTY-NINE

Greensleeves

I don't remember much of what happened next. I'm too tired to read Alpha's mind, but I remember being dragged… Althea's face…soaring through the sky…

I curl into Alpha listening to the thrum of her heart, feeling the tight dryness of tear stained cheeks.

"Thank you, Freya."

She bends down and places a bowl of my favourite fruits in front of me, but I can't face anything.

I imagine Gran's face in the flames of the fire we've gathered around.

"Gaia's had her revenge, alright," begins Elric sipping a rosy coloured juice.

Jack, wrapped in a blanket and curled under Elric's wing, sleeps soundly, as Constance cradles her sister, rocking her from side to side, humming a tune I recognise instantly.

Greensleeves. Mum's favourite.

Evelyn stretches against the stiffness from clinging to little Harriet for hours and hours on end. *At least we have her back.*

Freya moves to sit with Watton. They continue whispering their worries.

"It was a trap," I say sitting up.

"Freya was meant to see the Volkhas. Whichever Lord it

was delivered Harriet's body to Gaia. It's part of the plot. They'll have used Harriet to convince Gaia they were on her side and that Evelyn would come for her. They knew you'd never give your children up. Certainly not without a fight. I think the furies have been listening without us knowing."

"At least they're dead now. And Galtonia," says Elric.

"Yes, but Gaia's revenge is incomplete. She will try to find me and Mum and she'll annihilate Gaian and Earth to do so."

"She believes humanity deserves their fate," says Althea tossing another load of berries into her mouth.

"I could feel it in her. The furies and Galtonia succeeding in poisoning Gaia against us all," I add.

"But Gaia doesn't see the manipulation. I can only put it down to the fever. There's no way the Gaia that I know, that I served for dozens of years would ever fail to realise what was happening to her," says Althea.

"Her revenge has only just started," I admit realising I'm next. Or Mum. "You have to help me find my mother. We've got Harriet back, but this is far from over." I press the golden collar Gaia clasped around my neck. It still won't come off.

"We will!" exclaims Watton. "We'll get your precious mummy back with you. I's promise that. And I never breaks a promise, once made."

I smile. *He is so sweet.*

I choke back tears and many, many fears.

I'm just a teenager.

"What aren't you saying, Hannah?" asks Evelyn now sitting at my side. "Please tell us. Anything you say to us will not be repeated. I, now, as mother of the Elementals pledge myself to you and your protection."

My lip quivers.

"Thank you." I pause, the words sit in my mouth waiting to be released. Once said, they can never be unspoken. But they deserve the truth. "I felt Gaia's soul and for a moment I saw inside it. If what I saw was true and everything I'm feeling is right...then...somehow...I'm going to have to destroy Gaia."

Enjoyed this book?

I do hope you have enjoyed this instalment of Hannah's story and are looking forward to reading Book Three in this series *Hollow's End*.

If you have enjoyed it and are happy to share your thoughts about it, then leaving authors a review on places like Goodreads or Amazon.co.uk or Amazon.com really do make a difference to all authors, not just an independent like myself. You see, if you have enjoyed it, then other readers and book lovers like yourself may well do, too. Honest reviews matter. It's like getting a personal recommendation that it's time well spent investing in this book and myself as a potential new favourite author.

So, if you do have a couple of minutes and have enjoyed the book, then writing a review is something we authors appreciate more than words can say...

If you'd like to receive my timely newsletter, secret chapters, advanced news of events and promotions, then you can join my community at www.jabrowne.com

Happy reading!

About the author

J. A. Browne is the author of the environmental fantasy series *The Earth Chronicles*. She released her debut novel *Hannah and the Hollow Tree* in 2018. She continues to teach part-time in Yorkshire as well as visiting schools to share her passion for the environment, trees and all things nature. As an independent author, J.A. Browne also loves speaking about her transition from full time teaching to building her indie author brand.

She would love to hear from you, so do get in touch!

Her online home is www.jabrowne.com

You can email her using: author@jabrowne.com

Alternatively, you can find her on:

Instagram - @jabrowneauthor

Twitter - @JABrowne2017

Facebook – www.facebook.com/AuthorJABrowne

Acknowledgements

It's fair to say that I have completed *Gaia's Revenge* a tad quicker than I did *Hannah and the Hollow Tree*. I have taken inspiration, not only from those closest to me, but from the beauty of our incredible planet, our home. In particular, from trees that breathe life into us, their ability to protect not only themselves but their offspring and all inhabitants of the planet as well as having an intrinsic ability to communicate which humans actually mimic. I see trees as teachers, silent warriors and as guardians of our planet.

The inspirational and invaluable humans I wish to thank begin with Darran Holmes. A true visionary. His ideas, illustrations and cover artwork often go above and beyond. I could never have done this 'indie' thing without him.

Which leads me onto my editor, Carly and book designer Nicola from Peahen Publishing. Their guidance, creative input and attention to detail, I am truly grateful for.

A very special thank you goes out to Paul 'Oz' Hardwick, Martyn Bedford and Amina Alyal whose tremendous support and wisdom is difficult to quantify and from whom I have learnt so much. Leeds Trinity University is a very special place, my academic home.

To Joanna Penn – the matriarch of indie publishing whose advice is always golden.

To my beloved husband Aaron, my wonderful brother Stephen and all my cherished family and friends, each of whom imprint upon my heart in ways I am forever grateful for. And finally, to those loved and lost. My Grandmothers, Mabel and Eva – Eleanor wouldn't exist without you. To 'Dangerous' Daddy Brian who taught me the power of charity to others and to Mummy-B who taught me that family is everything. My heart misses yours. Love stays.